'I am sure I have done nothing wrong!'

Her cheeks were hot. She knew very well what people might say of her, and for a moment she was conscious of a deep regret, because clearly Hal thought she was ruined.

'My dear girl, you must be an idiot if you truly believe that,' Hal said. 'And I know you are not, which means you have been reckless and foolish with no thought for your reputation—or mine.'

She knew herself in the wrong, but pride kept her from confessing it. 'I do not mind if some think ill of me, for Mama and my sisters will not. I have no desire to mix in high society. Nor do I wish to marry…'

'That is besides the point…' He gave a sigh of exasperation.

'If anyone thinks ill of me they may do so,' Jo said hot-temperedly. 'I am sure I do not give a fig!' It was not true, because she saw now exactly what she had lost. Any faint chance that Hal might have married her had gone, and the regret was sharp.

Author Note

Jo Horne considers that she is not as beautiful as her sister Marianne, who married a marquis, or her darling Lucy, who has her head full of dreams. She does not believe in love, and thinks that she will stay home with Mama and Aunt Bertha and write her stories, but first of all she must accompany Aunt Wainwright to Bath. Jo does not like her mama's sister, but she has no choice, for a promise was given. She is not looking for love, but when she meets the handsome Hal Beverley her 'wicked earl' suddenly begins to behave like a hero—and then Jo is swept away into an adventure that may ruin her.

I hope that you will enjoy Jo's story—and Lucy's, which is still to come.

Look for Lucy's story
MARRYING CAPTAIN JACK
Coming soon!

MARRIED BY CHRISTMAS

Anne Herries

MILLS & BOON

Pure reading pleasure

First published in Great Britain 2007
Harlequin Mills & Boon Limited,
Eton House, 18-24 Paradise Road, Richmond, Surrey TW9 1SR

© Anne Herries 2007

ISBN: 978 0 263 85198 4

Set in Times Roman 10½ on 13 pt.
04-1007-90013

Printed and bound in Spain
by Litografia Rosés S.A., Barcelona

Anne Herries, winner of the Romantic Novelists' Association ROMANCE PRIZE 2004, lives in Cambridgeshire. She is fond of watching wildlife, and spoils the birds and squirrels that are frequent visitors to her garden. Anne loves to write about the beauty of nature, and sometimes puts a little into her books, although they are mostly about love and romance. She writes for her own enjoyment, and to give pleasure to her readers.

Recent novels by the same author:

A DAMNABLE ROGUE*
RANSOM BRIDE
MARIANNE AND THE MARQUIS†

Winner of the Romantic Novelists' Association
  ROMANCE PRIZE
†*The Horne Sisters*

and in the Regency series *The Steepwood Scandal*:

LORD RAVENSDEN'S MARRIAGE
COUNTERFEIT EARL

and in *The Banewulf Dynasty*:

A PERFECT KNIGHT
A KNIGHT OF HONOUR
HER KNIGHT PROTECTOR

and in *The Hellfire Mysteries*:

AN IMPROPER COMPANION
A WEALTHY WIDOW
A WORTHY GENTLEMAN

Chapter One

'Damn you, Harry,' Lord Beverley said and glared at his son. 'I should have thought that you would want to do your duty by the estate now that your brother is dead…' Pain showed briefly in the father's eyes, for the death of his elder son coming on top of their estrangement was hard to bear. 'You have hardly been in this house since you left the army, sir. I demand that you spend more time here learning about the way the estate is run. It will come hard to you when I am gone and it is all on your shoulders.'

Hal bit back the angry words that rose to his lips. A part of him wanted to tell his father exactly why he had no time to waste languishing at the estate, but he knew that his mission would not find favour in Lord Beverley's eyes. If he knew that Hal was searching for Matt's wife he would quite probably forbid him to go on—and it was impossible to tell him about his suspicions that Matt's death had not been an accident. As yet he had no proof, just a feeling that there had to be some other reason for an excellent horseman like Matt to die in a fall from his horse…that and some small inconsistencies in the stories that had been told him when he first learned of his brother's death. It had left a shadow hanging over him in all he did, though none would have guessed it, for outwardly he was the smiling carefree young man he had always been.

Lord Beverley's health was not all it should be and Hal was too dutiful—indeed, too fond—a son to cause his father unnecessary suffering, even if he did not agree with the way that he had treated Hal's brother and his wife. He shrugged, hiding his true feelings behind a careless manner.

'As to that, sir, I doubt you intend popping off just yet, which means I have plenty of time to learn. Besides, we have a very capable agent to run things at the estate and several good men who know their job.' He grinned engagingly. 'If I were to interfere with anything, you would soon send me packing. And I have arranged to meet some fellows at Newmarket. You wouldn't have me break my word?' He had no intention of going to Newmarket, but better that his father believed he was wasting his time and money on the horses than that he should know the truth.

'You imagine that everything is a joke,' his enraged father said. 'I sometimes think that you will laugh as they put you into your grave, sir!'

'It is something I picked up in the army, Father. We all learned to laugh at life, otherwise we should have cracked up.'

'You should never have been in the army at all,' Lord Beverley said. 'It was bad enough that your brother defied me—and as for marrying that girl!' He shook his head. 'He could have done much better than that, Harry. Her father is a rogue and a fool! I want your promise that you will find yourself a decent girl and marry her before six months is out. We need an heir for the estate.'

'Yes, Father. I am aware of your feelings on that matter. I can only say that I will do my best to oblige you if it is at all possible.'

'Surely you can pick a suitable girl from all those you must meet in the best drawing rooms in London?' his father said, clearly displeased with his answer. 'Your brother defied me and married a girl I could not welcome into the family. I disowned him. Don't make me do the same to you, Harry.'

'What you did to Matt was your own affair, sir,' Hal said, meeting his father's eyes with a challenge of equal determination. 'If you can live with your conscience then do so, but I should have thought you had learned a serious lesson.'

Ignoring the spluttering anger coming from his father, he turned and walked from the library, which was often the warmest room in this cold and sometimes bleak house. Hal had his own smaller estate, which had been left to him by his rather notorious grandmother, whom he had adored. It was a modern, comfortable house and was by far his favourite. He had never expected to inherit Beverley House or the estate, for he was the younger son and it should all have gone to his brother, Matthew. Matt would never have been in the army at all, except for the quarrel with his father. Matt had fallen in love with Ellen Rowley, the daughter of a wealthy wool merchant, and, as such, beneath his notice, according to Lord Beverley. He had advised his son to bed her and forget her, or keep her as his mistress and marry a girl from the right kind of family. Matt had ignored his father, marrying the girl he loved and taking her with him when he joined the army.

Ellen had become a camp follower, going wherever Matt

went and accepting all the hardships of the campaign as if they were a natural part of a woman's life. Hal had liked her. Had he been there when Matt had died, he would have taken her under his guardianship and looked after her. He had a useful income of his own, and was not financially reliant on his father. He could have afforded to see that she was able to live decently. However, he had been in England on leave when Matt had been killed in a riding accident. By the time he could get back to Spain, his brother had been buried and his sister-in-law had disappeared.

Hal had been looking for her ever since. He knew that she had a little money, for she had sold various possessions of her husband's, and he had been told that it was her intention to return to England—but where she had gone since then, he had not been able to discover. He had been to her parents' home, but her father had disowned her when she ran away with Matt Beverley. He had been equally as opposed to the marriage as Lord Beverley, and told Hal that they would not accept her if she returned home. He knew that she had not approached her father-in-law—and that meant she was trying to support herself by her own efforts. That might not have been so difficult, for Ellen was an attractive, intelligent woman—but Hal had been told that she was carrying a child.

The thought that his brother's beloved wife was alone, perhaps in trouble, had given Hal many sleepless nights. He knew that he was running the risk of being disinherited if he continued to spend all his time searching for Ellen, but at this moment he didn't care. He had already made up his mind that he would marry a suitable girl for the sake of the heir that his father so desperately wanted, but felt that it was more important to discover Ellen's whereabouts first. And there was also the matter of his brother's death. He had been broken-hearted when he discovered what had happened, and the suspicion that his brother's death had been no accident had been gnawing at him for a while now. He must do what he could to discover the truth.

He had heard something from a friend of Matt's, which had led him to hope that Ellen might be living in Bath. If that were the case, he might be able to kill two birds with one stone, because Chloe Marsham had just gone down to Bath with her mother and aunt.

Hal had almost decided that he would speak to Chloe. He wasn't in love with her, but he liked her. She seemed to be a good-natured girl with a nice smile, and she liked horses. Since it was Hal's hope to breed race horses once he had settled, either at his own estate or his father's, having a wife who enjoyed riding and would not complain too much if he smelled of the stables sometimes would clearly be an advantage.

Matt had been head over heels in love with Ellen. Hal asked him once why he had thrown everything away for the sake of the girl he loved. Matt had just smiled in that easy way of his.

'If you're ever lucky enough to find the right girl for you, Hal, you will understand. Love isn't something you choose— it comes along and knocks you for six and there's nothing you can do about it. Father thought that I should have chosen to put my duty above my feelings for Ellen, but I couldn't. That damned house he is so proud of is an empty barn as far as I'm concerned. I know it has been in the family for centuries, but if I had my way I would pull it down and build something newer. Without Ellen, I should have nothing to live for. She is my life, Hal, and I am hers.'

And now Matt was dead and Ellen had lost all that she loved—unless it was true that she was carrying Matt's child. Hal was thoughtful as he went out to his curricle, where his groom was waiting. If the child was a boy, he would be the rightful heir, and he was welcome to the house and the estate for all Hal cared. It would be difficult to make Lord Beverley accept it, but Ellen had the papers to prove that she was Matt's wife and in law he would be forced to accept her child as his heir—and that would cause one hell of a row.

Hal would face that when it came to it. First of all, he had to find Ellen and make sure that she was well and had sufficient money to live on. Everything else could wait.

Jo Horne kissed her mother's cheek and then hugged her sister, Lucy. Mama smiled and told her to be a good girl, but Lucy had tears in her eyes and was reluctant to let her go.

'I shall miss you dreadfully,' Lucy said and blew her nose on the handkerchief her mama handed her. 'But I do hope you have a lovely time in Bath, Jo—and write to me often, please, to tell me what is happening in your story?'

'Yes, of course I shall,' Jo promised, 'and when I come home I shall read you all the new chapters I've written for my novel.' She glanced over her shoulder, knowing that her Aunt Wainwright was impatient for her to join her in the carriage. 'Goodbye, Aunt Bertha. Thank you for having me here—and please take care of Mama and Lucy for me.'

'Of course I shall, Jo,' Lady Edgeworthy said, though in truth she knew that Mrs Horne was taking care of her. She pressed a little purse of money into the girl's hand and closed her fingers over it as Jo protested. 'Write to all of us as often as you can. Have a wonderful time with Lady Wainwright, and come home to us whenever you wish.'

'Thank you,' Jo said and kissed her cheek. 'You are so generous, but I must go now. Aunt Wainwright has called for me twice.'

She walked to where the heavy travelling coach stood ready, turning for one last look at her family lined up in front of the house. A brave smile in place, she waved and then climbed into the coach. Lady Wainwright gave her a sour look, her harsh features bearing the stamp of irritation.

'So you are ready at last, Josephine! I thought you would never make up your mind to leave. I hope this isn't a sample of what I may expect from you in Bath. I think I deserve some consideration from you!'

'Yes, of course, Aunt,' Jo said. 'Forgive me if I kept you waiting, but Lucy did not want to let me go. She has lost both her sisters now that Marianne is married, and it has upset her. She will have no one to share her pastimes.'

'No doubt you will be returning at the end of a few weeks,' Lady Wainwright said with a sniff of disapproval. 'It will do her good to learn to be alone for a while. She is no longer a child, and must learn to employ her time usefully rather than playing foolish games.'

Jo was tempted to retaliate, for she did not like to hear Lady Wainwright speak so harshly of Lucy, but remembering what her elder sister had said to her before she married, about not quarrelling with their aunt, she held her tongue. It was to have been Marianne who was taken to Bath by Lady Wainwright, for she was the beauty of the family. Instead, Marianne had come down to Cornwall to be with Great-aunt Bertha, and by being there had saved her from a rogue who had tried to cheat her out of her estate and might have murdered her. Lady Edgeworthy had been so grateful that she had asked Marianne's whole family to come and live with her. Now Marianne was married to her marquis and Jo was the one to accompany Aunt Wainwright to Bath.

Jo was under no illusions that her aunt was satisfied with the arrangement. She would have much preferred to take Marianne, but Jo's beautiful sister had made an excellent marriage with no help from anyone. Jo suspected that Aunt Wainwright was a little annoyed about that, because she had told them that, as Marianne had no dowry, she would be lucky to marry a baronet, but might do so if her aunt introduced her into society. It had piqued her to know that Marianne had made an even better marriage than her daughter Annette, and her uncertain temper seemed sharper than ever.

'Well, has the cat got your tongue?'

Jo looked at her aunt, considering her reply carefully. 'I was just wondering where Marianne and Lord Marlbeck are now. I believe they were to travel to his estate for a few days before going on board the ship.'

'Yes, I dare say,' Lady Wainwright said and sniffed again disapprovingly. 'In my day we did not bother with long honeymoons. Your uncle took me to Devon for two weeks and then we returned to his estate. I do not think that I should care to be jolted over foreign roads.'

'It would be exciting to see Italy. I have seen pictures of various treasures of art and architecture, of course, but to visit them…to see Venice…would be wonderful.'

'I dare say you will have to content yourself with pictures,' Lady Wainwright said. 'Marianne may have married a marquis, but it is not likely to happen to you, Josephine. That hair of yours is much too wild to be attractive. You must hide it or pull it back into a knot so that it is at least tidy.'

'Yes, I know it is awful,' Jo replied. The one thing she could agree with her aunt about was her hair, which was a flame red and curled into tight ringlets about her head. No matter how she scraped it back or pinned it up, it always escaped and came tumbling down, and she hated it. She wished that she might have had Marianne's honey gold hair—or Lucy's, which was a pale shining silver, almost like moonbeams. Lucy was going to be a beauty to rival Marianne one day, but Jo knew that she was the plain member of the family. Her features were regular and she looked well enough wearing her bonnet, but her hair made her look like a gypsy. Papa had always said so, though he said it with affection, which had taken the sting from the truth of his words. 'I do try my best, Aunt, but it is difficult to control.'

'Well, I dare say it does not matter,' Lady Wainwright said. 'You are not likely to take Bath by storm and must settle for a respectable gentleman of small fortune if you wish to marry.'

'As I do not wish to marry,' Jo replied with as much dignity as she could muster, 'I agree that it hardly matters what I look like. I shall stay at home, do good works and be a comfort to my mother and Great-aunt Bertha.'

Lady Wainwright gave her an awful look. Jo knew that she had aroused her aunt's ire once again, but it seemed that she did so all the time, even when she tried to be uncontroversial. She turned to glance out of the window. This visit to Bath was going to seem very long!

'We shall stay here for the night,' Lady Wainwright announced as she looked round the comfortable inn parlour. 'It was my intention to go straight to Bath, as you know, but that unfortunate business with the horse going lame has made us late. I am too weary to go further this evening. Tomorrow will do well enough.'

'Yes, Aunt, of course,' Jo said for she too was a little tired from the journey. 'Does the landlord have rooms for us?'

'Millicent will have to sleep in your room,' Lady Wainwright told her. 'But that is a small thing. Besides, in a public place like this it is better if a young girl does not sleep alone.'

Jo sighed inwardly, but knew that she could not refuse to have her aunt's personal maid in her room. It would be inconvenient, because she knew that Millicent snored, but, listening to a burst of laughter from across the room, she thought it might be as well. There was a party of young gentlemen enjoying their supper, and by the sound of it they were drinking a little too much wine.

One of them was staring at her very hard, and she drew her eyes away, annoyed that he should look at her in such a way. It was rude and made her uncomfortable, for she had not put up her hair; now that she had removed her fashionable bonnet, the hair fell about her face and tumbled down her back in a riot of untidy curls. She had seen Lady Wainwright glance at it twice, and put her hand up defensively, wishing that she had scraped it back in her usual style.

As the evening progressed, the noise from the young gentlemen increased and Jo was glad when her aunt said that they ought to go upstairs. She was not in the least tired, but she could amuse herself with her scribbling for an hour or so before she slept.

One of the young gentlemen had left the dining parlour, but came back in as she and her aunt were leaving. His eyes seemed to mock her and he stood deliberately in her path so that to pass she would have to squeeze by him.

'Would you mind allowing me to pass, sir?'

'I might,' he said, the suggestion of a leer on his lips. 'Then again, I might not…'

'Please, I must follow my aunt.'

Lady Wainwright became aware of her predicament and looked back. 'Kindly allow my niece to pass, sir—or I shall call the landlord and ask for his assistance!'

The gentleman scowled at her but stood aside, though Jo could feel his eyes following her as she began to walk up the stairs to the room her aunt had reserved for her. At that moment she was very glad that her aunt's maid was to sleep in her room—there was something about the man's eyes that had sent shivers down her spine. She was certain that he was not a very nice person at all. She heard a shout of laughter as he rejoined his friends, and blushed, knowing that she must be under discussion.

Lifting her head, she hurried up the stairs. She had not liked the gentleman one little bit and hoped that she would never have to see him again, but he would make a perfect villain in the book she was planning. He was a role model for her wicked earl if ever there were one!

'Well, what did you think of her?' Ralph Carstairs asked of the gentleman sitting to his right as he sipped his wine. 'Not a true beauty, perhaps—but something out of the ordinary, I think. There was pride in her eyes and a hidden fire beneath that cool exterior.'

'Yes, attractive enough, I grant you,' Hal Beverley said. 'But she is not for you, Carstairs. That dragon will keep all but those of pure heart and mind from her door. I assure you that you will not be allowed to get near—and rightly so, my dear fellow.'

Carstairs gave a shout of coarse laughter. 'You are right about the aunt. I know Wainwright slightly and I believe she leads him a dog's life. No wonder he kept a high flyer in town for years!'

'Well, we've all done that,' Hal agreed, though he had not done so for some months, since he left Spain and returned home to search for his sister-in-law. 'But you have a taste for the forbidden, Carstairs, and I can tell you now that she is not for you—or any of your ilk. It will be marriage or nothing for that young lady, as it should be.'

'Don't turn the prude on me,' Carstairs said with a frown. 'Madeline was a hot-tempered beauty. We all envied you her favours.'

'And sampled them as soon as my back was turned,' Hal said, for he knew that the Spanish beauty had taken lovers as and when she desired. 'I did not grudge her to you, my friend. She was too much of a firebrand for me—a man would have to give his soul to satisfy her needs.'

'But the little redhead has something of her look, did you not think so?'

'I saw nothing of it,' Hal said, 'but then I did not stare at her all evening as you did, Carstairs.' He grinned lazily. 'I dare say you have given her nightmares. And now you must excuse me, my friend. I think I shall go for a walk before I retire.'

Hal left the others to continue their roistering and went outside into the cool of the night air. It was a cursed nuisance coming across Carstairs and the others. He did not want to become involved with them, and hoped they were, as they had told him, en route to a mill and would not turn up in Bath.

Carstairs had begged him to join them on their expedition, but Hal had pleaded business. Indeed, he had business of his own in Bath, but it was of a personal nature. Carstairs would know Matt's wife, as would one or two of the others, and for the moment he wanted to keep his mission a secret. He would help Ellen if he found her, but the news that she was expecting Matt's child would need to be broken gently to Lord Beverley, for a sudden shock of that nature might kill him.

Jo looked out of the window before she was ready to sleep. Her aunt's maid had not yet come up, but it could not be long now. It was a clear night, the moonlight falling on the inn yard and turning it golden, hiding all the scars of daytime so that it looked mysterious and vaguely beautiful.

She saw a man standing alone in the yard. He seemed to be staring at the moon, or perhaps he was just taking the air before retiring, which she would have liked to do had it been possible. She thought that he was one of the young men who had been making so much noise earlier, though not the one who had stared at her. He had been quieter than the others, thoughtful, though their eyes had met once before she looked quickly away.

She turned as the door of her bedchamber opened and Millicent entered.

'Not in bed yet, miss?' the maid asked. 'I am sorry to disturb you, but it was the only room available.'

'Not at all,' Jo said with a smile, because she liked the woman. 'I am glad to have you here. Some of the gentlemen downstairs are a little the worse for drink.'

'Ah, yes,' Millicent said. 'Well, I shall be here—and we'll make sure to lock the door, miss.'

'Yes.' Jo smiled at her and ran to get into bed because she had turned cold. Thankfully, it was a large feather mattress and they would not be too cramped.

Jo was up early in the morning. She had not slept well, for Millicent had snored most of the night, and she was glad to get up and go downstairs. It was not yet time for breakfast, but she wanted to walk outside for a little to clear a slight headache.

She saw some of the servants beginning their work as she went out into the yard and began to walk towards what looked like a pleasant garden at the rear. It was still chilly for the sun had not yet come out, and Jo hugged her shawl about her shoulders. As she entered the garden, she saw that the man who had blocked her path the previous evening was sitting on a bench, and looked as if he had just doused his head in water. He was stripped to the waist, his tanned skin exposed to the elements.

'Oh…' She hesitated as he looked up and saw her. 'Forgive me…'

Jo turned away immediately, for it was embarrassing to come upon a gentleman in such circumstances.

'You don't get away that easily, my lovely,' the man said and stood up. Before Jo could move away, he came up to her, taking hold of her arm, grinning at her in a manner she could only think of as suggestive.

'Please let me go,' Jo said. 'I did not realise that anyone was here.'

'Spying on me, were you?' Carstairs said, a mocking grin

on his face. 'Don't run away, little witch. I saw you looking
at me last night. Your guardian isn't here now. We could have
a little fun together…'

'No!' Jo was suddenly aware that no one else was about
and a sliver of fear went through her. 'I have no wish to
know you, sir. I must go in or my aunt will look for me…'

'You shall pay a forfeit before I let you go,' Carstairs said
and grabbed hold of her. 'I'll take a kiss at least for my
trouble.'

'Let her go, Carstairs!'

Jo heard the voice behind her. She had not realised that
anyone was there, but his command had an instant effect for
the man let go of her and she pulled away. Turning, she found
herself looking at the gentleman she had seen contemplating
the moonlight the previous night. Seeing him close to for the
first time, Jo realised that he was very good looking with his
dark hair and eyes, and a firm chin that spoke volumes of his
determination.

'Thank you, sir,' she said. 'I must go in before I am
missed.'

'You would have done better not to come out at all,' Hal
told her sharply. 'An inn yard is not the right place for a young
lady alone—especially at this early hour when few are about.'

'I dare say you are right,' Jo said and walked quickly
away. She did not dare to look back, though she knew that a
heated exchange was going on behind her.

'Damn you for interfering,' Carstairs said. 'I only meant
to kiss the girl!'

'I know what you intended, and a kiss was the least of it,'
Hal said. 'We are in England now and there is no war—no
excuse for that kind of behaviour. I know what occurred at

Badajoz and we don't want that kind of thing happening here.'

'You can't blame me for what happened there,' Carstairs said, but he could not meet Hal's stern gaze. 'The men were out of control, driven by bloodlust and the needs of a long campaign.'

'I blame no one for anything that happened out there,' Hal said. 'We were all driven a little mad by it—but that was war. The girl you were molesting is innocent and deserves to be treated with good manners and respect.'

'Well, no harm was done,' Carstairs said, giving him an uneasy look, for he knew that he wasn't up to Hal's weight and would go down under a hammer blow from him. He would need a pistol in his hand to stand a chance against him. And the time might yet come when he would need it. 'She has run back to her dragon of an aunt and I dare say that is the last I shall see of her.'

'Take my hand,' Hal said. 'We should not be bad friends over this, Carstairs.'

'Come to the mill with us,' Carstairs invited again as he took Hal's hand in a show of friendship that was not felt. 'I can promise you a good time.'

'Thank you, but I was on my way,' Hal said. 'Perhaps we shall meet in town?'

'Yes, perhaps,' Carstairs said, an angry glint in his eyes as he watched Hal walk away. Arrogant devil! Beverley and his clique had always thought themselves above everyone else— but that hadn't saved Matt Beverley from breaking his neck in a fall from his horse. A fall that might just have had a little assistance... 'And perhaps you may meet with a similar fate to your brother's one day, my fine fellow.'

* * *

Jo glanced round the Pump Room, sighing as she saw that almost everyone was of her aunt's age. This was the fourth time they had been here in a week, and she was finding it tedious, but at least they were to attend the Assembly that evening, where she hoped at last to meet some young people.

'I think I shall bathe,' Lady Wainwright announced suddenly, surprising Jo out of her reverie. 'There is no need for you to stay, Josephine. You may visit the library or do some shopping if you wish. I shall take my nuncheon here and we shall meet for tea at home.'

'Thank you, Aunt,' Jo said feeling grateful that she was not required to accompany her aunt into the baths. 'I hope you enjoy your bathing.'

'It is not a matter of enjoyment,' Lady Wainwright told her. 'I am doing this for my health.'

'Yes, Aunt,' Jo said. 'Is there anything I may fetch you from the shops?'

'Yes, I should like half a pound of peppermint creams from the teashop near the library. Make sure they give you fresh stock and not something that has been tucked away under the counter for weeks.'

'Yes, Aunt. I shall ask for fresh.'

Jo made her escape before her aunt could change her mind. It was only rarely that she was allowed to go off on her own, though she had managed to join a ladies' debating circle and had attended their weekly meeting. Her aunt had allowed it because one of her friends had suggested that Jo might like to join, and had entertained Lady Wainwright while Jo was visiting a house just a few doors away. It was a treat to have the freedom to do as she wished for most of the day.

She lingered to look in a few of the fashionable shop windows, admiring the expensive items on display, but was not tempted to buy anything. Her aunt had seen that she had an adequate wardrobe for their visit, and Jo thought that the two bonnets she and Marianne had made were equally as stylish as anything that could be bought in the milliner's. One shop had a display of gold and silver articles, and a little silver box caught her eye, because it had a singing bird that popped up when it was opened and sang a tune. She had seen one like it at the house of Lady Eccles, who was here for her health like Aunt Wainwright. She had admired it when she was shown how it worked, and thought that, if she could have afforded it, she would have loved to buy one for Lucy. She had spent only a few shillings from the purse Lady Edgeworthy had pressed on her before she left. If she had sufficient when it was time to return to Sawlebridge, she might ask the price of the fascinating trinket.

As she turned away from the window, she almost collided with a gentleman. He grabbed her arm to steady her, and she found herself gazing up into his face as she thanked him, the words dying on her lips as she saw that he was looking at her very boldly, his dark eyes warm with laughter, his mouth curving wickedly at the corners. For a moment she had the oddest notion that he wanted to kiss her, and her eyes widened in surprise, because it was the man she had seen gazing at the moon—the same one that had saved her from a rough handling by that other one in the inn yard.

'Forgive me. I was not thinking…' Jo's cheeks flushed, for she was a little embarrassed because of what had happened at the inn, but he did not seem to recall it—he was behaving as if they had never met before. 'I am sorry.'

'Take care, sweeting,' he said. 'I might have knocked you down and I should have been grievously sorry for that—indeed, I should never have forgiven myself.'

'It would have been my own fault, sir,' Jo said. She stepped back and he let go of her arm. She decided that she would follow his lead. Perhaps he had already forgotten her. 'I was thinking of my sister, Lucy, and how much she would like that singing bird in the window and I did not realise that you were there.'

'Ah, yes, a pretty trinket,' the man said glancing into the shop window. 'Is your sister partial to trinkets of that kind?'

'She has never had such a thing,' Jo replied. 'But she is a dreamer, a romantic, and I think she would love it, but I am afraid it may be too expensive.'

'Yes, I dare say. Perhaps she has a birthday soon? Shall I buy it for her to make up for startling you?'

'Oh, no!' Jo was mortified. What kind of a girl did he think she was? 'I could never accept… What an extraordinary thing to ask! How could I possibly accept such a gift from a stranger?'

'How can we be strangers?' he said a wicked twinkle in his eye. 'I already know that you have a delightful sister called Lucy, and I am sure we could soon know each other better, if you would permit me to buy you some…hot choco-late, perhaps?' His eyes were filled with devilment, a chal-lenge that she found confusing.

'Sir! I think you must have mistaken me for…' Jo was torn between outrage and astonishment. 'I am a perfectly re-spectable person! What happened that morning at the inn was not of my making, I do assure you.'

Hal looked thoughtful. He had not immediately recog-nised her, for she had acquired a little town bronze over the past few days, and his mind had been occupied elsewhere. He had merely been flirting gently with a pretty girl. Seeing the outrage in her face, he was suddenly overcome by a wicked desire to tease her, to see how far she would go.

'Oh, yes, I am very sure of it,' he said and she saw that he was laughing inside. 'Perfectly respectable, if a little reckless. But Carstairs is a brute and a fool. If I spoke harshly to you then, I am sorry. My anger was for him, not you. You are a lady of quality and deserve respect. You are also irresistible when your eyes take fire. I feel that I have always known you, though not your name—for you have not given it to me. Mine is Hal Beverley, should you wish to know it.'

Jo gave him a straight look. 'Are you inebriated, sir?'

His laughter shocked her, because it was so honest and appealing. 'It is a question that is often asked. My father says that I am an irreverent rascal, but I assure you that my offer was made in good faith. You have a sister who would love a pretty trinket and I have money in my pocket—but forgive me if I have offended your sense of propriety.'

'No, you have not,' Jo said and surprised herself. 'Do you know, that is exactly what Papa might have done had he been able to afford it. He often gave his sixpences to the village children.'

'Perhaps another day we shall talk again,' he said and tipped his hat to her. 'Excuse me now, I must go, for I am already late for an appointment. Take care and watch where you tread. I should be most distressed if harm were to come to you.'

'Yes, I shall…' Jo watched as he walked away. His hair was very dark brown and he had such bold eyes—just like the wicked earl in the story she was writing. She smiled—

she had written of just such a meeting in her story only that morning.

Jo shook her head. She must not let her imagination run wild—that was for her stories, not for everyday life. She walked on, tired of window-shopping. She must hurry, for she was not perfectly sure what time the library closed. Jo paused to cross the road, waiting for a dray wagon drawn by four magnificent chestnut horses to pass by. A woman had just come out of the library; as Jo watched, she gave a little sigh and collapsed on to the pavement.

Jo hurried across the road now that it was clear and knelt down beside her, feeling for a pulse, which was still beating strongly. Even as she wondered what she ought to do, the woman moaned again and opened her eyes.

'Oh, I must have fainted,' she said. 'Forgive me, but could you help me to get up?'

'Yes, of course,' Jo said offering her hand. The woman took it and pulled on her as she struggled to stand up. As she did so, her shawl fell from her shoulders and Jo saw that she was quite obviously carrying a child. She retrieved the shawl and placed it about the woman's shoulders. 'Are you still feeling a little unwell?'

'Just a little,' the woman replied in a faint voice. 'If I could sit down for a few minutes…'

'Let us go into the teashop.' Jo said and offered her arm. 'Lean on me and we shall drink a dish of tea together—and perhaps a cake, if you feel able?'

'Yes, that would be nice,' the woman said. 'I was in a hurry to come out this morning and did not eat anything. I believe that may be the reason for my faintness.'

'Yes, I dare say,' Jo said. 'You really ought to eat properly in your condition, ma'am.' She had noticed the wedding ring on the woman's left hand. 'Would you like me to fetch someone for you—your husband, perhaps?'

For a moment her eyes were dark with pain. 'My husband is dead and there is no one else. I am forced to fend for myself, and that is why I was in such a hurry this morning. I am working as a seamstress from home, and I had promised to deliver some embroidery I had finished to one of the shops here. I ought to have gone straight home afterwards, but I wanted to look for a book in the library. Let me introduce myself—my name is Ellen Beverley.'

'I am very sorry to hear about your husband,' Jo said. She had found a table for them by the window and they sat down. 'It must be awful for you, especially in your condition.'

Ellen placed a hand on her swollen belly and smiled. 'Oh, no,' she said. 'Matt's child is a joy to me. Had it not been for the baby, I think I might have given way to despair when he died, but I had to live for my child's sake—because my husband would have expected it of me. He was a brave, kind man, and I shall love his child as I loved him.'

'Yes, of course,' Jo said. She had wondered for a brief moment if she might be related to the man she had met briefly outside the jeweller's that morning. His name was also Beverley, but it was clearly not so—Ellen had said she was alone. Her name was simply a coincidence. 'But is there no one who could help you?'

'I ran away to marry the man I loved,' Ellen told her with a wistful look. 'My parents disapproved and so did his—but we loved each other and there was never any question of giving each other up. We had almost a year of complete happiness, but now…' She sighed and shook her head.

Jo thought she looked very young and vulnerable, though exceptionally pretty with softly waving fair hair and green eyes.

'Perhaps we could be friends, at least while I am in Bath,' she offered impulsively. 'I know it will only be for a short time, but we may write to each other when I go home—and if you are ever in trouble I would try to help you.'

'Oh, how kind you are,' Ellen said. 'I do not believe you have told me your name.'

'How silly of me,' Jo said and laughed. 'I was too concerned for you to think of it. I am Jo Horne and staying here in Bath with my aunt, Lady Wainwright. I used to live in Huntingdonshire, but when I leave here I shall be living with Great-aunt Bertha in Cornwall.

'My whole family has gone to live with her, because Papa died and we had to leave the Vicarage. We were offered a home at the Lodge, but Mama did not like it there and poor Lucy was ill, and so we shall all live with my great-aunt from now on, but I was promised to Lady Wainwright for this visit.' Jo pulled a face. 'And now you know all there is to know about me, and very dull it is, too, compared with your life—' She broke off as the waitress approached and ordered tea and cakes for them both. She held up her hand as Ellen reached for her purse. 'No, you shall not pay a penny, Ellen—I may call you that, I hope?'

'Yes, of course,' Ellen said, her smile lighting up her face. 'I am so very pleased that we have met, Jo. I was feeling very alone—I do not go out much, except to deliver my work or look in shop windows. I have no friends, for my old companions were left behind, though of course we had many friends in Spain.'

'Was your husband a soldier?'

'Yes,' Ellen replied her eyes soft with memories. 'Captain Matthew Beverley. He always took a little house for us wherever we were, and all his friends would come and dine with us. It was such fun, for they were all so brave and gallant…and it broke our hearts when some of them died. Not many of them had wives with them, but one or two did, and another had his sister and mother. They used to follow him from place to place, as I did Matt, staying wherever there was a house that was safe and away from the fighting.'

'It must have been exciting,' Jo said. 'Though I should think it was hard having no proper home for all that time.'

'I would have been content to lie with him beneath the stars,' Ellen said. 'Indeed, once or twice I did when there was no suitable accommodation to be had. I do not know what would have happened if Matt had lived, for I should have had to stay behind somewhere because of the child. Though perhaps he might have sold out like some of his friends did…' A tear trickled from the corner of her eye and she dashed it away with her hand.

'Are you able to make a living with your sewing?' Jo asked, for she did not like to see her new friend cry, but could think of no way to comfort her.

'I am quite good at embroidery and bead work,' Ellen told her. 'It is the kind of work that takes a lot of patience and time, and the French lady I work for has been generous so far. Besides, I have some money I raised by selling things that belonged to my husband. I shall manage for the moment, though I am a little anxious about when the child comes.'

'Yes, you must be,' Jo sympathised. She wished that Mama was still living in the Vicarage, for she knew that her mother would have befriended Ellen, even if only until the child was born and she was able to work again. 'But you must find a woman who will come in and care for you, Ellen.'

'I shall have to make inquiries,' Ellen agreed. 'It is so good to talk to someone, because it helps to make up your mind. I hope we shall meet again, Jo?'

'Oh, yes,' Jo said. 'If you agree, I shall walk home with you once we have had our tea, and then I shall know where to visit you.'

'Will you really?' Ellen's cheeks turned a little pink. 'I know that some ladies look at me and wonder if I was ever truly married, but I promise you that it was so.'

'I did not doubt you for a moment,' Jo said, and then, boldly, 'Even if you had not, I should still have been your friend, Ellen.'

'Then you would be a true friend,' Ellen said. 'These cakes are delicious. You must come to tea with me another day, to let me say thank you for your kindness today.'

'I need no thanks,' Jo told her. 'But I shall be very pleased to come to tea with you, Ellen.'

She smiled as they left the teashop together, for she had made a friend, someone she could truly like and relate to, which was not true of many of her aunt's acquaintances. At least she now had someone she could visit whenever she had the time.

Chapter Two

Jo was thoughtful as she walked home after leaving the rooms where Ellen was lodging. They were respectable, though a little cramped, and were bound to be more so once the child was born. Ellen had put her individual stamp on them, her table covered in a pretty lace cloth, and her books and sewing on the table she used for her work. She had not apologised for her home, and Jo thought she was very brave to have accepted her circumstances the way she had, for she had clearly been used to better.

They had talked for a long time, and Ellen had told her about her parents' home, which was a substantial house in Hampshire. Her father was the son of a wealthy merchant, and had been well educated, becoming even richer than his father had been.

'He was determined that I should be properly brought up and I had a French governess,' Ellen told her. 'Father wanted me to be a lady—but when I wanted to marry Matt he was angry, because Lord Beverley would not accept me. He said that he was the equal of any aristocrat and that he would not allow me to marry the son of a bigot—and so we were forced to run away.'

'Do you not think that your father would welcome you home?'

'No, for we married at Gretna Green, and my father said that it was no true marriage. He said that I would be living in sin and that he wanted no more to do with me—and if he knew about the child he might demand that I give it up. He is a very religious man, Jo—and I think he would punish me for going against his wishes.'

'I see…' Jo felt sympathy for her. She realised how fortunate she had been in her parents, for Papa would never have behaved in such a fashion. He would have offered love and understanding, and forgiveness if it were necessary. 'But what of your mama?'

'Mama might forgive me,' Ellen said, 'but my father would not allow her to see me. I have wanted to write to her and tell her that I am well, but I am afraid that she might show him the letter.'

'Surely she would not,' Jo said. 'Besides, you need not tell her that you are in Bath, Ellen. I am sure she worries about you, even if she dare not show it.'

'Do you think so?' Ellen looked wistful. 'Perhaps I should write her a brief letter—as long as I do not tell her where I am, Father cannot come after me.'

'It might be of comfort to her, and you,' Jo said and on impulse kissed her cheek before leaving her to walk back to the house in Queen Square.

It was as she was nearing their lodgings that Jo saw a gentleman walking towards her. She could not mistake him, for he had immense presence and such an air of command.

'We meet again,' he said, a twinkle in his eyes. 'This must be my fortunate day…'

Jo laughed—there was a distinct challenge in his eyes, and it made her feel ridiculously pleased with life. 'I do not see why, sir, for I almost trod on your toes the last time.'

'I would gladly suffer such torments a thousand times to have the pleasure of your company, sweet lady. I must call you that, for you have not yet given me your name.'

'I think you are flirting with me, sir.'

'Perhaps, a little.' Hal grinned suddenly. 'No, I should not tease you, but there is something about you that is most delightful to tease. However, I shall not delay you—I dare say you are supposed to be somewhere else.'

'My aunt is waiting for me,' Jo told him. She felt the desire to laugh as he looked at her so expectantly, and yet she did not give him her name. He was a wicked flirt and she would not be drawn by his teasing. 'Excuse me, sir. Perhaps we shall meet again in company…'

He doffed his hat to her with a flourish, but made no attempt to prevent her going on. Jo smiled because he had lifted her spirits once more, lifting the slight cloud that had hung over her since she had learned of Ellen's sad story.

As she entered the house, Jo saw that her aunt's hat was on the sideboard in the hall and suddenly realised that it was past four. She had completely forgotten both the time, and, she realised guiltily, her aunt's peppermint creams. All thought of them had flown as she talked to Ellen. She had not even visited the library, which she had particularly wanted to do.

'Josephine!' Lady Wainwright said coming out into the hall. 'Where have you been all this time? I particularly asked you to be here for tea. Mrs Marsham brought her daughter, Chloe, to meet you, and she was most offended that you had not bothered to be here.'

'I am sorry, Aunt,' Jo said. 'I met someone and stayed talking to her. She was a little unwell and I walked home with her. Forgive me.'

'Who was this person? Respectable, I hope?'

'Oh, yes, Aunt, very respectable,' Jo said. 'Mrs Ellen Beverley.'

'I have not heard the name. One of the Hampshire family, I dare say. Well, you may introduce her to me and I shall decide if she is a fit person for my niece to know.'

'Yes, Aunt, certainly,' Jo said, though she had no intention of it. 'We are bound to meet one day, I dare say.'

Lady Wainwright's brow clouded, for she suspected something, though she did not know what. Her niece looked too innocent to be true! 'Did you buy my peppermint creams?'

'They did not have any fresh ones,' Jo lied, crossing her fingers behind her back. She did not like lying to her aunt, but had decided it was best in the circumstances. 'I may get them tomorrow—they should have some in by then.'

'Very well,' Lady Wainwright said. 'You had better go up and change, Josephine. We are going to the Assembly this evening, as you know. We shall meet Mrs Marsham and Chloe there. Now *she* is a very well-behaved young girl and exceptionally pretty. If she decides to take you up, you will move in her circles and may meet a gentleman of property. The Marshams are quite well to do, though they do not have a title—which is a pity because there is a son, I believe, of somewhere around your age. Though I dare say he is looking to marry a title to improve his chances.'

'If he is my age, I imagine he will not look to marry for some years,' Jo said. 'Drew is several years older than Marianne—and Papa was five years older than Mama.'

Lady Wainwright sniffed. 'Do not imagine that every woman marries for love, Josephine. Most make marriages of convenience, which is as it should be, for how else would they live? You must be prepared to accept something less than your sister. Marianne was very pretty—and her temper was good.'

'And mine is not, of course,' Jo said, for she could not deny that she was inclined to be hasty at times. 'I am aware that I am not pretty, Aunt, but I do not mind. If I married, it would be to someone I liked and respected, because I agree with you that it is not always possible to find love.'

Her head high, Jo walked up the stairs and along the landing to her own room. Her aunt's comments were hurtful, but she would not allow them to dampen her spirits. She had not been enjoying her visit until today, despite all the delights that Bath offered, but now she had a friend, and she was determined to meet Ellen as often as she could. Of her encounter with a rather bold gentleman, she would not allow herself to think for more than a minute or two. It had been amusing, of course, but she would probably never see him again.

'May I introduce my niece, Miss Josephine Horne,' Lady Wainwright said later that evening. 'Josephine, make your curtsy to Mrs Marsham and Miss Chloe.'

Jo dipped respectfully to the older lady, who was dressed in a gown of dark green velvet and looked very handsome for her age. Her daughter, standing elegantly beside her, was stunningly beautiful, her hair a shining gold, her eyes deep blue and her mouth softly pink. She was dressed in white as most young girls were that evening, the skirt embroidered heavily with pearls and pink crystals, a pink ribbon holding her fan from her wrist, and a spray of pink roses in her hair, fastened by a pink velvet band. About her neck she wore a double strand of expensive pink pearls with a diamond clasp.

Jo was wearing white also, and her mother's pearls. Her hair had been dressed back in a strict knot and she wore some white silk flowers in her hair. Had she known it, she made the perfect foil for Chloe's pretty pink looks, her red hair escaping in little tendrils about her face. She was Chloe's opposite: a wild gypsy, her expression a little mutinous whereas Chloe's was demure, her eyes clouded with mystery whereas Chloe's were open and innocent of guile.

'I am sorry to have missed you this afternoon,' Jo said. 'I was not aware that we were to have guests for tea.'

'Oh, it did not matter,' Chloe said. 'I am glad to meet you, Miss Horne, for it is nice to have lots of acquaintances, is it not?'

'Yes, I dare say,' Jo answered. 'This is our first visit to the Assembly. I have met only a few friends of Lady Wainwright thus far—and please call me Jo, if you will.'

'Oh, yes, that is so much better,' Chloe said. 'Shall we walk about a little together, Jo? Now that you are here I need not stay with Mama all the time and I want to see what is going on.'

'Yes, why not?' Jo said and the two girls walked away from the older ladies, gazing about the room with interest. It was a very large room and had only just begun to fill up. At one end there was another door, which led into what Chloe told her was the refreshment room, and another after that where ladies might go to refresh themselves. A small curving stairway led up to a second floor and there were seats and small tables set out so that chaperons and those who had come merely to greet friends and observe might do so in comfort. 'Have you been here before?'

'Oh, no,' Chloe said. 'I have been sort of out for a few months, for I attended some private balls at the homes of neighbours and friends, and my own ball will take place when I am eighteen next month. How old are you, Jo?'

'I was eighteen this spring,' Jo told her. 'Do you have any sisters, Chloe?'

'No, only a brother, who is a year older,' Chloe replied with a sigh. 'I have always thought it would be nice to have a sister—do you have one?'

'I have two,' Jo said. 'Marianne is nineteen and was married only a week or so ago, and my sister Lucy is not old enough to come out yet.'

'Oh, yes, I believe Lady Wainwright told Mama that your elder sister had married the Marquis of Marlbeck.' Chloe turned her wide eyes on Jo. 'How fortunate she was to make such a good match. I hope that I shall be as fortunate, though I am not sure…' She frowned. 'I have met someone I like, but I am not sure that he likes me. He is four and twenty, and I think he may not wish to be married just yet.' She sighed and pulled a wry face. 'Mama says there is plenty of time, for she intends to take me to London next spring for a season, but…' She shook her head. 'I should so like to fall in love, should you not, Jo?'

'I am not sure what being in love is,' Jo said truthfully. 'I love my family, of course—but to be in love with a gentleman would be something quite different, I imagine.'

'I think it is the most wonderful—' Chloe caught her breath, and suddenly her face lit up with excitement. 'Oh, *he* is here.'

Jo's gaze followed the direction of her new friend's. She could not see who Chloe was looking at for a moment, and then she saw a gentleman who had apparently just entered the ballroom. He was perhaps a little under six feet in height, of slim build with dark brown hair, and as he turned to look in their direction, Jo realised that she had seen him before. He was the gentleman who had come to her aid in the inn yard and then, only that morning, asked if he might buy the singing bird for Lucy! Mr Hal Beverley!

'He has seen me,' Chloe said and smiled. 'He is coming this way.'

Jo said nothing. She watched the gentleman make his way towards them, and her pulses raced, but at the last moment, her attention was turned to a young man who addressed her from her right.

'Miss Horne,' he said as she turned towards him. 'You may recall that we met at the Pump Room when you accompanied your aunt there two days ago?'

Jo turned her gaze upon him, struggling to recall his name. Her aunt had introduced them, but she had not been paying much attention, which was very rude of her. He was perfectly polite and quite respectable, though his sandy hair and pale eyelashes were not particularly attractive.

'Good evening, sir,' she said. 'How nice to meet you again.'

'Will you dance, Miss Horne?'

'Yes, thank you,' Jo said, accepting his hand as she struggled to remember his name. 'Mr…Tanner.' She felt relieved as it came back to her. He was the nephew of one of her aunt's oldest friends, she recalled, and one of the few younger gentlemen of her aunt's acquaintance. 'How kind of you…'

Jo saw from the corner of her eye that Chloe was now dancing with Hal Beverley. She was smiling up at him, and he seemed to be responding in an equally pleased manner. Jo did know why that made her feel a little envious, for they made a handsome couple and were clearly good friends.

Jo's dance with Mr Tanner was enjoyable, for though he was not the best of partners he did not tread on her toes. She thanked him when it was over and rejoined her aunt, who had moved on to another of her acquaintance. Jo was not asked for the next dance and stood with her aunt watching the more fortunate girls who had partners. Her toe tapped in time to the music, but she was content enough for the moment, and did not expect that she would dance every dance. After all, there were so many pretty girls for the gentlemen to choose from. However, just as the third dance was about to begin she heard her name spoken and turned to find herself looking at Chloe and the gentleman she had been dancing with earlier.

'This is Mr Hal Beverley,' Chloe said. 'He says that he does not know anyone else here this evening, and as he cannot dance with me all the time, I suggested that he dance with you, Jo.'

'Miss Horne,' Hal said and grinned as she made him a little curtsy, a hint of mischief in her face. 'Will you take pity on me for this dance? I find myself a stranger here, apart from Chloe and Mrs Marsham.'

'Oh…' Unaccountably, Jo's heart fluttered. 'Yes, of course. How kind of you, sir.' She gave him her hand, allowing him to lead her out on to the floor. Chloe was following with another partner—a rather dashing young man in a scarlet uniform.

'I do not think it particularly kind,' Hal said, his eyes quizzing her. 'It is odd that I should know so few of the company here this evening—but I believe that at this time of year mothers bring their youngest daughters for a taste of social life, before they have their first Season in town.'

Looking up at him, Jo surprised laughter in his eyes. 'You are perhaps used to more sophisticated company in London, sir? I dare say the company in Bath is a little slow for your taste.'

'Perhaps,' he agreed, but his bold look mocked her. 'I was fortunate that Chloe had a friend or I should have had to sit this dance out.'

'Oh, I think you might have found someone willing to introduce you to some of the other young ladies, sir.'

'Yes, but I am not sure that I wish to dance with any of the other young ladies here, Miss Horne.' He was giving her one of his wicked smiles again!

Jo hid her amusement and gave him a straight look. 'I cannot think why, for there are some very pretty girls here tonight.'

'Indeed, you are right. I would not doubt it for a moment.'

'Then why—?' She shook her head, her eyes sparkling. 'No, do not answer, for I am sure I should not have asked.'

Hal chuckled. 'I see no reason why not,' he said. 'I do not know why it should be, but I find that very young ladies either talk endlessly about nothing of consequence or say nothing at all—and I am not sure which is more tedious.'

'Pray tell me which category I belong to,' Jo said, her chin up. 'Then I may amend my behaviour.'

'Oh, I do not think that you belong to either,' Hal told her, a teasing glint in his eye. 'Indeed, my experience tells me that it cannot be so, for we are already acquainted, are we not?'

'You mean because I almost trod on your toes earlier today? Or perhaps because you came to my rescue at the inn?' She was deliberately provoking. 'And, of course, we met again this afternoon…'

'Yes, so we did,' he agreed, matching her for wickedness. 'Who knows, Miss Horne, we may be destined to meet wherever we go, like ghostly spirits passing in the night. Are you truly Miss Josephine Horne or but an apparition, a sprite sent here to tempt men to destruction? I believe it is the latter, for you have a touch of mystery that intrigues me.'

'I think you are a terrible flirt, sir, and talk a great deal of nonsense!' Jo could hardly keep from laughing.

'Indeed, my father would agree with you,' Hal replied, mock solemn. 'But it seems that we are destined to meet for another reason—but not one that we ought to discuss this evening.'

Jo was puzzled. 'I am afraid that I do not understand you, sir.'

'Why should you?' He smiled enigmatically as their dance came to an end. 'Alas, I cannot say more this evening. I must thank you for the pleasure of your company. I should take you back to your friends, and then I must leave.'

'Are you leaving so soon?' She felt a pang of disappointment, for he had brought a touch of magic to the evening that had been lacking before his arrival.

'I have another appointment,' Hal said, his mouth quirking irreverently. 'But I hope that we shall meet again soon, Miss Horne…if you are Miss Horne, and not a siren sent to lure my ship to the rocks.'

Jo inclined her head, but made no comment as he led her back to where her aunt was standing with Mrs Marsham and two other ladies. She thanked him, watching thoughtfully as he walked from the room.

Chloe came back to join them. 'Has Mr Beverley gone already?' she said looking disappointed. 'We danced the first two dances, but I had hoped we might dance again later.'

'I believe he had another appointment,' Jo said. 'But he must have come simply to dance with you, Chloe.'

'Oh…' Chloe blushed and looked pleased. 'Yes, perhaps he did.'

Jo understood that she had hopes of Mr Beverley asking her to marry him. She knew nothing about him other than that he seemed to have an irreverent sense of humour, which she liked, and was extremely attractive. She supposed he must come from a good family, though she did not like to ask.

It had crossed her mind that he might be in some way related to Ellen's late husband, but naturally she had not asked him. He might consider it impertinent, and, besides, she knew that Ellen did not wish it to be known that she was at present residing in Bath. However, she would ask Ellen when she next saw her if Mr Hal Beverley was in anyway related, for it seemed to her that if it were so he might do something to help her.

Lady Wainwright had decided that bathing had done her a great deal of good and she graciously told Jo that she might leave her after they had reached the Baths and go to the library or visit friends.

'But on no account are you to be late for tea, Jo. I shall be most displeased if you let me down again. I cannot help you to make friends if you behave in such a shockingly careless manner.'

'I know that it was very bad of me,' Jo admitted. 'I promise I shall not be late again.'

After leaving her aunt, she went first to the little teashop and bought some peppermint creams, which were packed in a pretty little box and tied with ribbon. Jo visited the library next and took out two books, one a novel and one on embroidery that she thought Ellen might like to see. She had also bought a smaller box of violet creams as a little gift for her friend, and was feeling pleased with herself as she made her way to Mrs Beverley's lodgings.

As she reached the top of the slope leading to the house, a gentleman came out of Ellen's house and turned away in the opposite direction. Jo stood watching him for a moment. She could not be sure, but thought it might have been Mr Hal Beverley. Perhaps he had discovered that Ellen was in Bath for himself.

Ellen answered the doorbell almost at once. Jo could tell from the look on her face that something momentous had happened, and she was pleased for her friend.

'Oh, I am so glad you have called,' Ellen told her. 'I have some news to tell you.'

'Exciting news?'

'Yes, I think so. I have just received a visit from my husband's brother Hal. He served in Spain at the same time as Matt, at least for a few months, and we knew each other. He says that he has been looking for me and wants to help me.'

'Oh, Ellen, that is good news,' Jo said. 'Did you not think of asking him for help before this?'

'No, for why should he take on the burden of my expenses?' Ellen said. 'I dare say I might have approached Lord Beverley if he had not been so set against the marriage, but Hal has his own expenses. I told him that I should be grateful for his help in practical ways, but for the moment I have sufficient funds to pay my way.'

'And what did he say to that?' Jo frowned, for in her opinion Mr Beverley should have ignored Ellen's scruples and given her a handsome present so that she had no need to work so hard.

'He said that I was to think of him as a friend and as my husband's brother. He was angry that his father had done nothing for me, and indeed, he says that he regrets it, but we must keep our meetings a secret for the moment, because Lord Beverley might be angry or upset by them. I believe his father might disown him as he did Matt, and it is very brave of Hal to risk so much for my sake.'

'Lord Beverley sounds disagreeable,' Jo said and pulled a face. 'I think it was very unfair of him to disown his son— and to treat you so harshly.'

'Hal was angry about it, but says that his father has been unwell for some months and because of that he does not wish to quarrel with him. He has independent means and does not care so much for the estate—but he does care for his father.'

'Yes, I see,' Jo said and looked thoughtful. 'I do not like Aunt Wainwright very much, but I must admit that I should not want to see her ill—and I should be distressed if I were the cause of that illness.'

'I understand his feelings completely,' Ellen said. 'Matt always hoped that he might settle his differences with his father one day. Hal is very good to search for me, and I should turn to him if I needed help, but I prefer not to accept charity unless I need it. I shall continue to use my married name to which I am entitled, but I shall not mention the connection to Lord Beverley—and the name is otherwise common enough.' She smiled at Jo. 'Have you come to take your nuncheon with me?'

'I must not be late for tea this afternoon. My aunt scolded me yesterday. I do not mind that—but she is paying for my visit here and she bought me some very nice clothes, so I must not disoblige her.'

'Well, we shall eat a light nuncheon and then you may leave,' Ellen said. 'I want you to look at some embroidery I am doing for a client. She saw some of my work at a fashionable shop in town and asked for me to work on her ballgown. She will be eighteen next month and is to have a special dance, I am told.'

Jo looked at a panel of exquisite embroidery that Ellen was working on, feeling amazed at both the beauty and intricacy of the design and the skilled workmanship.

'Oh, this is wonderful,' she said. 'You are so clever, Ellen. Who taught you to do something like this?'

'I am self-taught,' Ellen said looking pleased. 'My governess taught me the rudiments of the art, of course, and I begged my father to buy me books about it. He was pleased to do it, for he thought embroidery a ladylike occupation. He would not be so pleased if he knew that I was using my skill to earn my living.'

'It is such a shame that you are estranged from your family,' Jo said. 'Did you make up your mind to write to your mama?'

'Yes, I have written her a few lines,' Ellen confirmed. 'Just to tell her that my husband is dead and that I am with child and quite well. I gave her no forwarding address—and I intend to send my letter today.'

'I am sure she will be relieved to have it,' Jo said and smiled at her. 'I took out a book for you from the library, but I think you are too advanced for it. I shall take it home and study it myself. I am ashamed to say that I could not produce anything even half as fine as this panel.'

Ellen laughed softly. 'I studied for years, Jo. I was not particularly happy at home, for my father is a cold man, and Mama is afraid to displease him. When Matt came into my life it changed so much… I can never regret what I did, even though I lost him too soon.'

'I am glad that you were so happy,' Jo said. 'I have never been sure that real love existed—not the very romantic kind that you read about in books—but Marianne fell in love with her marquis, and you obviously loved your husband very much.'

'Yes, I did,' Ellen said. 'You may think my story tragic, but I would rather have had a year with Matt than a score of years with a man I did not love.'

Jo nodded and looked thoughtful. She was beginning to think that perhaps true love really did happen to the fortunate few.

'Ah, there you are, my dear,' Aunt Wainwright said and gave Jo a nod of approval as she walked into the parlour at half-past two that afternoon. 'I am glad you are back. You must go up and change, put on one of your prettiest gowns and tidy that hair.'

'Yes, Aunt,' Jo said and placed the small box of peppermint creams on the table beside her. 'I have been assured that they are very fresh.'

'But to buy them in a box like that,' her aunt said and frowned. 'So extravagant! A paper twist would have been adequate.'

'I bought them as a gift for you, to thank you for your generosity towards me,' Jo said, giving her a straight look. 'I shall go up and change now.'

'Do not be long. We have a visitor I particularly want you to meet, Jo.'

Jo nodded, but made no reply. She noticed her aunt staring rather oddly at the box of sweets as she left the room.

As she changed out of her walking dress into a silk afternoon gown in a pale green colour, the skirt flounced but otherwise quite plain apart from a sash of darker green, Jo was thinking about what Ellen had told her concerning Hal Beverley. It seemed that he was an exceedingly generous man—as indeed she had known before, for she believed that his offer to buy her sister the singing bird had been genuinely and with no thought of reward.

She thought that of late her wicked earl had stepped out of character, and was becoming a true gentleman, for she could no longer write of him as she had in the past, and must think of a way to redeem him in her novel.

The idea of changing her story so radically entertained her thoughts until she went downstairs. She heard voices coming from her aunt's drawing room and her heart beat rapidly for a moment, wondering if the caller might be Mr Beverley, but as she entered she discovered that their visitor was unknown to her.

'Ah, Jo, my dear, how delightful you look,' Aunt Wainwright said. 'You must come and meet the Reverend Mr Thomas Browne. Sir, this is my niece, Miss Josephine Horne, of whom I have already told you.'

'Mr Browne,' Jo said, coming forward. She held out her hand to him and smiled, for she was prepared to be welcoming to anyone who followed her papa's calling. 'I am very pleased to meet you, sir.'

'And I you, Miss Horne. I am a little acquainted with Lady Wainwright, and when I spoke to her of my difficulty, she was kind enough to say that she thought you might be willing to help.'

'If it is possible,' Jo replied. 'But I am not acquainted with your difficulty, sir—in what way would you like me to help you?'

'Oh, I thought…but no matter. I am holding various fundraising events this coming week, and I need a helper. The lady who was to have performed certain little tasks—helping to make banners, write notices, and assisting with a bring-and-buy stall at the church hall—is unwell and finds herself unable to help as she usually does.'

'Oh, yes, of course I shall be pleased to help you, Mr Browne—if my aunt permits. I must not neglect her, but otherwise I should enjoy being of assistance to you.'

'I have said that you may go in the mornings,' Lady Wainwright told her. 'You know that I have taken up bathing for the sake of my health. I shall not need you until teatime, Jo. You may wish to visit other friends, of course, but I am sure you can spare two or three mornings this coming week.'

'Yes, certainly,' Jo said. She was very accustomed to such tasks and willing to be of service. 'I shall enjoy it, though on

Tuesday mornings I have the debating society, and on Thursdays I visit a friend, as I have today.'

'What friend is that?' Lady Wainwright asked. 'I know it was not Chloe—she was at the Pump Room with her mama and inquired after you.'

'Mrs Ellen Beverley, Aunt. I told you. She is a widow and I went to her aid her when she was unwell. We have become friends.' Jo knew that if she told her aunt that Ellen was related by marriage to Lord Beverley her attitude would change completely, but her friend was determined not to trade on her husband's family and Jo must keep that part of her identity a secret until she was given permission to reveal it.

'Well, as long as you do not spend all your time with her. We are promised to Mrs Marsham and Chloe this evening. You have not forgotten?'

'They are holding a card party,' Jo said. 'I had not forgotten, Aunt.'

'Tomorrow is Friday,' the Reverend Browne said. 'Perhaps you would come to the church hall at ten—if that is not too early for you?'

'No, that will do very well,' Jo said and smiled. She could leave after two or three hours and perhaps call to see Ellen on her way home. 'I shall enjoy helping you, sir. Please tell me something of your good causes—are they here in Bath or elsewhere?'

'I have several causes I feel worthy of my attention,' he replied, giving her a look of approval, for not all young ladies would wish to spend their time helping the poor when they might be enjoying the delights of Bath. 'I support a home for orphaned children in Bath itself, and similar ones in

London—but I also send money to overseas missions, Miss Horne. We must do what we can to educate the heathen and alleviate their ignorance.'

'And their poverty, I hope, sir? Papa told me that the people live in terrible circumstances in some countries, perhaps even worse than in the slums here.'

'Ah, yes, I believe your father was also a man of the church, Miss Horne?'

'Papa was a wonderful man,' Jo said, her eyes lighting up. 'He taught all of us that it is our duty to be charitable and caring towards others—and he said that we must see it as a privilege to help them. I am proud to be his daughter.'

'Ah, yes, a worthy sentiment,' the Reverend Browne said and beamed with pleasure. 'I have seldom met a young woman who thinks as deeply as you have on these matters, Miss Horne. It is a delight to have made your acquaintance.'

'Oh, do not praise me too highly, sir,' Jo said. 'I enjoy helping with these things, and therefore it cannot be held a duty.'

If anything, the Reverend looked more approving. However, he abandoned the subject in favour of others, speaking with some intelligence about the political situation, which was quite troublesome for it seemed certain that there must be yet another war with the French. After thirty minutes he took his leave, touching Jo's hand for a moment as she escorted him to the door and thanking her once again for her promise of help.

'I am only too glad to be of help,' Jo said and meant it sincerely, for she liked doing the kind of task that he had asked of her and had often assisted her papa in much the same way. 'Thank you for calling, sir.'

Jo returned to the drawing room, where her aunt gave her what could only be a look of respect.

'That was very well done,' Lady Wainwright said. 'You showed yourself to be just the sort of gel that a man in his position would wish to know. I am sure that he liked you. If you continue in this way I believe he may make you an offer, for I have it on good authority that he is looking for a wife. It would be just the thing for you, Josephine—and you could hardly expect to look higher. I believe he has a small allowance from his family as well as his stipend, which means he can afford to marry.'

Jo stared at her in disbelief, for her aunt seemed to think that it was a perfect match. 'I hardly know Mr Browne, Aunt. He seems pleasant enough and speaks well of many things, but I am not certain we should suit one another. Indeed, I do not yet know if I wish to marry anyone.'

'That is ridiculous! Every gel must marry. It is expected and the only possible future—unless you wish to remain at home for ever?'

'I should like to be sure that I could be happy in my life, and I do not think that the kind of marriage you envisage would bring me happiness, Aunt. I think that I might find his company tedious if I were obliged to live with him.'

'How can you possibly know that?' her aunt demanded, the familiar look of annoyance returning to her face. 'You said yourself that you do not know him.'

Jo realised her mistake. She could not possibly tell her aunt that she would never marry the Reverend Browne, even if it meant that she remained single all her life. Lady Wainwright would simply become angry, and it made life so uncomfortable. For once it might be better to brush over it as easily as she could. After all, she did not dislike Mr Browne, and he was just the kind of man she had once thought her sister Marianne might have married.

'Yes, as you say, Aunt. I cannot know. We have hardly met and one should be certain about these things, for to marry in a rush would be both unseemly and perhaps foolish—do you not think so?'

Her aunt looked at her suspiciously, for the answer was too measured to be Jo's true sentiments, unless she had changed her ways overnight.

'Do not imagine you can fool me, Josephine. I am merely pointing out a possible chance to you, and one that you would be well advised to consider. You will not get a second chance for a visit like this, and you may grow bored with being at home. Most women prefer their own home—and children. I know that you like children, Jo. How can you content yourself to think that you might never hold your own child in your arms?'

'But what of liking and respect, Aunt? You notice that I do not speak of love, for I am not sure it exists, though Marianne was certainly in love. But one should at least like the man one marries—do you not agree?'

'Yes, of course, and I should never dream of suggesting that you marry a man who was not worthy of your consideration—but I believe Mr Browne is a man that many girls would be glad to marry. Especially those who have no fortune.'

'I expect you are right, Aunt. Would you excuse me now, please? I think that perhaps I should change for the evening.'

Jo went upstairs to her own room. After she had finished dressing, she sat down at her dressing table and looked at her hair. If only it was a pretty honey blonde like Marianne's and straighter!

Picking up her brush, she tugged at the tangled curls, pulling them back and securing the knot at the back of her head with pins, into which she pinned a spray of silk flowers. Tendrils of flame-coloured hair had escaped to curl attractively about her face. She sighed, because she knew that nothing she could do would tame it completely.

What did it matter? Jo fastened her mother's pearls about her throat and applied a dab of cologne to her wrists and behind her ears; the perfume smelled faintly of violets, a very soft delicate scent. Satisfied that she could do no better with her appearance, she went downstairs to wait for her aunt in the parlour. It was a chance to read for a few minutes, which was a treat, because Lady Wainwright did not like to see her with her nose in a book too often. She was just becoming engrossed in the story when she heard the sound of footsteps and looked up to see that her aunt had arrived.

'Reading again?' Lady Wainwright looked annoyed. 'I hope you haven't spoiled your gown sitting there. I do hate to see girls in creased gowns when they arrive for the evening. You should have walked about the room until I came down.'

'I do not think that sitting here has harmed my dress, Aunt.'

'Well, you are fortunate if it has not. Are you ready? It is already past six and we are engaged for half-past.' She looked about her and made a sound of annoyance. 'I have left my fan. Please go upstairs and fetch it for me. It lies on my bed.'

'Yes, Aunt.' She ran upstairs, and found the fan on the dressing chest after some few seconds of searching. Her aunt gave her a hard look when she came back down, but said nothing, taking the fan without a word of thanks.

They went out to the carriage, neither of them speaking to the other during the short ride, Jo because she did not have anything in particular to say, and Lady Wainwright because she was annoyed about something. Jo wasn't sure whether she had caused her aunt's mood or whether it was to do with something quite different, but it was clear to her that the best course of action was to remain silent.

Mrs Marsham had taken one of the larger houses in Bath, but her rooms were already overflowing with guests when they arrived. Jo was surprised for she had expected a small card party, but she soon discovered that cards were to be only a part of the evening's entertainment. A quartet was playing music as they entered, and Chloe told her that one of the drawing rooms had been cleared so that the younger people could dance.

'There is room for no more than ten couples,' Chloe said, her eyes glowing. 'But the older ladies do not dance and will content themselves playing cards or simply listening to the music.'

'I am not sure that I am dressed for dancing,' Jo said, because she was wearing a very simple evening gown. 'I did not expect it.'

'Oh, but you look very nice,' Chloe said. 'You always do—though I think it is a shame that you scrape your hair back so tightly. Do you never think of wearing it in a softer style?'

'Never! I should look like a gypsy,' Jo said and Chloe went into a fit of the giggles.

'Oh, you do say such droll things, Jo!' she cried. 'A gypsy, indeed. Mama would have a fit if I were to say such a thing.'

'But you always look so elegant,' Jo said and Chloe gave a pleased nod of her head.

Chloe had only waited for Jo to arrive. Her mother had released her almost at once, and the two girls went into the long room together. Jo saw that several young men she had met at the Assembly rooms were present, including Mr Tanner, and it was not long before both girls were dancing. Surprisingly, Jo found that she was sought after almost as eagerly as Chloe, and she did not sit out one dance, which might have been because Mrs Marsham had cleverly invited more gentlemen than young ladies.

It was not until an hour later that Jo felt a tap on her shoulder and turned to find herself looking at Mr Hal Beverley. She had not noticed him come in, because she had been enjoying herself, and her eyes were bright with laughter.

'Good evening, Mr Beverley,' she said. 'Chloe did not tell me that she expected you this evening.'

'Did she not, Miss Horne?' Hal's brows rose. 'Now why should that be, I wonder? For it must be an object of great public interest if I am to attend a card party, must it not? Indeed, had I thought, I should have had a blast of horns announce me.'

'You are a wicked tease, sir,' Jo said. 'You knew very well what I meant.'

'Did I?' His eyes gleamed with unholy amusement. 'Pray give me the pleasure of this next dance, Miss Horne—unless it is promised to another?'

'No, it is not,' Jo replied. She had planned to slip away to find herself a cooling drink, but could not give up the opportunity to dance with him. 'Oh, listen, I believe this is a waltz.'

'Yes, so I believe,' Harry said and gave her his hand. 'I trust you are a lady of your word, Miss Horne? You will not refuse?' His eyes quizzed her. 'Perhaps you are but an illusion and will disappear in a puff of smoke rather than waltz with me.'

'I… No, of course not,' Jo said. She was a little unsure, because the waltz was not yet thoroughly approved of everywhere, though she had heard that it was no longer frowned on at most venues and was certainly allowed at private parties. 'Yes, Mr Beverley, I should love to dance the waltz with you.'

Her heart fluttered as he placed his hand at the small of her waist, and she looked up at him, her eyes widening as she saw the challenge in his eyes.

'Why do you look at me that way, sir?'

'Because I am waiting,' Hal said. 'Most young ladies would have come out with it at once, but then, as I have observed before, you are different from most young ladies of my acquaintance.'

'Are you speaking of Ellen?' Jo asked.

Oh, he danced divinely! She had not realised that a waltz could be this much pleasure. She felt as if she were floating on air, the music filling her soul as she followed his lead effortlessly, their steps perfectly in tune.

'Ellen informs me that you have become her friend.'

'I believe we are friends,' Jo replied. 'She tells me that you have been kind enough to offer her help should she need it.'

'I would do more if she would permit it.'

'Yes, I know…' Jo smiled. At this moment she felt as if she were filled to the brim with content and happiness. 'Ellen is proud and does not wish for assistance. But she works very hard, and I am not sure it is good for her in her condition.'

'No, I am very sure you are right. I shall do what I can for her.'

'She would not accept anything she saw as charity.'

'It would not be charity. She and my brother's child are entitled to a decent life, and I wish that she would allow me to help her with her expenses.'

'I think you must be clever in how you offer help.'

'Yes, I am sure you are right. I must think of something, for at the moment she will not let me help her.'

The music was coming to an end. Jo found herself wishing that it might go on for much longer, but she knew that she must be satisfied with the one dance, for it was unlikely that he would ask her again.

'Perhaps she will when she needs you,' Jo said, as the other dancers began to leave the floor. 'I believe it may be time for supper, sir. Yes, I see that everyone is making a move in that direction.'

'Are you hungry?' Hal asked, and Jo shook her head. 'Come out into the conservatory for a moment or two. I should like to speak to you further on this matter.'

'I…' Jo was about to say that she was not sure if she ought to do that when she saw Chloe coming towards them. 'Perhaps another time. I may call on Ellen at something after noon tomorrow.'

'Oh, there you are, Jo,' Chloe said, but her eyes were on Hal. 'Are you coming into supper with me?'

'Yes, I was just about to,' Jo said, and looked at Hal. 'Shall you join us, sir?'

'Yes, of course, why not?' he replied. 'It shall be my pleasure to look after both of you. The two prettiest girls here this evening—what a damned lucky fellow I am!'

Jo smiled and shook her head, but Chloe had slipped her arm through his. She knew that his compliment was for Chloe, but he was being gallant, of which she approved. It was due to Chloe's efforts on Jo's behalf that she had not sat out one dance that evening. All the young gentlemen were happy to oblige Chloe. If a small voice told her that she had only chosen Jo as her special friend because she did not wish for competition, she ignored it.

'You are a determined flirt, Mr Beverley,' Chloe told him, eyes sparkling. 'I do not think you deserve us, but you may fetch our supper to prove that you were not merely mocking us.'

'How could you think such a thing of me?' Hal replied and turned to look at Jo with an expression of innocent appeal. 'Miss Horne knows that I mean everything I say—do you not? Please support me against this tyrant, Miss Horne.'

Jo merely smiled and shook her head, for it was obvious that they were comfortable together, and she would not be surprised if they were to make a match of it. She was almost certain it was in Chloe's mind to accept him if he made an offer—but would he? Jo had no way of guessing what was in his mind. He was a charming companion, and she liked him, but she did not know him well enough to have formed an opinion of his character.

If Jo's thoughts were in some confusion, it was as well that she could not know or even guess at what Hal was thinking. She would doubtless have been shocked to know that his thoughts were in turmoil, and his plans for the future had been turned upside down.

Hal's mind had been more or less made up before he came down to Bath. He would find Ellen, set her up in a decent house with enough money to allow her to live in comfort, if not luxury, and then ask Chloe Marsham to marry him. He had hoped that when his brother's child was born, Lord Beverley would accept his grandchild and then perhaps Ellen would be given the attention and consequence she deserved. His plan had gone sadly wrong, for Ellen had stubbornly refused his help with her finances, and he was no longer sure that he wished to marry Chloe.

He was not precisely sure why he had changed his mind—or, indeed, if he *had* changed his mind. Chloe was very lovely and she was a nice girl, just the sort of wife his father would approve. Harry had previously decided that she was the one he would feel most comfortable with of all the suitable young ladies he had met since his return from the army, but now he was wavering, and he was not certain why.

It could not possibly be anything to do with Chloe's friend…could it? Hal wrinkled his brow as he discarded his cravat. The hour was late, but he was not in the least tired. In London he would probably have gone on to his club from the Marshams' card party, but although he was acquainted with most of the gentlemen staying in Bath at present, none of them was his particular friend.

He thought about his old friend, Drew Marlbeck, feeling regretful that he had not answered his recent call to help capture the traitor who had betrayed so many of their friends in Spain. At that time he had been following a lead that had taken him to Amsterdam and which had turned out to be completely wrong. He had visited Drew in Truro before leaving, and on his return from abroad sent him and his new wife a wedding gift, though he had not gone down to the wedding, because his father had had one of his turns just as he was about to leave. By the time he had recovered, the Marquis and Marchioness had departed on their honeymoon.

He wondered if Drew ever thought about the old times. There had been a special companionship between the men out there…a bond that only shared grief and the knowledge that death hovered at one's shoulder could forge. Hal sighed. There was little point in repining, for he had made his decision when he sold out. Lord Beverley's health was uncertain, which was why Hal was doing his best to keep his quest for Ellen a secret. He knew that his father felt that Matt had let him down, and he had wanted to make things right by marrying well and giving his father an heir. It was his duty to do just that, but somehow it wasn't proving as easy as he had imagined.

Why? Hal was damned if he knew. It could not be because of Miss Horne, could it? She had remarkable eyes and he liked her straight way of talking, but she wasn't beautiful…at least in the conventional sense, though there was something about her. Hal sat in a high-backed chair by the window and looked out at the night sky, which was sprinkled with stars. Josephine Horne was a respectable girl with good connections, but he sensed instinctively that she would not be his father's choice of a bride. Lord Beverley expected him to marry an heiress of good family and would take some persuading if he were to suggest a match with the daughter of a parson.

Did he wish it himself? Damn it, what on earth was he thinking? Hal smiled ruefully. He hardly knew the girl whereas he had known Chloe slightly for some years, because her parents were cousins to their nearest neighbours at Beverley, and, although not close friends, at least on nodding terms with his father. He had not taken much notice of her as a child, but they had met a few times at small gatherings since his return from the army, and he did like her. He believed Chloe would be a comfortable wife, and she was certainly beautiful—so why had he dragged his feet? He believed that she would accept an offer from him, and if he were able to tell his father the good news, he might also be able to break it to him that Ellen was having Matt's child.

It was the sensible thing to do. He knew that he owed his father the surety of a grandchild, and he must not delay his decision for too long, because Chloe was an heiress and would probably receive an offer very soon. She might decide to wait until after her Season next spring, of course— but her mother would possibly agree to an engagement and a wedding next summer.

'Damnation!' Hal knew that he would never sleep a wink with this on his mind. He needed a drink…

Jo spent a very happy morning helping out at the church hall the next day. She had found several companions of like minds, young women who found pleasure in helping others, and in the friendship that could be found at such affairs. They painted banners to hang at the sale and wrote out neat price tickets, sorted through piles of unwanted items that people had given and helped to set up stalls ready for the bazaar the following weekend.

'Would you be kind enough to help at the sale itself, Miss Horne?' Mrs Henderson asked. She was a young matron of perhaps five and twenty, with two small children, who were at home with their nursemaid. 'We need someone to serve at the stall selling cakes and homemade sweetmeats.'

'Yes, of course, providing my aunt can spare me that day,' Jo said. 'What hours would you need me?'

'Oh, from just before noon until perhaps five,' the woman said. 'I shall be working on it myself, but we are usually very busy.'

'Then I shall ask my aunt and let you know next time I come—which will be on Monday, I think?'

'Yes, we are to meet here again on Monday,' Mrs Henderson replied with a smile. 'I dare say your aunt may spare you for once, my dear.'

Jo said that she hoped so and took her leave. She walked swiftly in the direction of Ellen's lodgings, not bothering to linger over shop windows. However, as she neared the end of the street, she saw Hal Beverley coming towards her. He smiled as he saw her, lifting his smart beaver hat and smiling as they met.

'Good morning, Miss Horne. I trust you are well?'

'Yes, sir, thank you.' Jo's heartbeat quickened, because his quizzing smile was so appealing. She thought that, of all the gentlemen she had met in Bath, he was the one she liked best. He was undoubtedly a tease and a flirt, and it would be foolish to take him seriously, but she liked him very well.

'It is a beautiful day, is it not, Miss Horne?'

'Yes, though the wind may be a little chilly.'

'What does a chill wind matter in the company of an enchanting young lady?'

'Sir, I think you like to tease for devilment.'

'Indeed, I do, Miss Horne—but only when the company is this charming.'

'You are wicked, sir!'

'You are right to chastise me. It is a fault.' His eyes were warm with amusement. 'Are you not shopping today?'

'I am on my way to visit a friend. Perhaps the same one as you have been visiting?'

'Indeed? Yes, it may be if you speak of Ellen. I called to see her for a few minutes and she said she hoped to see you later. I must not delay you, for I know she looks forward to your visit. Perhaps we shall meet again this evening?'

'Yes, perhaps.' Jo smiled, her heart beating rapidly as she walked on. She hoped that she would see him again soon, for he was a very pleasant young man. Arriving at Ellen's lodgings, she rang the bell firmly, waiting until her friend answered the door and invited her in.

'I was wondering whether you might come,' Ellen said, looking pleased. 'I hoped you might, because I wanted to tell you that I have sent the letter to my mother. Just to let her know that I am well.'

'I am sure that is all she needs to know,' Jo said. She considered Ellen, who was not as pale as she had been the first time they met. 'Are you feeling better now?'

'Oh, yes, I keep quite well most of the time,' Ellen said and placed a hand on her bump, smiling contentedly. 'It is a comfort to know that I have at least two friends now. Hal was here a few minutes ago.'

'Yes, I met him on my way here. It must be better, knowing that your husband's brother is there if you need him.' Jo followed her into the small but comfortable parlour. Ellen had been working at her embroidery and a panel of blue silk lay on the sofa. She moved it to one side and sat down.

'Hal was always a little wild when we were in Spain,' Ellen

said and laughed softly. 'Matt used to say he was the maddest prankster of them all—but they were good friends, and I am grateful that he took the trouble to look for me. He has even been as far as Amsterdam in his search, though I was never there, of course. It is odd how these tales get about, is it not?'

'Mr Beverley seems very pleasant,' Jo said thoughtfully. 'We met last evening at a friend's house, and he asked me to dance a waltz with him. He dances very well.'

'Oh, yes, all Old Hooky's favourite officers did,' Ellen said with a wistful expression in her eyes. 'They were an elite corps, Jo—young and dashing, brave and clever. The very best of the English aristocrats, a breed apart, I think. We had some good times as well as the bad ones.'

'You must miss all your friends?'

'Yes, I do,' Ellen agreed. 'I was lonely until I met you—and then, on the same day, Hal came, and I am not lonely any more.'

'But it is so unfair that you have had to fend for yourself,' Jo said, a flash of anger in her eyes. 'Lord Beverley should be ashamed of himself. If your child is a boy, he will be the heir to the estate.'

'Yes, in law, perhaps,' Ellen said, 'for I believe the estate was entailed—but I should never demand my rights. Besides, Hal told me that his father's health is uncertain. He has not told him that he was looking for me, nor will he tell him that he has found me—at least until the baby is born. He thinks that a grandchild may mellow Lord Beverley, and if Hal makes the kind of marriage his father asks of him…'

'Yes, I see,' Jo said. 'I suppose Lord Beverly will expect him to marry an heiress or the daughter of landed gentry?'

'Oh, yes, I imagine so. My grandfather was in trade,

though Father had bought land and was what they call a warm man—but that was not enough for him.' Ellen looked sad. 'I know it hurt Matt to be estranged from his father, but it was Lord Beverley's own fault.'

'Yes, indeed it was,' Jo agreed. 'Well, we must hope that he will relent in time, because it would be so much nicer for you to have your own home and enough money to live on.'

'Hal has offered that,' Ellen told her. 'But I have refused him, at least for the moment. If I cannot manage, I shall ask for help. It may be more difficult to work when I have a child.'

'Yes, I expect so,' Jo said. She sipped her tea. 'I have been working with the ladies of the church community. There is to be a bazaar next weekend and I have been asked to help with the preparations, and on the cake stall…though I must ask Aunt Wainwright about that, for she may not allow it.'

Ellen nodded her understanding. 'She may not think it quite proper for her niece, because of course there will be persons of all sorts there on that day, I imagine.'

'If you mean there will be poor folk, ordinary women, working men and their children, I am sure you are right. I always used to help Papa at home—he considered it was good for his daughters to see how other people lived. We were fortunate, because we always had food on the table, and we often gave some of it to beggars who came to our door. He would say that it was my duty to help, but Aunt Wainwright may wish me to accompany her somewhere.'

'Well, you must ask her,' Ellen said and frowned. 'Does she know you visit me here?'

'Oh, yes,' Jo said airily, because she would not offend her friend by telling her she was keeping her visits a secret for the most part. 'I think I should be going now. I shall come again as soon as I—' They heard the doorknocker at that moment and Ellen went to answer it. Jo pulled on her York tan gloves and picked up her reticule. Hearing the voice in the hall, she hesitated, her heart thumping madly of a sudden.

She stood waiting as the door from the hall opened and a gentleman followed Ellen into the small parlour. He looked at her, his eyes quizzing her in that bold way of his and she smiled.

'I was just about to leave, sir,' she said. 'I must not be late back or my aunt will worry.'

'Oh, must you go so soon?' Hal asked and frowned. 'I hope it is not on my account. I had thought of something I wanted to tell Ellen, but I can leave and return later if you have not finished your gossiping.'

'We were not gossiping,' Jo said. She had a feeling that his return was an excuse to see her again, but she told herself she was being foolish. He was almost engaged to Chloe! Besides, he would never think of her in that way. 'It was merely a discussion of the activities concerning the church bazaar next weekend. I have been helping with the preparations.'

'Have you, indeed? How industrious of you,' Hal said, a glimmer of laughter in his eyes. 'Most young ladies would find something more pleasurable to employ their time while in Bath, I imagine.'

'Oh, I have time enough for all I want to do,' Jo told him, a spark of defiance in her eyes. 'I assure you, I prefer to be busy rather than to sit idle—and one meets friends.'

'Yes, I dare say,' Hal said a hint of devilment about him. 'Tell me, Miss Horne—are you given to good works?'

'Papa taught us to consider others,' Jo said. 'Marianne and

I used to make lots of clothes for the poor children in our village. There were always offcuts that could be used for something, and she was a marvel at cutting a pattern from the odd bits of cloth. We wasted nothing at the Vicarage.'

'The Vicarage…yes, your father was a parson, I believe.' Hal frowned, looking at her thoughtfully. Her name had seemed oddly familiar from the first. Something had been hovering at the back of his mind, but he had not put two and two together until this moment. 'Drew married a girl called Marianne Horne and *her* father was a parson…' He stared at her incredulously. 'Can it be? I recall that you told me your elder sister had been recently married…did she by chance marry Drew Marlbeck?'

'Yes? Why do you ask?' Jo stared at him in bewilderment.

'Drew is a friend,' Hal said. 'He sent me an invitation and I should have been at the wedding had my father not been taken ill at that time.'

'Oh…' Jo nodded '…how odd that we should meet in Bath—but there, it is a small world, they say. I am sorry your father was ill. Is he recovered now?'

'He is very much better than he was, of course, but his health is not good. I believe it may be his heart, though he speaks of his illness as a slight turn and dislikes a fuss.'

'That is a worry for you,' Jo said. She wrinkled her smooth brow. 'Do you not think it might be a comfort to him to know that Ellen is to have your brother's child, sir?'

'It might,' Hal agreed. 'If broken to him gently, it might well give him something to live for…but I think it best to keep it a secret until the child is born.'

'I do not see why,' Jo said, anxious to defend what she saw

as Ellen's rights. 'Surely any right-thinking man would want to help his son's widow at such a time? Indeed, it must be his duty to his son's wife and unborn child—do you not agree?'

'Please do not,' Ellen said and threw her a look of appeal. 'I have no intention of approaching Lord Beverley for anything. I shall manage very well as I am—but if he wishes to see his grandchild when he or she is born, he will always be welcome in my home.'

'I believe he may relent when he sees the babe,' Hal said, but looked thoughtful. 'It is not right that Ellen should still be working in her condition, but I am here if she needs me.'

'Well, I must leave,' Jo said, reluctantly tearing herself away. 'I dare say you have things to discuss. No, do not come to the door with me, Ellen. I can see myself out.'

'Then I shall accompany you, Miss Horne. For I may return later to speak to Ellen.'

Jo looked at him uncertainly, but he seemed determined to accompany her. They walked in silence for a moment.

'I mean to call at the library, sir. I do not think that you can wish to visit it yourself.'

'Do you not think me bookish?' His eyes quizzed her. 'You wrong me, Miss Horne. I can sometimes sit for an hour or so at a time with a good book.'

'Indeed? As long as that? You surprise me, sir.'

'Now *you* are teasing *me*, Miss Horne.'

'Yes, I am—do you mind?'

'Mind?' Hal smiled oddly. If he were to tell her what was in his mind at that moment, she might be shocked. 'It delights me, Miss Horne. It seems that you are full of surprises. But we are at the library and I shall leave you here for the moment.'

Jo gave him her hand. He raised it to his lips to kiss it. Her heart raced, and she turned away, her cheeks flushing to go into the library.

Jo walked home swiftly afterwards. The day had fled again, and she would be back only just in time to change for tea.

Chapter Three

The next few days were busy ones for Jo, because she suddenly found that she was in demand; taken up by Chloe, she had been noticed by several indulgent mamas who thought that she was a pleasant girl and no threat to their prettier daughters. It meant that she was invited to go walking and shopping, and to take tea, sometimes with Lady Wainwright and sometimes without her. She particularly enjoyed her debating society and being able to visit the library whenever she wished, but Ellen was still the friend she liked the best.

However, Jo found that every part of her day was spoken for and it was not until the following Thursday when she received a note from Ellen that she managed to slip away to visit her.

'Oh, Jo,' Ellen said as soon as she had admitted her to the house, 'I am so glad that you came today. I have had a letter from my mama. She says that my father has had agents searching for me since my letter reached her. Apparently, he was able to discover that it had been sent from Bath and then it was an easy matter to trace where I was living. She says that he has asked her to write and tell me to return. He is prepared to give me a home, providing I behave properly in future.'

Jo was stunned for she had never expected this. 'How could he have discovered where the letter was sent from?' she asked. 'You did not give her your address?'

'No, of course not,' Ellen said. 'The letter was franked when I took it to the receiving office. I suppose it must have carried the word Bath or some such thing in the official stamp…and my father sent his agents to look for me here.' She gave a little sob of despair. 'What shall I do? If I write and refuse, he may come here himself and force me to return home.'

'Would that be such a terrible thing?' Jo wrinkled her brow.

'Yes, it would, because my father is so very strict, Jo. You have no idea how unkind he can be when he wishes.' Ellen's face was pale, her eyes anxious. 'Mama would not be unkind, but she dare not stand up to him, and he says that I am not married in the eyes of God. He believes that I lived in sin with Matt, and that my child is a bastard. I know that he would not let me keep it and shame him. He would hide me somehow until the baby was born, and then give my child away to some worthy person to care for. I should never be allowed to see my baby. It would be like living in prison after the life I have led here and with Matt. I was so happy then. I cannot bear to return to my old life.'

'Oh, that is too cruel!' Jo said and looked at her in horror. 'Is he really so very unfeeling, Ellen?'

'Yes. It is the reason I did not go home after Matt died. I would rather scrub floors than live in his house again!'

'Then you must not,' Jo said. 'You must go away some-where that he cannot find you. I am sorry, Ellen. I should never have persuaded you to write to your mama. I did not think that he could trace it back to you so easily.'

'Nor did I—but I suppose I should have known that it might be possible.' Ellen looked anxious. 'I think I must go away, but I am not sure where—and it is so difficult. I have a piece of work that will not be finished until Monday, and I must finish it, for I shall need whatever money I have to support myself. I have done well here and it may not be as easy to find work elsewhere. If I spoke to Hal, he might have some idea of where I could best find a refuge, and if he took me in his curricle it would be much better, because I cannot afford to spend money on travelling.'

'Yes, you must do so,' Jo agreed. 'I may see him this evening because we go to a private dance and I believe he is to attend. Chloe is to be there and he seems to attend most affairs at which she is present. I shall speak to him and hear what he thinks about this affair.' She gave Ellen a look of apology. 'I feel that I am to blame for this, because I encour-aged you to write to your mama.'

'I should not have done so had I not wished to set her mind at rest. I did not think she would show him the letter, but ap-parently he saw it first and she was allowed to read it only after he had opened it himself.'

'What beasts men are!' Jo exclaimed. 'I have always said that I shall not marry and what you have just told me makes me more certain that I was right to make that decision.'

'But it was not like that for me with Matt,' Ellen said. 'It is just that one must be very careful what kind of man one marries.'

'Yes, you are very right,' Jo said. 'Well, I must fly, for I have an appointment this afternoon. But I shall try to speak to Mr Beverley this evening, and I shall visit you tomorrow if I can, but without fail on Saturday, even if I have to make some excuse to Mrs Henderson and leave the bazaar early.'

'You are a good friend,' Ellen said and took her hand. 'Thank you for being here, Jo. It makes things easier just to talk to someone who understands.'

Jo was thoughtful as she left her friend's lodgings and walked back to the house in Queen's Square. Ellen was very brave, but she was in some danger. Her father was a cruel man who would not spare his daughter. She could not be allowed to return to his house! Somehow they must get her away to safety.

She was thinking of Mr Beverley, Jo realised. She met him almost everywhere she went these days. It was because she was always in Chloe's company, of course, and he was one of the little court that clustered about her. She did not think he had spoken to Chloe yet, but it seemed obvious that it was his intention. However, she believed that he would do what he could to help Ellen despite his own plans.

What part she could play in all this, Jo was not yet certain. She wished that she could help her friend, but in truth she had only a few more days in Bath and then it would be time to return home.

Jo's brow wrinkled as an idea occurred to her. It was a very bold plan, and quite shocking—but she felt that her papa might just have approved.

So lost was she in her thoughts that she did not see the gentleman staring at her from across the street. Nor did she realise that he was following her as she walked home.

* * *

Carstairs watched as the little witch went into the house, an unpleasant smile on his lips. He had not thought to see her again, but here she was and it seemed that he was in luck. If it was her habit to walk out alone he would make it his business to meet her one day, and then they would see.

Hal Beverley had interfered the last time, but next time he would make sure that the girl was alone. She was not the most beautiful girl he had ever seen, but there was something about her that had stuck, haunting him.

She was undoubtedly of a respectable family, as Beverley had insisted, but that mattered little to Carstairs. He and his cronies had abducted more than one girl of good family. He would have to be careful, of course, because he could not afford a scandal. His debts had been mounting steadily since he sold out of the army, for he had been drinking and gambling carelessly. If the girl had a fortune he might even marry her—but if she had not…

Carstairs grinned at the thought of the pleasure it would give him to bed her, with or without her consent. For him the pleasure was all in the chase, in the moment of conquering— after that she could go to the devil for all he cared.

'Ah, there you are,' Lady Wainwright said when Jo walked into the house. Her expression was one of frosty disapproval. 'I have been hearing something that disturbs me, Josephine.'

'I am sorry for that, Aunt,' Jo said, a sinking feeling inside. What had she done now? 'Is it something that concerns me?'

'Of course it concerns you. Who else should it concern?' Lady Wainwright scowled at her. 'I have been told that you are in the habit of visiting a woman—a widow of uncertain reputation.'

'Do you mean Ellen? I do assure you that she is perfectly respectable, Aunt. Her husband was killed while in the army and she is forced to support herself.'

'She says that she is a widow,' Lady Wainwright said waspishly. 'But you have only her word for that—and gentlemen have been seen leaving her rooms. I think she is not decent and you should not know her. Indeed, I am forbidding you to visit her again.'

'You cannot do that,' Jo cried, holding on to her temper by a slender thread. 'Ellen is my friend and she is perfectly respectable, whatever your informer says. The only gentleman who visits her to my knowledge is her husband's brother.'

'Indeed? How would you know such a thing?' Lady Wainwright said. 'You cannot know what goes on when you are not visiting her and I have it on good authority that she has gentlemen callers. You will please do as I ask and strike her from your list of acquaintances, Josephine. If you refuse, I shall have no alternative but to cut this visit short and send you home to your mama in disgrace. I know that she had high hopes for you. Do you wish to disappoint her?'

'No, Aunt, of course not.' Jo hesitated, the words trembling on her lips. She wanted to defend her friend against the wicked slander that had been levelled at her, but knew that she must not. Hal Beverley had told her why he wanted to keep his sister-in-law's true identity a secret until the child was born. If rumours reached his father's ears it might do untold harm, and Jo had no right to go against his wishes.

'Very well,' Lady Wainwright said. 'I shall let the visit

continue as long as I have your promise that you will cease to visit this wretched woman?'

'You must know that I would never willingly do anything to distress Mama,' Jo said. 'So for the moment I must do as you ask, though I cannot give my word that I shall never see her again, for we might meet in the street and I should be loath to cut her.'

'You may acknowledge her if you meet,' Lady Wainwright said. 'But there are to be no more visits to her house.'

'As you say, Aunt.'

Jo escaped and went up to her room to change for the evening. She had not exactly promised to stop visiting Ellen, though her aunt thought it—but she would not go to the house for the moment. She would send a note and ask Ellen to meet her at the library.

It was so unkind of Lady Wainwright to say that she must stop visiting her friend, and especially when Jo knew that Ellen was distressed about the possibility of being forced to return home by her father. Jo decided that she would not give in to her aunt's bullying, even if it meant that she must deceive her.

Lady Wainwright maintained a cool silence as they were driven to the house where a private dance was being held that evening. However, her manner became several degrees warmer when they met Mrs Marsham and Chloe. She greeted them with smiles and gave her gracious permission for the two girls to go off together.

'You look beautiful this evening,' Jo said, admiring Chloe's new gown. It was a pale blue and had a panel of exquisite embroidery at the front of the bodice, which Jo recognised as Ellen's work. For some reason it made her a little cross, because Ellen had worked so hard for very little money and Chloe took it for granted that she should have such expensive clothes. 'That embroidery is very fine.'

'Yes, it is,' Chloe agreed, 'though it is not quite as I ordered it. I wanted more beading. Mama said that we should refuse to pay as it was not exactly as we ordered, but in the end she paid half…and it is not so very bad after all. Indeed, perhaps it would not have looked so well if it had been as I asked.' She looked pleased, as if she was glad that she had obtained the gown for less than its true worth.

'Yet still your mama refused to pay the full price. Do you not think that was a little unfair to the seamstress who laboured so long and hard to make it pretty for you?' Jo could not help thinking of Ellen, who worked such long hours and was too proud to take Hal's money.

'You are so droll sometimes,' Chloe said with a little laugh. However, the laughter did not reach her eyes. 'Really, Jo, everyone does not concern themselves with the fate of the poor. She ought to have done as I asked, and it is her own fault if she was paid less than was promised her.'

Jo felt very angry, but did not say anything more, for it was not the proper place to argue the rights and wrongs of social conscience. Besides, both she and Chloe were asked to dance at that moment, and it was some little time before they met again.

Chloe was still cool towards her, and Jo wondered if something more than their disagreement was on her mind, but once again they were parted by eager partners, and after the dance ended, Jo went to stand near the open door, which led out to the garden. It was dark outside, for the moon was shaded at that moment, but it was dry and not particularly cold. She decided to venture out of the stuffy ballroom if only for a few minutes. Her head had begun to ache and she realised that she was not particularly enjoying herself. She had been asked to dance several times, but Chloe was obviously withdrawn, and Jo had made no other real friends, apart from Ellen, who did not attend such affairs.

'Why so pensive?' a voice asked from just behind her, and she turned, looking up into Hal's face. 'Is something the matter?'

'Have you heard from Ellen?' Jo asked, turning eagerly, for she had been hoping to see him, though did not know if he was expected that evening.

'No. I believe there may be some letters waiting for me at home, but I was in too much of a rush to open them. I have been busy all day and returned to my lodgings only in time to change.'

'Ellen's father knows where she is,' Jo said as she walked out onto the terrace. It was much cooler and she shivered, pulling her thin silk stole around her shoulders. 'Her mother has written to tell her that she must return home at once.'

'She will never do that,' Hal said and frowned. 'I spoke to her father. He is as cold as ice—a harsh disciplinarian. He would make her life a misery. No, she must not allow him to bully her into returning to his house, for he would keep her a prisoner to punish her for running away.'

'Yes, that is what Ellen says,' Jo agreed. 'She wrote to you asking for help. She cannot stay where she is for much longer. She has some work to return on Monday, and after that…'

'She ought to be spirited away somewhere.' Hal nodded, looking thoughtful. It would fit in very well with his own plans if Ellen were to leave Bath. 'But where—that's the point, is it not?'

'Could you not take her to your father's house? Surely he ought to help her in the circumstances?'

'I have told you, I dare not tell him just yet.'

'Surely that is a cowardly attitude,' Jo said, speaking harshly because she was concerned for her friend. 'Your father must wish to know he has the prospect of a grandchild?'

'Yes, perhaps—but I have told you that he has been ill. I had another letter this morning, asking me to visit him. I think he has taken a turn again.'

'Oh, Mr Beverley,' Jo cried because she was in too much distress to think clearly, 'you are afraid to face him with the truth!'

'Are you calling me a coward?' Hal demanded and now he looked angry. 'Had you been a man, I should have taken retribution for that remark!'

'Oh…' Jo looked at him, suddenly aware of where her hasty words had led her. 'No, of course I did not mean that— not as it sounds, sir. No, I do not think you a coward. Forgive me, I spoke thoughtlessly, as I often do. It is a fault in me. I should be more careful.'

Hal glowered down at her, and then suddenly reached out, taking hold of her upper arms. He drew her towards him, lowering his head to kiss her. His kiss was demanding, powerful, as if he meant to punish her for her thoughtless words, and then he drew back and smiled a little strangely.

'Now I have behaved despicably, have I not? Forgive me, Miss Horne. I had no right to do that—but you aroused the beast in me and I reacted in response to feelings that would be better denied.'

Jo shook her head. For a moment she was robbed of the power of speech. She sensed that his kiss had been an angry impulse, and that she had unwittingly forced him to step over an invisible line.

'I think that perhaps it is I who should apologise, sir. I had no right to speak to you that way and am well served for my behaviour.'

'You did so out of concern for Ellen, and I admire that in you,' Hal said. 'But I cannot tell my father just yet. I think the shock might kill him. I have to go home for a few days, but I shall return on Tuesday, or the following day at the latest. You will please tell Ellen to be ready to leave. I shall arrange for a carriage to take her to…' Hal smiled as the solution came to him. 'Yes, I know just the place. She will be comfortable and well hidden. I shall have to arrange for her to have a companion, for the house is a little isolated and I do not wish her to feel abandoned, but that may be arranged when I have her safe. Tell her that she will be picked up on Tuesday afternoon from her lodgings. My driver will know where to take her if I am not back in time.'

'Yes, of course I shall,' Jo said. She gave him a tentative smile. He was generous, and she regretted that she had almost quarrelled with him. 'Thank you for your care of her—and forgive me?'

'I think there is nothing to forgive,' Hal said. He reached out to touch her cheek. 'Ellen is fortunate to have such a friend. I must say farewell now, Miss Horne. I came only to say goodbye to Chloe and her mama—and to you.'

Jo nodded, lifting her head proudly as she gave him her hand. 'We may not see each other again, Mr Beverley. Our visit is over soon and I shall be returning home. I should like to say that it has been a pleasure to know you, sir.'

'Indeed, I shall be sorry for that,' Hal said. He hesitated, then inclined his head. 'Goodbye.'

Jo turned her head to watch as he walked into the ballroom, looking to neither right nor left as he made his way through it and out of the door at the far side. Realising that she was cold, Jo went back into the ballroom. She stood watching the dancers for a moment, and then became aware that someone was staring at her. She turned to see that Chloe was there, her eyes cold and hard, her pretty face tight with anger.

'I saw you,' she hissed. 'How dare you go out there with him like a scheming slut? I thought you were my friend, and I asked Hal to dance with you—I asked all my partners to dance with you and this is how you repay me. You kissed him!'

'No, Chloe, you are mistaken. He kissed me,' Jo said. 'I promise you that I did nothing to encourage it. Indeed, we had quarrelled and I think he meant to punish me. I do not think he likes me very much.'

'Do you think I have not seen him look at you?' Chloe demanded. 'I am not such a fool as to believe you. A man does not kiss a girl to punish her—and you did not slap him or push him away. You are disgraceful and I do not wish to know you.'

Jo watched her unhappily as she walked off, her back straight. She had not wished to quarrel with Chloe, because she knew that her visit to Bath had been very much more pleasant than it might have been—and that was due to Chloe's kindness in taking her up. Now she felt guilty and a little ashamed of her behaviour, for though she had not encouraged Hal Beverley's kiss, her rash words had provoked it.

'Miss Horne,' a man's voice said. 'May I have the pleasure of this dance?'

Jo looked up. She was surprised to see the Reverend Browne, because she had not expected him to be there that evening. 'Thank you, sir, that is very kind,' she said, accepting his hand.

As he led her out to the dance floor, she closed her mind to all that had happened that evening. It would be time enough to think about that later when she was alone.

Jo stared out of the window at the sky. It was cloudless and the moon was waxing full, casting its magical light over the wet pavements. It had rained earlier but now it had stopped, which was a blessing for Jo needed to slip out early in the morning. Her aunt had forbidden her to visit Ellen again, and she had meant to ask her friend to meet her, but things were a little different now. Hal Beverley had given her a message for Ellen, and she ought to deliver it as soon as possible. If Ellen had to be ready to leave by Tuesday, she ought to start packing her things at once.

Mr Beverley had spoken of a companion for Ellen. Jo wondered if she dared to offer herself, just as a temporary arrangement. After all, by Tuesday there would only be a couple of days remaining of their visit to Bath, and it could not affect her aunt so very much if Jo left her. She could send a letter to her mama, and explain some of the situation, enough so that Mama would believe her to be with a friend and safe and not worry.

Yet it was a rather bold act, for it would be thought scandalous if people believed she had run off with a lover— but why should they? She would send her mama a letter and put her mind at rest. Jo knew that she must consider her plan carefully before making up her mind. She would risk losing her reputation, which meant that she might no longer be accepted in polite society. It was a considerable risk— and Jo knew she had to think of the consequences if she did suffer some loss of reputation. She would not be returning to Bath with her aunt, and must settle to the idea of living at home with her mother and Lady Edgeworthy. If there was a little scandal in Bath, it would probably not reach the remote corner of Cornwall where her family was living, and would soon be forgotten if it did. She smothered her doubts, for as yet it was only an idea that she might consider if necessary…

Satisfied that she could do nothing for the moment, Jo went to bed and soon fell deeply asleep, dreaming of a kiss and a man's face…though when she woke again the dream had faded into the mist.

Ralph Carstairs looked moodily into his wineglass as he sat in the corner of the seedy inn, which smelled of sweat and stale ale, but was the best that he could afford. He had seen the little witch in Beverley's arms, kissing him. Damned little prude! Neither of them had noticed him—he had gone out to the garden previously to smoke a cigar in the shrubbery, and left immediately afterwards.

He had wanted to take his pleasure with the girl, but now everything had changed. He had not been close enough to hear what they said, but from the way they looked at each other it seemed obvious that there was something between them—and that was worth thinking about. To abduct and ravish a girl merely for the hell of it was one thing, but if he could punish Beverley for being a self-satisfied devil at the same time that was quite another matter.

It was Captain Matthew Beverley whom he had quarrelled with over a game of cards. Hal's elder brother had accused him of cheating, a crime which could have led to a court martial if he had lived long enough to give evidence—but he had made sure that it would never come to that by arranging for Beverley's horse to be spooked. It had ended better than he had hoped, though he had, in private, been advised by a superior officer that it would be better if he sold his commission, which he had.

Since then his luck had gone from bad to worse, and he was barely running ahead of his creditors. Perhaps there might be a way to take his revenge on Hal and gain some profit from it. For the moment he would watch and wait and see what the future held…

Jo set out early to visit her friend the next morning. She saw a smart curricle being driven at a spanking pace in the direction of the Abbey. As it drew closer, she realised it was being driven by Hal Beverley. He lifted his whip in salute to her, but drove past without stopping his horses.

Jo felt a pang of regret that he was leaving Bath, and wondered if she had offended him the previous evening. After all, she had practically accused him of being cowardly, and that had been unfair of her, because it was perfectly proper of him to be concerned for his father's health. And yet he had kissed her afterwards, and his kiss had seemed to say so much that words could not—but she would be a fool to dwell on it. A kiss was just a kiss to a man of his character.

She frowned, but then put it from her mind as she approached Ellen's house and knocked at the door.

'Oh, thank you for coming so early,' Ellen said when she answered the door to Jo. 'I have been working very hard to complete this panel, because it is for a special customer and Madame wanted it to be perfect. Apparently something I did for her was not quite right last time, and I did not want to disappoint again. I shall take it today and ask for my money. Hal called on me late last night. I have asked for his help, and he is eager to give it, but I do not want to be dependent on him for my living and I hope to continue with my sewing after I leave Bath.'

Jo looked at her intently. She looked pale and there were shadows beneath her eyes. 'Is something wrong, Ellen?'

'Oh, it is nothing…' Ellen sighed and then gave a wry smile. 'No, I must be truthful. I have not been feeling well again—and I feel nervous. I am being watched, Jo, and it frightens me. He stands outside, watching the house, and follows me when I go out. I think my father must have sent him.'

'Is he there now?' Jo went to the window to look out, but could see no one. She turned to look at Ellen. 'You must be very careful, dearest. Hal will return soon and then he will take you away.'

'Yes.' Ellen looked upset. 'I shall be glad to leave Bath now, but I shall miss you, Jo. Sometimes I think that when my child comes I shall die.'

'No! You must not think it!' Jo said. She hesitated, because the cold light of morning had made her realise how much she would be risking, but Ellen looked so distressed that she could not hold back. 'Supposing I were to come with you— live as your companion? At least until after the birth.'

'Jo—you would not?' Ellen stared at her, hope dawning

in her eyes. Jo knew that her sacrifice would be worthwhile, for Ellen had become as another sister to her—and, after all, it was unlikely that she would ever have the chance to marry.

'Yes, Ellen, I shall if you want me,' she said. 'But we must wait until Hal returns and make our plans then.'

Jo ran all the way home. She was afraid that her aunt might have come down and noticed that she was absent, but fortunately no one seemed to have noticed and she was eating her breakfast when Lady Wainwright entered the parlour.

'And what are your plans this morning, Josephine?'

'As you know, I am going to help at the bazaar this afternoon, Aunt,' Jo said. 'But until then I am quite free—if there is anything you wish me to do for you?'

'You are aware that we leave Bath on Wednesday,' Lady Wainwright said. 'I have some library books that need to be returned—and there is a package for me at the apothecary's shop, if you would be kind enough to collect it for me.'

'Of course,' Jo said. 'I also have a book that needs to be returned. I shall fetch it down and go at once.'

'I had hoped that you might have had a suitor by now,' Lady Wainwright said, her gaze narrowed and thoughtful. 'Not that I expected a great match, but you have been unfortunate. There are several very pretty girls in Bath at the moment. However, it may be that Mr Browne will speak. He has told me that he admires you—and that must be hopeful.'

'Yes, Aunt,' Jo said, deciding that silence was best in the circumstances. 'I am sorry to disappoint you.'

'It might have been different…' Lady Wainwright sighed '…but there it is. Mrs Marsham expects an offer for Chloe quite soon, but that is another matter, of course.'

'Yes, she is beautiful,' Jo agreed. 'Forgive me, Aunt, I must go if I am to finish my commissions and reach the church hall on time.'

'Go along with you. Why you are wasting time I don't know!'

Jo held her tongue. She had to endure her aunt's scolding only for three more days and then she could escape with a clear conscience. It would be such an adventure, and she was sure that her dearest mama would understand.

She walked directly to the library, returning her aunt's and her own books, reluctantly forgoing the chance of taking out a book she had been wanting to read, because she might not have time to read and return it.

Walking home, she had experienced the oddest feeling that she was being followed. She turned, looking back nervously. A gentleman was staring at her. For a moment she could not recall where she had seen him before, and then she suddenly realised that he was the man from the inn. The man called Carstairs! She sent him a haughty look and walked on, refusing to quicken her pace or show fear. He would hardly attack her on a busy street! But she would take care for the remainder of her visit to Bath.

As she entered the parlour of the house in Queen's Square, she saw a gentleman standing by the window looking out at the garden. Lady Wainwright gave her a peculiar look and stood up.

'I shall leave you alone, Josephine. Mr Tanner wishes to speak to you.'

'Mr Tanner…' Jo was startled, particularly when he turned to face her and she saw that he was distinctly nervous. 'I am sorry. Have I kept you waiting, sir? I do not think we had an appointment?'

'Oh, no, I called on the chance that you might be in,' he said. He glanced at her face and then away, his cheeks flushed. 'I know that we are only slightly acquainted, Miss Horne—but…well, I like you so much and Miss Marsham told me that you are leaving Bath soon. I wanted to ask if you would allow me to call on you, when you return home.'

'If you are in the area, I am sure Mama would always welcome you,' Jo said, a little puzzled by his words and his manner.

'Oh, no, I mean, of course…' He floundered. 'What I meant to say was…is there any hope for me? I do admire you so very much.'

He was asking her to marry him! It was so unexpected that Jo hardly knew what to say, and then her good nature came to the fore.

'If you are saying that you have formed an attachment, Mr Tanner, you must allow me to thank you for the compliment. I never expected it and I am flattered…no, I am warmed by your kindness, and it is a kindness, sir, for I know that you mean it sincerely. I have enjoyed knowing you and your friendship must mean a great deal, for true friends are precious, are they not? At this moment I have no thought of marriage, but if, one day… I must say no more, for it might mislead you. I cannot give you hope, sir, but I do thank you so very much for your offer.'

He moved forward, emboldened by her smile and her manner. Taking her hand, he lifted it to his lips and kissed the back, holding it for a moment as he looked at her.

'I have heard you say that you are not pretty, Miss Horne—

but I think you beautiful, in nature and form. I knew that it was unlikely that you had formed an attachment for me, but wished to make my offer before you left Bath. You have refused me so kindly that I will say this…if you should ever change your mind, a brief note will fetch me.' He took his calling card from his pocket and presented it to her. 'I shall go now, Miss Horne—but I shall never forget you.'

'Goodbye, Mr Tanner. Thank you so much for calling.'

Jo waited until he had gone, and then ran upstairs to tidy herself. She heard her aunt call to her as she was leaving the house, but did not stay to be scolded. She must hurry or she would be late!

Jo had a wonderful time at the bazaar that afternoon. She enjoyed serving her customers and it was not long before she had sold out, which was a triumph according to Mrs Henderson. Having handed her considerable earnings to that lady, she went in search of something to eat and drink herself, and then saw Ellen come into the hall.

'Oh, am I too late to buy something from you?' she asked. 'I had hoped to see you earlier, but there was a man following me this morning and he stood outside my house for ages. I was frightened, Jo. I thought he might try to grab me and force me to go with him.'

'Was it the same man as before?' Jo asked, because she could see how pale Ellen looked. 'You believe he is your father's agent, don't you?'

'Yes, I do,' Ellen said. Her hand was trembling and it was clear that she was very distressed. 'I know it is only three days before we leave, but I am so nervous. Supposing my father comes himself and demands that I go home with him?'

'Yes, I suppose that is a possibility,' Jo said. Any doubts or concerns she might have felt about the huge step she was taking vanished in her desire to protect the girl she had come to love as a sister. She looked at her anxiously. 'Would you like to leave sooner?'

'Could we?' Ellen looked at her. 'I have a little money, but not much.'

'I have some—and I dare say Mr Beverley would refund our fare. I think we should leave sooner, Ellen. I shall come to your house early on Monday morning with my bags, and I shall book us a passage on the mail coach. I do not think we could afford to go by post chaise.'

'But where shall we go?' Ellen asked. 'Perhaps we ought to wait for Hal to return.'

'It might be too late if this man was sent by your father,' Jo replied and frowned. 'Send a note to Mr Beverley's lodgings, for I am certain he means to return there. Tell him that we have gone to…the White Boar Inn. It is only a short distance from Bath, but respectable. We stopped there for some refreshment on our way here. It is not a busy posting inn, but quiet and out of the way. We may wait there for Mr Beverly to find us.'

'Supposing he does not?'

'Then I shall think of somewhere else,' Jo said. 'My great-aunt might take you in—or…but he will come, I am sure of it.'

'Yes, I am sure he will,' Ellen said. 'I suppose I am being foolish—that man cannot force me to do anything, can he?'

'No, but if he sends for your father, he might—and I dare say the law is on his side.'

'Yes, you are very right,' Ellen said and shivered. 'Let us

go on Monday as soon as I have delivered my work. I cannot wait to leave Bath.'

'I shall walk home with you now,' Jo said and then hesitated as the Reverend Browne came up to them. She smiled at him in a friendly manner. 'Are you pleased with the way things have gone, sir?'

'Yes, indeed. I understand that we have done very well with the cake stall, Miss Horne—which is partly due to you, I am certain.'

'Oh, I only sold them, but I think they were quite delicious—I bought one myself and ate it,' Jo said. 'May I introduce you to Mrs Beverley, sir? She is a friend of mine and we are just leaving. I am delighted that everything has gone so well. Please excuse us now.'

'Yes, of course.' He frowned as they walked away. 'I shall call on Monday, Miss Horne.'

'And I shall not be there,' Jo said in a low voice as she walked out of the hall with her friend. 'That will not please Aunt Wainwright, for she had settled it in her mind that Mr Browne was to be my only suitor.'

'Oh, no! She did not?' Ellen said looking at her in surprise. 'Why should she think that? I am sure that you will have offers of marriage one day, Jo—when you meet someone you truly like.'

'As a matter of fact I had an offer this morning before I came here,' Jo said. 'It was most kind of him, for he is a pleasant young man. I could not give him hope, of course.'

'Not because of your promise to me?' Ellen looked anxious. 'If you wish to marry him…'

Jo laughed softly, shaking her head. 'You goose! Of course I do not. I liked him as a friend, and I still do, for he took my refusal well—but I did not wish to marry him. I am not sure that I wish to marry at all. If I could find a way of earning my living, I should be quite content to remain a spinster all my life.'

'Would you really?' Ellen looked at her face. 'You might not wish to marry the gentleman who asked you earlier today—and perhaps not the Reverend Mr Browne, but might there be someone else you quite like?'

'Oh, I dare say there are any number of gentlemen I quite like—or would if I met them,' Jo said with a naughty expression. 'But marriage is another thing. I am persuaded that it is not for me and I shall not think of it…at least for the moment.' If a picture of a certain gentleman's face had intruded into her mind, she shut it out resolutely. Her promise was given to Ellen and there was no reason to think that Hal was in the least interested in her—despite the kiss, which had caused so much trouble!

Jo walked home with Ellen. She was relieved that they were not followed by anyone and that no one was lingering suspiciously outside her friend's house. Clearly the mysterious man had discovered as much as he wished to know—and had perhaps gone off to make his report to Ellen's father.

'I shall come early in the morning,' she said. 'Write your letter to Mr Beverley now, Ellen, and I shall deliver it to the receiving office on my way home. Mr Beverley will be certain to find it waiting for him when he returns.'

Ellen sat down. Taking up her pen, she dipped it into the inkpot and began to write, then signed and sanded it and sealed it with wax. 'There, I have told him that I was frightened by a man following me and that you came to my rescue.'

'Yes, that will explain why we did not wait,' Jo said and took the letter. 'I must go, for we are to attend the assembly this evening and I must not be late. This is my last but one evening in Bath, and I must find time to write a letter to my aunt. I am not sure that I shall be able to visit tomorrow, Ellen, but do send me a note—or come if you are frightened.'

Ellen glanced out of the window. 'There is no one watching me now, but I do not believe I imagined it. I dare say he has gone to report to my father.'

She looked so distressed that Jo took her hand and pressed it. 'Do not be upset, dearest Ellen. Tomorrow will soon pass and then we shall leave Bath. I promise you that everything will be all right. I shall look after you.'

'I believe that you would manage it somehow,' Ellen said and laughed. 'It was a fortunate day for me when we met, Jo.'

'And for me,' Jo said, 'because I have found a friend.'

She took her leave then and walked home very fast, feeling a little out of breath by the time she arrived. It was her intention to go upstairs and change quickly, but her aunt came out of the parlour as she entered the hall.

'So you are back at last. I thought you would be home sooner.'

'Forgive me, Aunt. I was very busy.'

'Well, no matter—but I wish to talk to you before you go up to change. I am most displeased with you, Jo.'

Jo's heart sank. What had she done now! 'I am sorry, Aunt. Have I done something to annoy you?'

'You have upset Chloe, and of course that has distressed her mama.'

'Oh…I did not mean to,' Jo said. 'Did Mrs Marsham say why Chloe was upset?'

'No, she did not, but she hinted that you had been behaving in a manner that does you no credit, Josephine. Am I to understand that you went out into the garden with a young man the other evening?'

'No, Aunt, that is not true. I went out for a little air and Mr Beverley followed me. It was not an assignation.'

'No, I do not think it. Mr Beverley is clearly intending to make Chloe an offer, so it is unlikely that he would have followed you. I told her that I thought she must have made a mistake. However, let this be a lesson to you, Josephine. It is unwise to put yourself into a position where others may think ill of you. You must apologise to Chloe this evening and tell her that it was an unintentional meeting.'

'I have already told her,' Jo said. 'She did not wish to listen. I am sorry if she is upset, but I assure you it was unnecessary, for I did nothing wrong, Aunt.'

'Very well. You may go and change. I shall change myself. Do not keep me waiting.'

Jo made no reply. She was not particularly looking forward to the evening. She knew that her special friendship with Chloe was at an end, and that she would quite possibly be left sitting out for most of the dances. However, there was nothing she could do, except to smile and behave as if nothing had happened.

Chapter Four

It was not quite as difficult an evening as Jo had feared, for she had gained her own admirers. Although not as conventionally pretty as Chloe, she had her own special charm, which appealed to several of the gentlemen, and she sat out no more than three dances in all. Mr Tanner was there and they danced together once, his manner as gentle and pleasant as it had always been. He did not give any indication that he was angry or distressed about her refusal of his rather hesitant proposal and there was no embarrassment on either side.

Once during the evening, Jo became aware that someone was staring at her hard. A shiver went through her as she realised that it was Mr Carstairs. It was a shock for somehow she had not expected to see him here, though as a gentleman he would obviously be invited to such affairs. She turned away swiftly and found that she was being asked to dance again. When she looked in that direction later, Carstairs had gone.

Since several gentlemen continued to ask Jo to dance she enjoyed her evening. However, Mrs Marsham gave her barely a nod in passing, and Chloe glared at her the whole evening. She could only be glad that she would not have to meet them in company again. It was something of a relief to her when Lady Wainwright said it was time to leave.

Alone in her room that night, Jo sorted out the things she could not bear to leave behind, which were not so very many and would be easy enough to carry with her. Before she retired that night, she wrote a very difficult letter to her aunt.

I am sorry to desert you, Aunt, and I know you will be angry, but Ellen was in some difficulty and I have gone to be her companion until she is settled. I shall write to Mama and tell her and I can only apologise for being so ungrateful as to run off like this. You have been generous and do not deserve such ill treatment. Forgive me, Jo.

It was done! She had made her decision and she would allow herself no regrets. She hid the letter in her trinket box and packed a few of her things, though most would have to be done on Sunday night, because otherwise one of the maids might notice something odd.

On Sunday morning she attended church with her aunt, and then they had lunch with another of Lady Wainwright's friends. She was accosted by the Reverend Browne as they came out of church. He spent a few minutes talking with them, saying how much he had admired her for helping with the bazaar and that he hoped to call soon.

In the afternoon her aunt retired to her room to rest for a while and Jo went upstairs to pack more of her things. She would only be able to take two small bags with her, because she could not carry any more, and most of her things would no doubt be sent back to Cornwall.

On impulse, she sent for one of the maids and arranged to have her trunk brought down, explaining that she thought she ought to start packing some of her things so that she would not have it all to do on their last day.

'Shall I help you, miss?' the girl asked.

'That is very kind,' Jo said. 'But I can manage. I know what I want to pack and what I shall need in the meantime, thank you.'

She packed all her smartest clothes into the trunk, along with most of her other things. It would be best to take two serviceable skirts with her and as many different bodices as she could squeeze into her bags. She would wear one of her favourite gowns and take sufficient underwear—everything else must be left behind. Reluctantly, she added her unfinished novel to the trunk. It was, in any case, in something of a muddle—she could no longer force her *wicked earl* to be wicked. He kept behaving like a hero and she had not written anything for some days. She thought that she would begin a new story when she and Ellen were settled.

That evening they had a small dinner party, because Lady Wainwright had wanted to thank friends who had shown them hospitality during their visit to Bath. Jo was glad that they were not alone, for she felt very guilty, and when her aunt smiled at her before they retired for the night it was like a dagger thrust to her heart.

'That was our last dinner party before we leave Bath,' Lady Wainwright told her. 'I have had a note from the

Reverend Browne saying that he intends to call tomorrow at eleven, Josephine. Please make sure that you are here. We are promised to Lady Russell for her card party tomorrow evening, and on Tuesday it is a musical evening—and then we shall leave Bath. I shall send you home by post chaise, I think, because I do not wish to drag all the way down to Cornwall. I trust you have enjoyed your stay?'

'Oh, yes, Aunt, it has been most enjoyable,' Jo said truthfully. 'I am grateful for the opportunity—and I do thank you sincerely for your generosity in bringing me here.'

'Well, it has been pleasant enough, apart from that little bother with Chloe,' Lady Wainwright said. 'I dare say that was irritation of the nerves on her part, because Mr Beverley left Bath without asking her to marry him. Mrs Marsham was sure he meant to return, but Chloe was naturally afraid that he did not mean to speak, and she suffered a disappointment.'

'Yes, I expect so,' Jo said. She hesitated, then kissed her aunt's cheek. 'Goodnight, Aunt.'

'Goodnight, Josephine. I wonder why Mr Browne wants to see you so particularly?' She gave Jo an oddly smug smile and turned away.

Jo went into her own room and locked the door. She took off the gown she was wearing and stuffed it into one of her bags. It would not close, but she thought that she ought to take at least one evening dress; although it would be sadly creased, it could be rescued once they were settled.

All her other possessions were now packed and she was ready to leave. She put on the dress she had decided to wear in the morning and lay down on top of her bed. She would slip out of the house at first light.

* * *

'Oh, my dear friend,' Ellen said as she opened the door to Jo the next morning. 'You are very early, but I am ready. I could not sleep a wink last night.'

'Have you seen any more of that mysterious stranger?'

'No. I am much relieved for that,' Ellen said and placed a hand to her back as if it ached, but made no complaint. 'Come, let me make you some breakfast. I am sure you have not eaten, and we cannot leave until I have delivered my work and received the money owed me.'

'No, of course not,' Jo said. 'I packed all my things and left a letter for my aunt, explaining where I had gone and why—and asking her to send my trunk to Mama. I shall write to her when we are settled, for I dare say she will worry, even though I have left a note in my trunk to tell her not to.'

'She is bound to be a little anxious even then,' Ellen said and gave her an anxious look. 'Are you sure you should do this, Jo?'

'My mind is quite made up,' Jo said. 'Aunt Wainwright will be angry when she gets my letter, but Mama will understand—she always does. I shall write to her almost at once.'

Ellen cooked them both some bacon, which she served with bread and pickles, and a pot of tea. They ate their meal in some excitement, for it was an adventure and seemed all the better because it involved the two of them, because, as Ellen said, she had not been looking forward to being hidden away on her own.

'We shall get on so well,' she told Jo as she put on her pelisse and hat. 'Now I think you had best stay here until I come back, Jo. I have arranged for my trunk to be collected by the carriers and they may arrive before I return.'

'Yes, of course. I shall clear up here and you will not be long,' Jo replied.

'No, I will be as quick as I can. I hope that Mr Beverley will have my trunk sent on. For the moment I shall have two bags like you, Jo.'

'I should have thought of that,' Jo said. 'But there, it would have aroused too much suspicion. Do not be long, Ellen. The coach leaves at eleven on the dot and we need to be early to be sure of a place inside.'

'I shall not be,' Ellen promised and kissed her cheek. 'I cannot thank you enough for being my friend.'

'Think nothing of it,' Jo said. 'I should not be a true friend if I had deserted you when you needed me.'

'I hope that I may do as much for you one day,' Ellen said. 'Do not be anxious, I shall be no more than half an hour at most.'

Ellen returned at half past ten, looking pleased. 'I have collected all the money that was owed to me,' she told Jo. 'Madame said that she would always have work for me, and would recommend me to anyone.'

'That was good of her,' Jo said. 'I believe we should leave now, for it will take us some minutes to walk to the coaching inn—' She was startled by a loud rapping at the door. 'I wonder who that is.'

'If that is my father, I shall refuse to go with him,' Ellen said, clearly in distress. She was trembling from head to toe. 'You must go to the door, Jo—if it is an older man you do not know, pray tell him that I am not here.'

'Do not worry,' Jo said stoutly. 'I shall not desert you.'

She went through to the hall, her heart racing, but determined not to let anything happen to Ellen. Taking a deep breath, she opened the door to see Hal standing there and gave a sigh of relief.

'Thank goodness it is you,' she said. 'We were about to leave for the coaching inn. The mail coach leaves in twenty-five minutes—and we were afraid that you might be Ellen's father.'

'*You* were to leave together on the mail coach?' Hal asked with a slight frown. 'Did Ellen ask you to accompany her?'

'Hal?' Ellen came out into the hall at that moment. 'Oh, thank goodness you have come. We were about to leave, because we did not expect you back. We had left a letter for you at the Receiving Office—'

'Were you running away from me?'

'No, of course not,' she said and gave a nervous laugh. 'Someone has been watching me these past few days. I was afraid that my father might force me to go with him if I delayed.'

'I am not surprised,' Hal told them. 'You must have known there was a risk in writing to them.' He shook his head. 'Well, it is no matter. We may as well leave at once. What about your trunk?'

'I have sent mine to the carrier,' Ellen said.

'I shall arrange for it to be sent on,' Hal confirmed, 'though not to our final destination. It can be delivered to an inn and collected from there.' He looked at Jo. 'What of your trunk, Miss Horne?'

'I shall arrange for it to be sent on at a later date,' Jo said. 'I have these bags for the moment.'

'I see,' he said, his expression thoughtful. 'This is a surprise—I had not expected to have two ladies in my charge.'

'I cannot leave without Jo,' Ellen said. 'Please do not ask it of me, Hal. I need her, because the birth is so close and I am afraid of being alone.'

'You would not be alone,' he replied, but, seeing her expression, shook his head. 'No matter. Since it is all arranged, Miss Horne is welcome to come with us. I suggest that we leave immediately, for we do not want to be followed.'

Lady Wainwright came downstairs at a quarter to eleven that morning. She was feeling pleased with herself, because she was certain in her own mind that the Reverend Thomas Browne was calling that morning to ask for Jo's hand in marriage, and it was all down to her, for she had encouraged him. He had been hesitant at the start, but she had given him a few hints and she was confident that he would come up to scratch.

'There are some letters for you, my lady.'

'Oh, thank you, Benson.' Lady Wainwright took the small pile of notes from her butler and went into the parlour. The visit to Bath had gone as well as she might have expected, given that she had been obliged to bring Josephine and not her elder sister. She laid her letters on a small table and sat down to read them.

There were the usual polite thank-you notes for the dinner she had given the previous evening, and two invitations that she would have to refuse. The letter at the bottom of the pile was written in a hand that made her frown. Surely that was Jo's writing?

She broke the seal and read the brief note that Jo had laboured over so hard, staring at it in disbelief for some seconds before giving an exclamation of disgust and anger. How dare the girl behave so badly?

She rang the bell for Benson, giving him a sour look as he entered in response to her summons. 'Have you seen my niece, Benson?'

'No, my lady, not this morning. I believe she may have gone out earlier.'

'What do you mean—you believe she may have gone out? Did you see her?'

'No, my lady. One of the maids thought she saw her go…she was carrying two soft bags, and her trunk is packed. She asked Maisie to have it brought down yesterday and packed it herself.'

'Indeed?' Lady Wainwright was lost for words. She was about to go upstairs to investigate when the doorbell rang.

'Shall I answer, my lady? Are you at home?'

'Only if it is the Reverend Browne.'

'Yes, my lady.'

Lady Wainwright stood up, Jo's letter in her hand. She was angry and embarrassed—what could she say to the man? She had encouraged him to believe that his suit would be welcome to her niece—and now this…

'Lady Wainwright…' Mr Browne came into the room. 'The most extraordinary thing… I believe I just saw Miss Horne leaving Bath in a gentleman's carriage.'

'What did you say?' She stared at him, shocked and disturbed. 'You had better read this, sir.' She held out Jo's letter to him. 'She says that she and this…woman she has befriended are to travel by the mail coach.'

'I am sure I saw her getting into a smart curricle just a few minutes ago,' he replied with a frown. 'They set off as if they were leaving town and there was another lady with her…and it may have been this friend. I believe she introduced her to me on Saturday after the bazaar.'

'But I do not understand,' Lady Wainwright said. 'If she did not go by the public coach…this letter might be a lie. Do you know who the gentleman was?'

'I am not sure—but it may have been Mr Hal Beverley,' the Reverend Mr Browne said. 'I cannot be certain, for we have only met a couple of times, but I think it might be so.'

Lady Wainwright gave a shriek of dismay. 'She has run away with him! Mrs Marsham told me that she had set her cap at him…that they were seen kissing in the garden…but I did not believe her. This is terrible. I cannot believe that she has done this to me. What will her poor mama say? It is such a scandalous thing to do. To run away like that…' She placed a hand to her heaving breast, giving a cry of frustrated anger. 'He will never marry her! She is ruined. Quite ruined!'

'But surely…' Mr Browne looked at Jo's letter again. 'She says that she has gone to be with a friend. It may be true, ma'am.'

'She is a wicked girl and I shall finish with her—and her family,' Lady Wainwright declared. 'Such ingratitude! I must leave Bath at once. I must tell her mother what she has done—to bring shame and disgrace on our family is wicked. Wicked!'

'Will you not wait and see if she is telling the truth?' Mr Browne said, reluctant to think ill of a lady he admired. 'She may have decided to help a friend in distress. It would be like her.'

'Yes, but if she went in a gentleman's curricle, after telling me that she was to travel on the mail coach—don't you see? It was all a lie to deceive me. She has eloped, or, worse still, simply gone off with him. He probably offered her *carte blanche* and she was foolish enough to accept it.'

'Are you sure, ma'am?' Mr Browne asked. 'Miss Horne does not appear to be that way inclined. I think I would give her the benefit of the doubt for now.'

'Then you are a fool, sir,' Lady Wainwright said, too angry to consider her words. 'She has betrayed me—and put herself beyond all decent society. I shall never speak to her again!'

'How fortunate that you should come just as we were about to leave,' Ellen said to Hal as he handed her down from his curricle outside a respectable country establishment where they were to take some refreshment. 'We did not expect you until Tuesday at the earliest.'

'So it would seem.' Hal raised his brows. 'Had I not come when I did, I might have had the deuce of a job finding you again. You are sure that you did not plan on disappearing once more?'

'Oh, no,' Ellen replied with a smile. 'I would not do that to you, Hal. It was merely that I was frightened—and Jo said that she would come with me.'

'Yes…' Hal frowned and took Jo's arm as she would have followed Ellen into the posting inn. 'Miss Horne, I would like a word with you.'

'Yes, sir?' Jo turned to him, feeling a little apprehensive, for he had not seemed to relish the idea that she had accompanied Ellen, though he had not refused to accept her. 'Is something the matter?'

'I am a little concerned,' Hal replied. 'Does Lady Wainwright know that you have agreed to leave Bath with Ellen and stay with her for some weeks—or months? And what of your mama?'

Jo's cheeks were warm as she looked at him. 'I left a note

for my aunt, telling her that I was with Mrs Ellen Beverley—and I shall write to my mama as soon as we are settled. Just to let her know that I am safe and happy.'

'Good grief!' He gave her a look of sheer disbelief. 'In effect you have run off without the knowledge and permission of your family, Miss Horne. As you are still a minor…do you realise that I could be charged with abduction or at least aiding an under-aged girl to leave her family?'

'Oh, no, sir, surely not?' Jo said, because she could see that he was torn between concern for her and annoyance that she had caused him an added problem. She had considered her own disgrace if a scandal should ensue, but not his, and now she realised that she had been too reckless, for it was not only her own reputation that might suffer. 'I came of my own free will to be with Ellen. She is a perfectly respectable married lady…' Her words died away as she saw his mouth harden. Regret washed over her, for she knew that he was right to censure her. She had behaved recklessly, though for the best of motives. 'Ellen was very frightened and we did not know if you would return in time, sir—and when you did, well, it was too late to go back. Besides, Ellen wished me to come with her. She has been unwell and needs a female friend at this time.'

'I do not fault your motives, only your actions,' Hal said and sighed. 'You must know that Ellen was becoming a little notorious in Bath. When people do not know someone's history, they tend to invent it for themselves—and I was seen visiting her…a widow living alone and keeping herself private of necessity. Naturally, many thought the worst.'

'How unkind people can be!' Jo said, angry for her friend.

'To make something of nothing! You are Ellen's brother-in-law and it is despicable that anyone should think ill of her, because you visited her.'

'I agree with you there,' Hal said. 'But I did not tell anyone that she was my sister-in-law, because I wished to keep her whereabouts a secret. Mrs Beverley might be anybody and Ellen will be living on my estate, which means people may talk. If there is scandal, it might reflect on you, Miss Horne.'

'I am sure I have done nothing wrong!' Her cheeks were hot, for she knew very well what people might say of her, and for a moment she was conscious of a deep regret, because clearly Hal thought she was ruined.

'My dear girl, you must be an idiot if you truly believe that,' Hal said. 'And I know you are not, which means you have been reckless and foolish with no thought for your reputation—or mine.'

'I am sorry if I have put you in an awkward position,' Jo said, lifting her chin. She knew herself in the wrong, but pride kept her from confessing it. 'I do not mind if some think ill of me, for Mama and my sisters will not—and they are all I care for. I have no desire to mix in high society. Nor do I wish to marry.'

'That is besides the point.' He gave a sigh of exasperation.

'If anyone thinks ill of me they may do so,' Jo said hot-temperedly. 'I am sure I do not give a fig! As long as Mama understands—and I am perfectly certain that she will once she has my letter.' It was not true because she saw now exactly what she had lost. Any faint chance that Hal might have married her had now gone and the regret was sharp.

'You must, of course, write to her immediately,' Hal said.

'Indeed, I think you should do it at the inn and I shall have it sent for you—but do not tell your mama where you will be situated. Until Ellen is settled and the child is born, I do not wish anyone to know where she is staying.'

'Yes, I understand,' Jo said. 'And now I think we must hurry, sir, or Ellen will wonder what has happened to us.'

'Yes…' Hal smothered his frustration. It was unlikely that she understood just what she had done, for despite her avowals she *would* mind if she were ostracised from society. Either that or her pride would not let her admit it! However, the damage had already occurred and there was little that he could do about it. Ellen had been in such a state, vowing that she would go nowhere without her friend, and Hal had had no choice but to bring her with them. There was nothing he could do now, except wait and see what the future might bring.

Jo went to join her friend, her feelings a little bruised. Mr Beverley had made her feel foolish, and she was more apprehensive than she had been about telling her mama what she had done. She was sure that her papa would have said it was the right thing, but mothers were naturally inclined to be protective of a daughter's good name. She hoped that her behaviour would not reflect badly on Lucy, but surely, even if she had caused a small scandal now, it would be forgotten by the time Lucy was brought out? Besides, there was no need for anyone to know outside the family. If Aunt Wainwright were sensible, she would not tell anyone that Jo had gone without her permission. She was always talking of propriety, and it would be quite improper of her to speak of family matters to anyone else. Jo must hope that she had been discreet for all their sakes.

* * *

'My dear Lady Wainwright,' Mrs Marsham said. 'I had to call on you at once. Such tales are circulating in Bath! I was sure that they could not be true but felt that I must ask. It must surely be wrong that your niece has run off with Mr Beverley?'

'Well, you have only just caught me, for I am about to leave Bath. However, you may as well know the truth. *She says* that she has gone with a woman friend of hers—a widow named Ellen,' Lady Wainwright said and pulled a sour face. 'But I have been told that Mr Beverley was with them. Well, she has ruined herself as far as I am concerned. I shall have nothing more to do with her!'

'Mr Beverley went with them? I am shocked. Utterly shocked,' Mrs Marsham said, her face tight with anger. 'It is just as well that Chloe did not receive an offer from him, for I should certainly never have allowed the marriage now. What can he have been thinking of to abduct your niece? It is quite disgraceful!'

'One cannot blame you for feeling distressed,' Lady Wainwright said. 'But it may be all perfectly respectable for all I know…' She had suddenly realised that her careless words had led to gossip; though she was angry with Jo, she did not wish to bring scandal on her own name. 'I hope I may trust you to keep this to yourself, Mrs Marsham? My niece may have been reckless, but I would not wish to cause her family more distress than necessary.'

'Oh, of course,' Mrs Marsham said. 'I was never one for gossip, my dear Lady Wainwright.'

She stood up, pulling on her gloves. She was on fire now to leave, for she could not wait to tell her friends what she had discovered that afternoon.

Lady Wainwright frowned after her visitor had gone. It was all such a nuisance! She really did not wish to have the trouble of posting down to Cornwall to give Mrs Horne such terrible news. Indeed, she would not. She would write a letter instead and simply go home. After all, if Marianne had not been so disobliging as to go off to Lady Edgeworthy's in the first place, this would never happened! For *she* would never have behaved so badly!

It was not her fault that things had turned out so ill and she simply could not be chasing all that way for no good reason! A letter would do very well.

Carstairs listened avidly to the conversation taking place between two ladies outside the Pump Room. He had come in the hope of meeting Miss Horne, for he had discovered that that was her name. If the plans he had been making these last few days were to proceed, he must make her acquaintance. He did not think she would remember him, for she had looked straight through him on at least two occasions.

He was not flattered to know that he was so easily forgettable, but it would make it easier to ingratiate himself with her—at least that had been his thinking. However, from the conversation he had just overheard, it seemed that she had caused a scandal by running off with Hal Beverley.

That was not quite in Beverley's style, Carstairs thought, because the man he knew would risk neither his nor an innocent girl's reputation by such reckless behaviour. Unless, of course, he was madly in love and there was some objection to the marriage—but who would object to such a match? Not her parents, unless they were fools…which meant it was more likely Lord Beverley who was being deceived. Unless, of course, the girl had agreed to become his mistress, which might perhaps be the case, if Beverley's father would not countenance the marriage.

It was an interesting development. He would have to change his plans once more, but first he had to discover where they might have gone. He puzzled over it for a moment and then smiled. Of course, the very place! It was so obvious that he wondered he had not remembered it at once.

He knew his way there well enough, and he would take his time, planning his revenge slowly, because he wanted to be sure that he inflicted as much pain as possible on Hal Beverley…for he sensed that Hal was not convinced that his brother's death had been an accident. It might be safer to dispose of him, too, but first he would see what profit could be got from this interesting situation.

'Oh, what a pretty house,' Ellen said when she saw that the carriage had stopped outside a cottage of a decent size. It had walls of red brick that had faded to a pale rose and a thatched roof. Climbing roses were growing up one wall, and would be glorious in summer. Indeed, a few blooms still clung to life in the pretty garden, for it was sheltered and on a sunny afternoon such as this seemed warm despite the season. 'Are we truly to have this house to ourselves, Hal?'

'Do you think you can be happy here?' he asked with a smile. 'It belongs to the estate and I have always kept it in good repair. The last tenant moved out two months ago, but I have had it aired and made comfortable for you. I have employed a woman to take care of you, Ellen—and Miss Horne, of course, now that she is to be your companion.'

'I am sure that we shall be happy here,' Ellen said and

turned to Jo, who was standing a little way behind them. 'Do you not think so, dearest Jo?'

'Yes, I am sure of it,' Jo said. She turned to Hal, her brows raised. 'You do not live here?'

'No, I have a house just through those trees,' Hal said and pointed out the direction. 'When I am here I shall expect you and Ellen to walk up and visit me for tea—or perhaps for luncheon? If you should care to give me the pleasure of your company, Miss Horne.'

'We should like it of all things,' Ellen said and gave him an odd look. 'Why do you not call Jo by her name, Hal? Miss Horne is so formal—especially when we are all together here.'

'I am not sure that Miss Horne would permit it. I believe she is a little bit cross with me—is that not so, Miss Horne?'

'Why should I be cross with you, sir?' Jo asked, giving him a straight look. The prospect of being able to see him often was one that gave her a great deal of satisfaction. 'I dare say it would not matter if you wished to call me by my first name—but you must do as you please, of course.'

'Then I shall,' he said. 'Would you like to go in first, Ellen? Mrs Stowe is waiting to welcome you to your new home.'

'Home…' Ellen said wonderingly. She smiled because it pleased her. 'It is so good to hear that word, Hal. I have not truly had somewhere to call home for a long time.'

She walked ahead of them into the small entrance hall, which smelled of roses and lavender. The floor was of polished wood that had a soft, mellow sheen to it, and the hall was furnished with mellowed oak pieces that belonged to an earlier century. There were some tall Chinese vases filled with dried flowers, and paintings of country scenes on the walls. As they walked into the small parlour, where a welcoming fire was burning, they saw that the furniture here was mahogany and much in the style of Mr Chippendale, but made by a country tradesman to suit the cottage rather than a town house.

The house had a warm feel to it, as if it had been lived in and loved, and, when the housekeeper came bustling in, she greeted them with a smile of genuine pleasure.

'Well, here you are then, my dears,' she said. 'I was delighted when Mr Beverley asked me to come and look after you, Mrs Beverley. I was a nursemaid to the Captain when he was a little boy, ma'am, and I remember that he was such a sweet child. I was so sorry to hear that he was killed. It is so sad for you.'

'Yes, it is,' Ellen said and for a moment tears misted her eyes, but she smiled through them. 'I am very pleased to meet you, Mrs Stowe. Mr Beverley told us that he had engaged someone to look after us—and now, may I introduce you to my friend and companion, Miss Horne?'

'I am very pleased to meet you, miss,' the housekeeper said, though she looked slightly puzzled. 'Mr Beverley did not mention that you were bringing a friend, ma'am, but I am sure it will be all the better. It is a little isolated here in the winter, though there is a village not far away. I am sure it is no more trouble to me to look after two rather than one. And the rooms are always kept aired, so I'll give Miss Horne the room next to yours, shall I?'

'Yes, thank you,' Ellen said. 'Shall we go up, Jo? I am a little tired. I think I shall lie down for an hour or so before I come down.'

'Yes, of course you must rest,' Jo said. 'I shall come up and make sure that you are settled and then I may try to find my way about the house and garden.' She looked directly at Hal. 'Shall we see you later this evening, sir?'

'I may walk down later,' he said, frowning slightly as he sensed he had been dismissed. 'Yes, of course. You will not want me here until you have settled in. Good afternoon, ladies. Ellen, I am nearby if you need me.'

'You have been so kind,' Ellen said. 'I can never thank you enough for bringing me here. I believe I shall be safe here in this place.'

'Yes, of course you will,' Hal said. 'You are on my estate and I have instructed my people to look out for strangers so you may feel quite free to walk where you please.' He nodded to Jo and turned away as the two ladies went out into the hall and up the stairs.

For a moment he listened to their chatter. Ellen seemed genuinely excited and pleased with the house, which was pleasing, for he hoped that she would make it her home for as long as it suited her. Jo answered her in measured tones, and he realised that he had offended her without meaning to— but she *had* behaved recklessly and he only hoped that they could brush through it without a scandal. Jo might say that she did not wish to marry or go into society, but he could not believe that deep down she truly meant it.

Having seen Ellen settled in a soft bed with everything she needed to hand, Jo looked around her own room. It was small, but adequate for her needs. She placed her personal possessions on the dressing chest near the window, and unpacked her clothes. She would have to be meticulous about getting her things washed—she had only been able to bring a few clothes. She still had a little money, and, if good plain cloth could be bought locally, might be able to make herself some lingerie and perhaps a new gown. In the meantime she would have to do the best she could with what she had.

Jo looked out of the window. It was a pretty view across a meadow to the woods beyond, and from this point she could just see the roof of Hal's house over the trees. In a way it reminded her of her old home at the Vicarage, though that had been much larger than this cottage, but it was just right for the two of them. A bigger house would have seemed wrong and they would not have felt comfortable.

She could see a small kitchen garden, and she knew that there was a pretty garden where they could sit on fine days at the front of the house. Going downstairs, she explored and found that there was a large dining parlour and a back parlour as well as the kitchens and the large front parlour.

Mrs Stowe looked surprised when she walked into the kitchens, but welcomed her with a smile. 'Getting to know where everything is, my dear?'

'Yes,' Jo said. 'When we were all at home in the Vicarage, we often used the kitchen as our dining parlour when it was just the family. I want to be of use to you, Mrs Stowe. You must not think that I expect you to wait on me. I shall be glad to do light housework or any little job you think suitable.'

'Now that is what I call handsome,' Mrs Stowe said with a nod of approval. 'If you could keep your own room tidy, it would be a help, Miss Horne. Perhaps the flowers and, if you should not object, some dusting—just the main parlours.'

'Yes, of course, I shall be pleased to do all of that,' Jo said. 'And I want to be of help when the baby is born, and afterwards, naturally. For the moment, I have some clothes that need washing, and I wondered if you would permit me to bring them here and wash them myself.'

'No need for that, my dear,' Mrs Stowe assured her. 'Bessie does the laundry for us and the big house, and she will collect it once a week.'

'Yes…but that may not be enough, for I have only a few things with me. If I could just rinse out some light things when I need…'

'Yes, of course, but Bessie will do the main wash for you, same as always,' the housekeeper said. She hesitated, then, 'I wonder if you would be interested in some clothing we have in the attic, miss? I don't wish to offend you, but Mr Beverley's grandmother sent a trunk of her things here to be stored some years ago, and, being dead, will not miss them. I don't know if anything would do for you, but you might be able to use a few bits and pieces—especially if you are good with your needle.'

'Are you sure the family will not want them?' Jo hesitated, for she was not sure that Mrs Stowe had the right to offer them to her, but they would be useful if no one wanted them.

'I dare say as they've forgotten they were ever here,' Mrs Stowe said. 'There may be nothing you fancy, but I'll ask George to bring the trunk down when he comes with our stores from the market tomorrow.'

'That is very kind of you,' Jo said and blushed. 'It would be a help until I can arrange something.' She was not sure that she would ever be able to send for her things, because it was important to keep her whereabouts a secret. But if she went to visit her mother after Ellen's child was born, she might bring a trunk on her return. 'Thank you, that was a kind thought, Mrs Stowe.'

'Well, it may be of use, but I can't vouch for the contents,' the housekeeper said. 'I was about to make a pot of tea for myself, Miss Horne. Mrs Beverley won't want hers for a while, but there's no need for you to wait.'

'Thank you, that is very kind,' Jo said and sat down at the kitchen table. 'This makes me feel that I am at home again.'

Waking to the sound of birds singing outside her window the next morning, Jo thought for a moment that she was back at the Vicarage and she smiled as she stretched, expecting Lucy to come running in at any moment. However, in a moment or two she had remembered where she was and she sat up, throwing back the covers. She dressed and then tidied her room, taking the undergarments she had worn the previous day downstairs with her to the kitchen. She had rinsed them out using some of her personal soap and was just about to take them out to hang them on a small clothes line that she had seen previously in the kitchen courtyard, when Mrs Stowe came into the kitchen.

'You are about early, miss,' she said. 'I was just about to make tea and send it upstairs.'

'If you prepare Ellen's tea, I shall take it up for her,' Jo said. 'But I shall come down and share my breakfast with you, if you don't mind?'

'I don't mind that at all,' Mrs Stowe said. 'You're not like most of the young ladies I've worked for in the past, miss, and that's a fact.'

'Papa brought us up to expect to do our share of the work,' Jo told her. 'Sometimes when I went visiting with him, I did chores for the poor folk we visited. Just small things— washing the plates if they had been left to pile up or sweeping and cleaning. I am quite used to it, you see.'

'Well, you go and put those things out,' Mrs Stowe said, shaking her head because Miss Horne was a bit of a mystery. Her manners and the clothes she had worn on her arrival seemed to say that she was quality, but it was clear that she did not have much money.

Jo was unaware of the questions in the housekeeper's mind as she took her clothes out to the line and pegged them to dry in the breeze. She had just finished when she became aware that someone was watching her, and she turned to see Hal standing a few feet away staring at her.

'What are you doing?' he asked. 'Did Mrs Stowe not tell you that one of the maids collects the washing each week?'

'Yes, she did tell me,' Jo said. 'But I am not above washing my own clothes. Besides, once a week will not do, because I do not have many clothes with me.'

'No, I suppose you could not order your trunk sent round,' Hal said looking thoughtful. 'Can you manage for the time being? I shall arrange something…there is a local seamstress, I believe.'

'Thank you, but I do not need her services,' Jo said with a lift of her head. 'I have enough for the moment and my needle will supply anything else I might require. I shall hardly need to wear my society gowns here, shall I?'

'No…' Hal looked doubtful. 'But you are used to wearing pretty clothes. You must have something to wear in the evenings.'

'I hardly think it matters, and I do have one gown,' Jo said. 'Besides, I enjoy making my own things, as I always did at home. It will not take me long to make what I need once I have the material.'

'Very well,' Hal said. 'You must do as you wish, of course—

but you are here as Ellen's friend and companion, not her maid.'

'I have washed only my own things,' Jo told him, though she had every intention of washing a few of Ellen's later that day.

'You will ruin your hands,' Hal said, looking at them. He took one, holding it and turning it as if he expected to see red marks. 'You are a lady, Jo, and even if you did take me by surprise when you came with Ellen, you are under my protection. I wish that you will allow me to take care of you.'

'I am grateful that you have given Ellen this lovely place to call home,' Jo said. 'It is so peaceful here. I believe we shall be quite content—and I like to be busy, sir. I should hate to sit idle all day, doing nothing.'

'Yes, I dare say,' he said. 'But do not spoil your hands with washing. Bessie may come every day to fetch your soiled linen. It is no more than half an hour here and back—and you are my guest.'

'But you must allow me to do something to earn my keep,' Jo told him, a glint of pride in her eyes. 'Ellen is your sister-in-law, but I am nothing to you, sir. I should feel most uncomfortable living here if I did not help in some way.'

'I have just said that you are my guest. Ellen needs a companion and she is fond of you, Jo. Your task is to keep her from fretting and look after her as the time for her confinement comes nearer. I think that will be difficult enough.'

'We shall not quarrel over that,' Jo said. 'I know that she is still a little nervous that her father will somehow find her and claim her—and she would hate to be forced to go home with him.'

'That shall never happen,' Hal said. 'She need have no

fears. It is perhaps a good thing that you came with her, Jo. She would not have settled without you. I am sorry if I was harsh to you at the inn, but I was concerned for your sake. If it is known in Bath that you ran away with Ellen—and me— you may have suffered a loss of reputation, which would be difficult to repair.'

'Yes, I suppose I may,' Jo agreed feeling a little uneasy. 'It is unfortunate, but I shall not let it weigh with me. I have made my decision now and Ellen needs me. I will be her friend and companion at least until she moves on or marries again in the fullness of time. After that, I will return to live with my mama, who I am sure will take me in.'

'I dare say something will be arranged,' Hal said, frowning. 'But there is no need to concern ourselves about that for the moment. Ellen will need you in the next few weeks. It cannot be more than a month before she is confined.'

'Perhaps not so much,' Jo said. 'I do not have much experience of these things, but Mrs Stowe told me that she would not be surprised if it is sooner than we think. And I believe she is well used to attending ladies in these situations.'

'Yes, indeed, so I believe,' Hal said. He was surprised at how easily she spoke of Ellen's confinement, for most young, unmarried ladies would blush and hide their faces if such a subject was mentioned in the presence of a gentleman. 'You said that you had little experience, Jo. I am surprised that you have any.'

'I believe I have told you that I went visiting with Papa?' He nodded. 'After Papa died, I continued to visit the poor of our village, and I have been present at the birth of a child on two occasions. Once I was the only other person there besides the mother, and I…helped her. She had seven children and she told me exactly what to do.' Jo's cheeks were warm, but she lifted her head proudly. 'I dare say you think that I should have run and got help, but she begged me not to leave her and I did all that she needed.'

'Do not imagine that I shall censure you for what you did,' Hal said and his smile was warm, almost tender, making Jo's heart race foolishly. 'I am sure you will be a great help to Ellen and Mrs Stowe when the baby comes. And now I must say what I came to tell you…' He paused, then, 'My father has sent for me. He has been unwell again, and I dare say he has something he wishes to say to me. I should be gone a little over a week. In the meantime, you must ask Mrs Stowe for anything you and Ellen need. She has money for housekeeping, but if you need more you may apply to Mr Bent at the house. He is my agent and has the authority to advance you money if you require it.'

'For myself I have all that I need at this moment,' Jo said. 'Ellen has plans to take in embroidery when she is over the birth of her child—and I shall write stories and articles, which I hope a periodical may purchase from me. I know it will take time to establish myself, but in the meantime I shall hope to be of use to Ellen and Mrs Stowe.'

'I have told you that you are *my* guest,' Hal said, a flicker of annoyance in his face. 'But if you wish to write, please do so. I shall always be pleased to send anything you wish to go to an editor—a fashion journal or a ladies' monthly, I dare say?'

'Yes, perhaps,' Jo agreed. 'Though I have recently thought

that perhaps my talents may lie in another direction.' She smiled and shook her head as his brows went up. 'No, I shall not tell you yet. I have settled nothing in my mind, sir.'

'Do you think you might call me Hal?' he asked. 'Sir is so very formal, and I think we are beginning to know each other. I had hoped we might even be friends.' His eyes were filled with wicked humour of a sudden. 'There was a moment when we might have been more.'

He was alluding to that kiss, of course! Jo's cheeks were on fire, but she would not respond to his teasing, for she was not sure what he meant by it.

'I hope that we shall continue to be friends…Hal,' she said. 'It would be most uncomfortable for all of us if we were not.' She missed his teasing, but knew that she had forfeited his respect by behaving so recklessly.

'Indeed it would,' Hal agreed. He reached for her hand, turned it over and kissed the palm. 'Keep these hands as soft as they are, Jo—for my sake, if not your own.'

And then he turned and walked away from her, leaving Jo to stare after him. Her heart was racing wildly, though she did not understand why it should. He had said nothing particular—and she knew that he had been annoyed by the decision that she and Ellen had taken without consulting him. In Bath there had been a moment in his arms when she had felt that he cared for her, but she must not hope for anything of that nature. He had probably been flirting with her all the time, as he perhaps did with countless other ladies. It would be very silly of her to put too much hope on his words, which might mean anything or nothing.

Returning to the house, she saw a speculative expression in the housekeeper's eyes, and a slight hint of disapproval.

Did Mrs Stowe think she was a designing hussy out to trap her master into making a misalliance?

'Mr Beverley is so kind,' she said. 'He says that Bessie will come more often for the washing in future, which will be better for all of us. His father has sent for him, and he may not be here again for a week or two.'

Mrs Stowe nodded. 'That will be much better for everyone,' she said with a grim look.

Jo was not certain if she meant the fact that Bessie was coming more often for the washing—or that Hal would not be here for the next week or so.

She could not help feeling a little disappointed that she would not see him, but she knew that she must not allow herself to look for him or rely on his coming to visit them. He was a young man and in time he would marry. After that, he would probably visit them on only rare occasions.

Jo's heart was heavy as she wondered how soon he would make Chloe an offer. If she accepted him, she would not be at all happy to discover that Jo was living here as Ellen's companion, and though she might accept his brother's widow, she was unlikely to tolerate a girl she thought had tried to take him away from her. Jo knew that if Chloe came here as Hal's wife, she would be forced to leave.

She would face that when she came to it, Jo decided. Ellen's breakfast tray was ready. She would carry it upstairs, and then come back to share hers with Mrs Stowe.

Chapter Five

Jo opened the trunk that had been brought down for her with a feeling of anticipation. She did not know why she should be excited, for it was unlikely that she would discover anything worth having inside. The faint smell of roses was tantalising; as she lifted the top layer of tissue, she saw a blue velvet cloak lying on top. She lifted it out carefully, for it was of wonderful quality, the material heavy and lined with fur. She half-expected that it would fall apart in her hands or be full of the moth, but it was as good as the day it had been placed in the trunk.

Why would anyone send a trunk filled with beautiful things to be stored in an attic? Jo wondered about it as she lifted out various garments. Only the cloak was wearable without a great deal of cutting and sewing, though there was plenty of fine material that she might use in all sorts of ways, and the lace was exquisite. Jo thought that she had never seen finer. However, she repacked everything carefully, except for the cloak, which fitted her well and could be used without alteration.

She had decided that she must ask Hal for a decision on the other things. Mrs Stowe had given them to her, but it was not truly the housekeeper's prerogative to give away such lovely things. Jo would use the cloak for she could clean and press it, and something about it was very appealing. When she put it on she felt like someone very different…she felt beautiful, like a butterfly newly emerged from its chrysalis.

She laughed as she laid it gently on the bed. She was not beautiful, but the cloak made her feel that way, and she thought that she would very much like to use some of the other things in the trunk, but she must wait until Hal returned and ask him.

A sigh escaped her, because he had been away for more than a week and she had missed him. It was foolish of her, of course, because she did not expect that he spent all his time in the country. Indeed, why should he? She was sure that he liked to visit London and Bath, or even Brighton when the weather was clement, and of course his father's estate. It was probable that they would see him only on rare occasions when he visited his own house.

Jo got up and went over to the window, looking out. She shook her head at her own foolishness, for wishing would not bring him here—and when he did come it was very possible that he would bring his new bride. She knew that Chloe Marsham had been expecting an offer of marriage, which he had perhaps delayed on account of Ellen. Now that she was safe, there was no further need for delay.

'Have you any news for me, Harry?' Lord Beverley asked, looking at his son with a frown. 'I had hoped that by now you might have settled things. Was there not a girl you thought might suit you?'

'Yes,' Hal said hesitantly. 'I have not got round to asking her yet. Forgive me, I have had other things on my mind.'

'It is not so very long to Christmas,' Lord Beverley reminded him. 'I had hoped for at least an engagement by then, if not marriage. If you continue to drag your feet, I may never see my grandson born.'

'You do not have to remind me of my duty, Father,' Hal said. 'But you must be patient for a little longer. I may have news for you soon—perhaps when I come next time.'

'And where are you going this time?' His father frowned at him. 'To London—or back to Bath?'

'Neither,' Hal told him. 'I am going down to my estate. I have business there, sir.'

'Are you telling me the truth—or are you off to the races again?' His brow furrowed. 'I do not wish to dictate to you in this business of your marriage, Harry—but I am not getting any younger, and you know my health is not good. I should like to see a grandson before I die, to know that the line goes on for at least one more generation.'

'Yes, I understand that,' Hal said. 'Perhaps you will, Father—and sooner than you might think.'

'What's that?' Lord Beverley glared at him. 'You haven't got yourself a bastard, have you? It would grieve me sorely, Harry. When your brother went off like that…but there, he is dead now and I rely on you to keep the name going.'

'I shall do my best to please you, sir,' Harry said and hesitated. Ought he to tell his father that Ellen was about to give birth to Matt's child or would it be too much of a shock for him? Surely he would be prepared to accept her if she presented him with the heir he craved?

'Yes, I dare say you will,' Lord Beverley said, his voice

thickened by emotion. 'I must not be harsh on you, my boy—but if you love me, marry well and do so soon.'

'Yes, Father,' Harry said, but he turned away to gaze out of the long windows at the garden with its vista of a lake and ancient trees. He could understand his father's obsession with the estate and the family name, even if he did not share it. 'It is just that I wish to choose my wife to please both you and myself.'

'It is so pleasant for November,' Ellen said as they were strolling in the garden a few days later. 'I know the breeze is cold and I dare say it will be bitter this evening, but the sun is warm, is it not?'

'Yes, it is beautiful in this sheltered spot,' Jo said and looked at Ellen in concern as she sighed and put a hand to her back. 'Does it ache very much, dearest?'

'Yes, it is rather bad today,' Ellen told her. 'I feel so big and so clumsy, Jo. I shall be glad now when it is all over and I can hold my baby in my arms.'

'Oh, yes, you will feel so much happier then,' Jo agreed. 'But I am sure it will not be long now, dearest. Mrs Stowe is expecting it to happen any day and I think she knows what she is talking about. We are very lucky to have her here.'

'Yes, I know,' Ellen agreed. 'And I am lucky to have you, Jo. You talk to me, tell me stories and make me laugh—and you fetch everything as soon as I ask for it. Poor Mrs Stowe would have had hard work of it if you had not been here. I think I must be a great trouble to you.'

'It is a pleasure for me to help you,' Jo said. 'I am so content here with you, far more than I ever was in Bath with my aunt.'

'I think Lady Wainwright is very unhappy,' Ellen said. 'It has been my experience that people grow sour and cruel when their own lives give them no joy.' She looked sad, and Jo knew that she must be thinking of her parents.

'Was it very bad for you at home?'

'Yes, quite bad,' Ellen said. 'I think Mama cared for me, but she was afraid to show emotion in front of my papa— and he never loved me. I was not the son he wanted and he could not forgive that. I feel so sorry for Mama. I have escaped, but she has not.'

'Perhaps she cares for him in her own way?'

Ellen shook her head. 'I do not see how—' She gasped and clutched at herself, the colour draining from her face. 'Oh…the pain…it must be the baby. It is sooner than I thought…'

'We had best go back to the house,' Jo said. 'Though I suspect walking will not harm you—it may help the birth to happen a little more quickly.'

Ellen nodded, but her face was white and she could not help giving a little cry as the pain struck her again. She held tight to Jo's arm, her fingers digging into the soft flesh as she struggled to control the painful spasms.

'It hurts…' she said through clenched teeth. 'Oh, God, it hurts. I wish…I wish Matt were here. I need him so much…' Tears were sliding down her cheeks. 'I need him so much, Jo. I loved him so and we had such a short time together.'

'Yes, of course,' Jo said, feeling sympathy for her. 'Any woman would want her husband at such a time. You must have loved him a great deal to risk all you did for him.'

'So much that I thought I did not want to live after he died,' Ellen told her. 'But I want to live now, Jo. I want to live for the sake of my baby. I don't want to die.'

'You are not going to die,' Jo told her and gave her arm a little shake. 'I am here to help you, and so is Mrs Stowe. We shall send for the doctor, but I am sure that we shall be able to manage. You are young and strong, Ellen, and even though this is your first baby, you will come through it. I know you will.'

'Yes, perhaps,' Ellen said and smiled as the pain eased a little. 'I have you to love me and my baby, Jo. Promise me that you will not leave me when the baby is born. I know that you must miss your family, but…'

'Hush,' Jo said because Ellen was getting very upset. 'You must not distress yourself, dearest. I shall write to Mama and Lucy again, and when Hal comes he will send the letter for me. They will not mind as long as they know that I am well and happy.'

'You are happy with me?'

'Yes, of course I am,' Jo said. 'Now, stop worrying about me. Think about your baby, Ellen. He or she will soon be here.'

'I had thought the child would be here before this,' Mrs Stowe said to Jo. 'Mrs Beverley has been in labour through-out the night and she is getting weaker. I think we should send for the doctor, miss. He said that he would not be needed for some hours when he came last night, but I fear that if the child does not come soon she may die.'

'No!' Jo's throat caught with emotion. 'She must not die. We cannot let that happen. You must send for the doctor again—' Hearing a cry from Ellen's bedchamber, she turned away from the housekeeper. 'Send someone for him at once and then come back to her. I shall do what I can, but she needs your help.'

'Yes, of course. Go to her—she seems calmed by your voice. In times like these there is not much any of us can do except wait and pray. I'll see that we have boiling water once the doctor comes.'

Jo went into Ellen's room, hurrying to the bed to look down at her friend. Ellen's forehead was beaded with sweat as she writhed in pain and clutched at the rope, which Mrs Stowe had tied to the bedpost.

'Dearest Ellen,' Jo said, bending over her to smooth her forehead with a cooling cloth. 'I know the pain is very bad, but you must not give up. Try to push once more, my love. Mrs Stowe is sending for the doctor again, for it cannot be much longer.'

'I think I am dying,' Ellen said and the tears trickled down her cheeks and into her mouth. 'I shall be with Matt, but my baby will be all alone. Promise me that you will not let my child die, too, Jo. Promise me that you will care for my poor babe…' Her hands clutched at Jo's, bruising her fingers as she writhed in pain again.

'You are not going to die,' Jo said, smiling down at her tenderly. 'I shall not let you die—but your child will be cared for whatever happens. I promise you that I would never neglect it.'

'Oh, God,' Ellen screamed out, her back arching as the pain ripped through her. 'How much more? Matt…please help me. Matt, I need you so…'

'What is happening?' a voice asked from the doorway and Jo turned to see Hal standing there. 'Is she dying? Mrs Stowe said that she was very weak.'

'She is weak,' Jo said, 'but she is fighting as hard as she can, Hal. Has Mrs Stowe sent for the doctor?'

'Yes, for I saw one of the grooms as I came here,' Hal said and approached the bed. His face twisted with pity as he saw Ellen's agony. 'Is there nothing we can do?'

'Ellen is concerned for her babe,' Jo said. 'It might help her if you told her that you will care for her child if…'

Hal nodded, bending over Ellen as she writhed once more. 'I am here, Ellen,' he said. 'I shall take care of the child— but you must try. Try for Matt's sake. He would want you to live for his child…try for Matt, Ellen.'

'Matt?' Ellen's eyes opened, but it was clear that she hardly saw him. 'Matt…you have come for me. My love…'

'No, Ellen, it is Hal, Matt's brother,' Hal said. He stripped off his coat, going to her and taking her hands in his. 'Give me Matt's child, Ellen. Try once more, my dearest sister. Try once more for Matt…he would expect it of you, Ellen. He wants you to be strong for yourself and the child.'

Jo's eyes misted with tears as she saw the change in Ellen almost at once. Hal had struck the right note, and it had given her strength to try again. Now, perhaps, there was a glimmer of hope that when the doctor came he might save her.

Jo looked at Hal and something moved inside her, for she saw a side of him that he normally kept hidden behind his mocking smile. He was strong and brave and generous, and she thought that she might be falling in love with him.

Ellen opened her eyes and looked at the child as Jo placed her in her arms. Her face was stained with tears, for she had suffered greatly, but in the end the doctor had delivered her baby without use of the forceps, and she was beautiful.

'She is lovely, isn't she?' Ellen whispered, her strength almost at an end. 'Perfect…she is perfect, Jo.'

'Yes, she is perfect,' Jo said and watched as mother and child bonded, a feeling of love and tenderness swelling inside her—after all the trauma of the night, it was good to see Ellen at peace. 'You were very brave, Ellie.'

Ellen looked up at her, a wistful expression in her eyes. 'Thank Hal for all he did for me, Jo,' she said. 'He made me remember how strong and brave Matt was and I knew I had to live for his child's sake.'

'Yes, I shall. I shall go down now,' Jo said, for Mrs Stowe was signalling to her that she ought to leave Ellen to sleep.

She left the bedchamber and walked down the stairs, feeling weary, for she had not slept at all the previous night. Hal was in the parlour. He was nursing a glass of sherry and sitting in a chair by the fireplace, his head back and his eyes closed.

'Ellen is sleeping now,' Jo said and he opened his eyes to look at her. 'She asked me to thank you for what you did, Hal. She says it helped her to bear the pain.'

'I am glad if it did,' Hal said as he stood up. He put his glass down, the contents hardly touched. 'But I did very little. You were with her all the time and you did everything. Your encouragement made her try again and again when she would have given up. I cannot thank you enough for what you have done this night, Jo.'

'I did only what I would for any woman in such distress,' Jo said. 'But Ellen is my friend and I wanted to comfort her, because I care for her. I should have been distraught had she died.'

'The doctor told me it was touch and go for a while,' Hal said and looked grim. 'Thank God she was here with us and not alone in some grimy back street in London! She would certainly have died without help.'

'Yes, she would,' Jo said and made a little choking sound. 'She should have had her husband and family about her—' Breaking off because she was close to tears, Jo found herself being cradled in Hal's arms. He did not attempt to kiss her or make love to her, but simply held her as she leaned her head against his shoulder, the tears of relief trickling down her cheeks. 'I was so afraid for her…'

'Hush now, dear Jo,' Hal said and kissed her hair. 'You have been so brave and it is all over now. The doctor told me that she will recover, though she must rest for a long time, and he does not think she should have more children.'

Jo drew away from him, wiping her eyes with the back of her hand. 'I am foolish to weep all over you. Forgive me, Hal. It was just the relief of knowing that the child is safely born and Ellen has come through her ordeal. It is sad that the doctor thinks she ought not to have more children—but she loved Matt so much that I do not think she will marry again.'

'I dare say not,' Hal said and looked thoughtful. 'Matt told me that he was very much in love with her, and I think she felt the same. They were fortunate, for such a love is not given to everyone.'

'No, I do not believe it is,' Jo agreed. She raised her head, looking into his eyes. 'I am very tired. I think I shall go up and rest for a little—and perhaps you should go home? You must have travelled a long way yesterday.'

'Yes, I did,' Hal said. He hesitated and then nodded. 'Yes, I shall go home. I shall call and see how Ellen goes on tomorrow, if I may?'

'Yes, of course. You must know that we are always pleased to see you here, Hal.'

She turned away before he could reply, going up to her

own room, where she lay down fully clothed and pulled the bedcovers over her. It had taken all her own strength to help Ellen through the pain, and she was tired—too tired to wonder why her heart was aching, though it might have been the way Hal had looked at her when he said that his brother and Ellen were lucky to have known real love.

She drifted into sleep, dreaming of her home and the time when she was young. It was a warm summer day and she was playing in the meadow with her sisters when they saw their papa coming towards them.

'Papa…' she murmured in her dream and her cheeks were wet with tears. 'Oh, Papa…I love him so…'

'Oh, how could Agatha say such a thing?' Mrs Horne screwed up the letter from Lady Wainwright. 'She has such a wicked tongue! If Jo found it unbearable staying with her, I am not surprised that she chose to run away with her friend. I should never have let Jo go to Bath with her! I knew they did not get on.'

Lady Edgeworthy took the letter, smoothing it out and reading it herself. 'I agree with you that this is most unkind,' she said and frowned. 'Some of the things she says are uncalled for—especially when you have Jo's own letter explaining how it was.'

They were sitting in the parlour at Sawlebridge House taking tea together and the letters had that minute been brought in. Lucy was upstairs busy with her own pursuits and it was a chance to talk about this business in private without fear of upsetting her. She had been distressed when Jo's letter arrived, announcing that she would not be coming home for some time.

'Yes. I am glad that I had that first,' Mrs Horne said, nodding, 'otherwise I should have been very distressed. My sister says that she wrote this in Bath, but I do not think that she can have sent it until she had returned home. It would not have been all of two weeks in coming.'

'That was remiss of her,' Lady Edgeworthy said and shook her head over it. 'Well, I should put these remarks from your mind if I were you, Cynthia. She does not deserve a reply, to my mind.'

'Oh, she deserves a reply,' Mrs Horne said. 'And would receive what she deserves had it not been for Lord Wainwright's kindness to us. To tell you the truth, Bertha, I should have said something sharp to her long ago had it not been for Wainwright. He has been generous and I would not be bad friends with him for the world. I have always liked him, and I think that my sister makes his life…difficult.'

'Well, I dare say you are right,' Lady Edgeworthy said and looked at her. 'You are not worrying about Jo, are you?'

'Just a little,' Mrs Horne confessed. 'Perhaps it is foolish of me—it has only been a matter of a few days since her letter arrived—but I must confess that I do worry how she is and whether she has settled with her friend. Last night I could not sleep for thinking of her, and I felt that she was in some distress, but I dare say it was merely an irritation of the nerves.'

'Yes, well, it is only natural that you should think of her in the circumstances,' Lady Edgeworthy said. 'But Jo is so sensible and so capable, my dear. I do not think that she will come to any harm—though it appears that she may have caused a little gossip in Bath. No matter, it will die down in time, I am sure.'

'Yes, I hope so for her sake,' Mrs Horne replied with a sigh. 'Jo is headstrong and on occasion thoughtless. She says that she does not wish to marry, but I think she forgets just what that means, for she loves children. It would be a tragedy if she were to have none of her own.'

'Oh, I do not think you need worry about that,' Lady Edgeworthy said with a smile. 'Jo is young and not ill looking. Indeed, I have sometimes thought her quite lovely in her own unique style. I believe that she will find a husband one day, Cynthia—even if he is not a member of the *ton*. I dare say she would be quite happy to marry a gentleman of her father's calling.'

'Yes, perhaps she would,' Mrs Horne said. 'I think she mentioned a gentleman in her letters. Perhaps there is hope that she may be happy one day after all.'

'Yes, I am certain of it,' Lady Edgeworthy said. 'If I know anything of Jo, she will write again as soon as she can.'

'Look at your beautiful daughter,' Jo said, bringing the baby to the bed so that Ellen could take her into her arms. 'Now she was worth all the trouble, was she not?' She made light of her friend's suffering, though they both knew that for a little time it had been touch and go. The doctor had arrived almost too late, for Ellen's strength had been all but gone, but he had come and the baby had been born with his help. Ellen was all the better for a night's sleep, though still weak and rather sleepy.

'She is wonderful,' Ellen said and took the babe into her arms. She smiled tenderly as her child nuzzled at her and began to suck eagerly. 'Oh, how hungry she is, poor little one—but she is so strong and clever, isn't she, Jo?'

'Very clever,' Jo agreed and laughed as the babe sucked greedily at its mother's breast. 'She knows exactly what to do, doesn't she? We were all novices at what we did for her when she was born, but she needed no telling and cried loudly at once. Now she knows just what to do even if you are not sure, Ellen.'

Ellen stroked the dark hair on the baby's head and kissed her. 'I have thought of calling her Matilda—what do you think, Jo?'

'It is a very pretty name—or you could name her for your mother. What was she called?'

'Rosemary,' Ellen said. 'I shall call her Matilda Rose Beverley. Yes, she shall be named for my husband first and then my mother.'

Matilda had done feeding and lay sleepily in her mother's arms. Jo bent to take her from Ellen, transferring her to the cot beside her mother's bed, where she smiled up at them for a moment before drifting off peacefully to sleep.

'She is such a good baby,' Jo said. 'Some of the children I visited in the cottages cried so much that they drove their mothers almost mad with it—but little Mattie is so very good.'

'Oh, yes,' Ellen said and sat forward. 'That is even better, Jo. We shall call her Mattie, for she is her father's daughter. She has his eyes and his nose—and perhaps my mouth.'

'Her hair is very dark now,' Jo said, 'but it may change. I think babies change a lot in the first few days and weeks.'

'I wish that Matt could be here to see her…' Ellen's smile faded as she lay back against the pillows. 'He would have been so proud of her, Jo—but he died before I knew that I was to have a baby.'

'That is very sad,' Jo said, sitting on the edge of the bed

and taking her hand. 'But you have told me what a good man he was, Ellen. If he is in Heaven, he can see her. Try to think of him as being there—and believe that he still loves you and his daughter.'

'Yes, I shall try,' Ellen said. 'If it is true that he is looking after me, I think he sent you to me, Jo. Your friendship has come to mean so very much to me. You cannot know how hard it was for me until I met you. I think I might have died had you not been here last night. If I came through, it was because of you.'

'I did very little,' Jo said. 'Mrs Stowe and the doctor did all that was necessary.'

'But you were here, giving me strength, making me try when I wanted to give up because it was too much to bear. I love you as the sister I have never had, Jo.'

'And I love you as another sister,' Jo said and bent to kiss her cheek. 'Now you must not tire yourself, dearest. The doctor said that you were to rest because you have had quite an ordeal.'

'Yes…' Ellen closed her eyes. 'I do feel very tired…'

Jo left the room quietly. She hoped that Mattie would sleep for a while. Ellen needed her rest. The doctor had been concerned that they might lose her even after the child was born. He had told them that she was not to get up for anything for all of three weeks, and after that they must just hope that she gradually recovered her strength.

Jo was still a little tired, too. Yet she was loath to sit around in the house all day. It was dull out and she suspected that the wind would be cool, but she would be warm enough wrapped in her beautiful cloak. Although a little tired looking when rescued from the trunk, it had responded to a thorough sponging and the flat iron, which Jo had wielded with a will. She had never owned a cloak of this quality and she liked its warmth and its weight, because it hung so well—and somehow when she put it on she felt as if she had become someone else, an exciting, vibrant woman who loved life and was willing to dare all for what she wanted.

Wrapping it about her shoulders, she went downstairs and out of the back parlour windows into the garden. She headed for the gate in the wall, because it was a long time since she had been for a really good walk. Ellen had not dared to venture far since their arrival at the cottage, and Jo had not wanted to leave her.

Now she was free to walk as far as she liked, as long as she was back in time for tea, when Ellen would look for her. She set off in the direction of the wood, and spent a pleasant half an hour or so finding her way up to the Hall, which was where Hal resided when at home.

Jo stood looking at the beautiful old house for a few minutes, which she knew had belonged to Hal's grandmother. It was tempting to go up and ask for Hal, but she resisted, for she must let him come to them. Though he had said they were welcome to visit, she was afraid of appearing too forward. It would be better to wait until she was invited or Ellen was well again.

She was completely unaware that she was being watched, for her imagination was weaving dreams about the house and the life she might have there if by some amazing chance Hal were to make her an offer. He would not, of course, and she shook her head, mentally scolding herself for allowing her imagination to become so wayward.

It was only as she turned and began to walk back to the

cottage that Jo began to think that she might have been followed. At first it was no more than a twig snapping and a feeling...but then, when she turned sharply once, she was almost sure that she saw a man's shadow as he hastily hid behind a tree, but it had happened so fast that she could not be sure.

'Is someone there?' she called out. 'Who are you? Please step out and say your name.'

There was no answer. Jo hesitated for a moment, listening, but there was no sound of any kind, and she decided that she must have been imagining it. Who would want to follow her—and why?

The man stood watching as Jo entered the cottage. So he had been right, he thought with a smirk of satisfaction. She was staying on Hal Beverley's estate, and it was clear that she had the run of the place. What did that mean, he wondered—and what use could he make of the information? Lord Beverley might pay good money for such information—but then, Hal might pay more to save it coming to his father's ears.

It would have been easy enough to snatch the girl in the woods if he had wished, but he was not certain where his best profit lay. He would wait and watch a little longer to see if he could discover just what was going on here...

Jo was in the garden when Hal saw her. She was wearing a midnight-blue velvet cloak with a hood that fell back from her shoulders, and her hair was loose about her face, a little ruffled by the wind. He saw that she had a basket on her arm and had clearly been picking greenery for the house.

He had never seen her look so well. She was always attractive, but she usually did her best to scrape back her lovely hair, leaving only a few tendrils to escape and curl about her face. At this moment it tumbled about her face and shoulders in a glorious tangle of red-gold curls that he found bewitching. She looked like a gypsy, he thought fancifully, but a very beautiful and elegant one.

'Jo?' He went forward eagerly, feeling a spurt of pleasure in seeing her this way, sensing that he had caught her in a private moment.

She turned, a look of alarm in her eyes, which faded as she saw him. 'Hal, you startled me. We expected you yesterday, but you did not come.'

'I had a visitor,' Hal said and frowned. 'He said that he was in the area and called out of the blue. I was forced to entertain him to dinner, though it went against the grain, but I could not refuse him. He stayed last night and I was glad to see him on his way.'

'You do not like him?'

'No…' Hal frowned. 'We are acquaintances, but not friends. You met him once—at that inn outside Bath.'

'Oh, yes, I remember,' Jo said. 'I had forgotten it until you reminded me. No, I do not like him. You had not invited him to call?'

'I may have said that he might in an unguarded moment,' Hal said. 'It was inconvenient, for he would know Ellen.'

'Would it not be best if you were to tell your father now that the child is born? Do you not think that he would like to know he has a granddaughter?'

'I had hoped the child might be a boy,' Hal said. 'I think he would have forgiven anything for an heir.'

'Yes, I dare say,' Jo said. 'However, I do not think Ellen would have survived the birth of a son, Hal. Mrs Stowe says that a boy child would have killed her.'

'Then it is as well she had a girl,' Hal said and frowned. 'I may tell him soon, Jo. He is growing a little stronger, I think, and I would like to have this matter settled—but I must be sure that the shock would not be too great.'

'Yes, well, I cannot argue with your judgement, for I do not know your father.'

'He is a good man, but inclined to be hasty-tempered.'

'You are not like him?'

'I am told I take after my mother. When roused to anger she was implacable, but she seldom lost her temper, for she was blessed with a sense of humour, as I am. Matt was like my father, which is why they quarrelled as often as they did.' She nodded and he saw that she had something on her mind. 'Is something the matter, Jo?'

Her brow wrinkled, a look of doubt in her lovely eyes. 'I am not certain. I think someone may have been following me on my walks these past few days, but I am not sure.'

'What do you mean—following you?'

Jo explained that she had walked as far as his house the previous afternoon, and believed she had been followed on her return to the cottage. 'Since then I have thought that I was watched as I went down to the village, and then again, early this morning, I glanced out of my window and saw a man staring at the cottage. I could not see his face clearly, but he was a tall man, and I thought a gentleman. He looked at me and then turned and walked away. He may have been here on legitimate business, but it was not George, for I have met him.'

'George is my head groom,' Hal said. 'He looks after my stable here and fetches the letters for us—but there are other men working on the estate. I dare say you may have seen one of them.' He frowned. 'At what time did you see this man?'

'Oh, it must have been not much more than seven, for I was up and dressed but had not yet come down.'

'I do not think it can have been Carstairs, for he did not leave his room until nine.'

'Oh…yes, it would have been like him to follow me, I suppose.'

'I cannot vouch for yesterday,' Hal said frowning. 'But I know he was with me from about five in the evening until late—and then, as I said, he did not leave before nine. You must have seen one of the estate workers.'

'Then why did he hide? Why did he not answer when I asked who was there yesterday afternoon?' Jo asked.

'This man…he made no attempt to harm you?'

'No, for I am not the one he wants. If he is here on behalf of Ellen's father, it is her he is interested in.'

'I am sure he is not. How could he have known where to find you?' Hal asked. 'I made sure that we were not followed on our journey. I think you have seen estate workers going about their business, Jo.' He smiled at her. 'How is Ellen this morning?'

'Oh…' Jo laughed. 'How foolish I am! She is a little less tired today, though she still has no energy. She has decided to call the child called Matilda. Mattie for short.'

'That is a lovely idea,' Hal said. 'I am so pleased for her, Jo. It must have been such a terrible time for Ellen these past months—and now at last she has someone of her own to love again.'

'I think she has suffered far more than she let either of us guess,' Jo agreed. 'Usually, she is placid and takes everything in her stride—but when she knew that the child was soon to be born she could not keep the mask in place and she told me how much she wished that Matt could be here. She told me how much she loved him and misses him still.'

'Yes, of course, she must,' Hal said and his expression became bleak, his eyes filled with grief. 'You don't know how much I wish that he could be here, too. He was my brother and my hero. I was always destined for the army or the church as the younger son, and to my mind it was always the army, though my father hoped I would choose the church. When Matt defied my father to marry Ellen, he joined, too. My father disowned him, but I believe he has deeply regretted it. We talked for some time when I was at the estate the last time, and I almost told him that I had found Ellen and that she was about to give birth to Matt's child—but he looked so frail that I was afraid the shock might be too much for him.'

'I am sorry that your father is ill,' Jo said. She wanted to reach out and touch him, but knew that she must not. 'But come in, Hal. Ellen is still resting in bed, because the doctor forbade her to get up for three weeks—but I am sure that she would wish to see you.'

'Yes, of course. I am anxious to see her and the child. You will take me up, Jo?'

'Of course.' She smiled at him. 'Perhaps you would care to take nuncheon with me after you have seen your niece?'

'Why not?' he said. 'I am here for at least a week, Jo. After that I may need to go up to London for a while, but I shall be back as soon as possible.'

'You must not think that you have to dance attendance on us,' Jo said. 'We shall go on very well as we are. Oh, there is one thing you might do for me, if you will?'

'Yes, of course—anything you wish.'

'I have some letters to post to my mother and Lucy, also one for Aunt Bertha,' Jo said. 'If you would be kind enough to frank them for me, it would save some sixpencees for things we need.'

'I shall always be pleased to send your letters, Jo—but if you need money you have only to ask.'

'You know that I shall not do that unless I have no other means of supporting myself,' Jo told him. 'You did not ask me here and I would not be a burden to you, Hal. You have taken Ellen under your wing and that is enough.'

'Nonsense!' Hal said and grinned at her. 'I may be a younger son, but in some ways I was luckier than Matt for I have independent means. My grandmother was quite an heiress and she left her property and money to me. She always said that Matt would inherit Father's estate and that I should have hers.' For a moment the bleak look was back in his eyes. 'Ellen is entitled to whatever I can give her—and one day she will have what is rightfully hers as my brother's widow.'

'Have you not thought that perhaps your father might like to make amends?' Jo asked. 'I know he disowned your brother, but he must have regretted it a thousand times. He cannot be a bad man—you would not care for him as you do if he were.'

'How wise you are for one so young,' Hal said and reached out to touch her hair, letting the silky soft strands of fire slip through his fingers. 'And beautiful with your hair like this. You should wear it loose more often, Jo.'

'Do not mock me!' she cried, jerking her head away. 'Even Papa told me that I looked like a gypsy when my hair was loose. Had I known you were coming, I should have tied it back as I usually do.'

'Well, you should not,' Hal said and there was an unholy light in his eyes. 'Your papa was right, it does make you look like a gypsy—but a very beautiful one. I like your hair, Jo. You should not be ashamed of it.'

'Oh, do not,' Jo said. 'Come, Ellen will have heard our voices and be waiting for us…' She ran ahead of him up the stairs, her cheeks heating. How could he say such things to her! It was unfair of him to tease her so when she knew that it could not be long before he was officially engaged to Chloe Marsham.

Jo left Hal talking to Ellen and went downstairs. She found Mrs Stowe in the kitchen and asked if she would serve a light nuncheon in the dining parlour, because Mr Beverley would be dining with her.

'Mr Beverley is staying to nuncheon, miss?' The housekeeper looked at her in surprise.

'Yes, he says that he will stay,' Jo said, lifting her chin a little. 'There is nothing improper in it, Mrs Stowe. We are merely friends.'

'If you say so, miss,' the housekeeper said. 'But young ladies of your class do not normally entertain gentlemen to nuncheon on their own.'

'We are not alone,' Jo said, a hint of stubbornness about her now. 'Ellen is upstairs and you are here, Mrs Stowe. I assure you that we shall do nothing of which you might have cause to disapprove.'

'Very well, miss,' the housekeeper said, but it was clear that she did not like the idea. 'I shall remain to serve you, unless you dismiss me.'

'As you wish,' Jo said and went away to put her flowers into water. She was in the small parlour putting the finishing touches to a vase when Hal came in. He watched her for a moment, smiling as she placed each bloom just so.

'You enjoy arranging flowers, I see—and you do it very well.'

'Thank you,' Jo said. 'It is one of the small duties I have taken upon myself to ease Mrs Stowe's work.'

He frowned. 'You have no need to work. You are my guest here. If Mrs Stowe cannot manage, I shall send one of the other maids to help her.'

'I pray that you will not do so on my account,' Jo said. 'As you remarked just now, I enjoy arranging flowers, just as I enjoy many other small tasks. Had we been sooner, I should have liked to help pick the fruit from the vegetable garden and bottle it. Mama sometimes allowed me to assist her in her stillroom and I enjoyed making up her recipes for many things.'

'You will make a remarkable wife for some fortunate gentleman,' Hal said, looking at her thoughtfully.

Jo blushed and turned away, for she did not want him to see that she was affected by his remark. 'Shall we go in? Mrs Stowe will serve as soon as we are seated.'

'Yes, of course, but I think we do not need her services,' Hal said. 'She may serve the soup, but after that we shall help ourselves.'

'Perhaps you would tell her that?' Jo said in such a manner that he looked at her.

'Oh, I see. Does she think that I mean to seduce you?' Laughter danced in his eyes and his mouth curved.

Jo shot him a wicked glance. 'I rather think that she believes I mean to seduce you, sir. She suspects that I am a designing hussy who is trying to entrap you into marriage.'

Hal threw back his head and laughed, delighted with her sally. 'Oh, no, does she?' he asked, a glimmer of tears in his eyes. 'Poor Mrs Stowe. I think we must put her out of her misery.'

'What do you mean to say to her?'

'Oh, nothing very much,' Hal said and smiled, 'but leave it to me and do not contradict what I say.'

Jo shook her head at him, but made no reply as they walked into the dining parlour. Mrs Stowe inclined her head respectfully, welcoming him back.

'I am sure Mrs Beverley was pleased to see you, sir.'

'Yes, I am certain she was,' Hal said. 'And I was very happy to see her and my niece. Yes, you may serve the soup at once, Mrs Stowe, but Miss Horne and I will serve ourselves afterwards, thank you.'

'Yes, sir…if you wish it,' the housekeeper said and looked at Jo suspiciously.

'Oh, before you leave, Mrs Stowe,' Hal said, 'I should like you to wish me happy. It is my intention to be married quite soon—perhaps before Christmas if the lady I care for accepts my offer.'

'Oh…Mr Beverley!' Mrs Stowe was suddenly all smiles. 'Well, sir, that is good news, I am sure.'

'Now, you must keep it to yourself for the moment,' Hal said. 'I have not yet spoken to the young lady, and I should not wish it to become common knowledge—but I wanted you to know my intentions.'

'I am sure I am honoured, sir,' the housekeeper said and flashed a smile of satisfaction in Jo's direction. 'Isn't that good news, Miss Horne?'

'Yes, very,' Jo said. Her heart felt as if a dagger had been plunged into it, but she managed to smile. 'I am sure we are all very happy to hear Mr Beverley's news.' His words confirmed what she had suspected—he meant to ask Chloe to marry him very soon.

Mrs Stowe nodded and went out, clearly feeling that she could leave them alone now that Mr Beverley had announced his intention to marry. He would obviously not begin a liaison with his sister-in-law's companion if he were on the verge of asking a young lady to marry him.

'Well,' Hal said as he picked up his spoon and looked across the table at Jo, 'I think that should cure her suspicions for the moment.'

'Yes, I am sure it must,' Jo said. 'She is flattered that you have seen fit to tell her in confidence. I should like to add my good wishes to hers.'

'Should you?' Hal smiled enigmatically. 'Why? You must know that I merely wished to ease her mind. At the moment, the matter of my marriage remains unresolved. I had thought that I knew my own mind, but…' Hal shook his head. 'Let us speak of other things.'

'Yes, very willingly.' Jo said. 'Have you heard from your father since you returned home?'

'No, not yet,' Hal said. 'But I have to go into Lavenham tomorrow on business. If Ellen will spare you to me, you could come with me. We shall see if any letters have come for you from your family—and you might wish to do some shopping?'

'Yes, that would be useful,' Jo said. 'I am sure Ellen will not mind—I shall see that she has all she needs to hand before we leave.' She smiled at him. 'Yes, I should enjoy that very much.'

Chapter Six

'You will enjoy a trip to Lavenham,' Ellen said when Jo told her about the forthcoming excursion. 'My father took me there once years ago, and there are some beautiful old buildings—and a very nice haberdashery shop. At least it was there when I visited, though of course it may not be now for it was some years ago.'

'Is there anything I might purchase for you in the town, Ellen?'

'Yes, I should like some embroidery silks and some beads—blue ones, I think, and jet if they have them. I feel a little better and I should like to begin work on a panel of embroidery, which I shall make up into a gown when I am up and about again. Once it is finished I shall take it into Lavenham and see if I can find a shop that would sell it for me.'

'Oh, what a good idea,' Jo said. 'I am sure there must be a seamstress in the town, and I shall see if I can discover her direction.'

It was good to see Ellen looking less tired and beginning

to think about the future again. Jo took little Mattie from her cot and gave her to her mother. She had begun to whimper, but quietened as soon as Ellen put her to the breast.

It made Jo's eyes moist to watch them together, and she thought that it must be a wonderful feeling to hold your own child. She enjoyed nursing Ellen's baby, and helping to keep her clean and sweet, and she took Mattie when she had finished feeding again, laying her in her cot once more.

'I dare say we shall be gone some hours tomorrow,' she said, 'but you will not mind being alone?'

'I shall not be alone, for Mrs Stowe will be here,' Ellen said. 'Enjoy your visit, Jo. We shall not often get the chance, for Hal will not wish to stay here for ever, and it will not be easy to go in on the public coach—though I believe there is one from the village once a week.'

'Yes, I believe so,' Jo said. 'But once I have the things I need, I dare say I shall not need to visit often.'

Mrs Stowe entered the room then with the tea tray. She gave Jo rather an odd look as she set it down, but said nothing. Instead, she bent over the cot and smiled down at the baby.

'Is there anything else you need, ma'am?' she asked Ellen.

'Nothing for the moment,' Ellen told her. 'I may need your help with the baby tomorrow, Mrs Stowe. Jo is going into Lavenham with Mr Beverley to purchase some things we need—is there anything you require for the house? I am sure she would be glad to order it for you.'

'Yes, of course,' Jo said. 'Just give me a list and I shall be pleased to do it, Mrs Stowe.'

'Yes, well, there might be a few things,' Mrs Stowe said. 'It was very good of Mr Beverley to take you, miss. I dare say he has plenty to do what with the wedding—'

'What wedding?' Ellen looked surprised. 'No one has said anything to me.'

'I dare say that is because it is not certain,' Jo said. 'Hal said that he intends to ask the lady he wishes to marry, but is not yet sure that she will accept.'

'Oh, but she will, of course she will, for he is such a charming man,' Ellen said and frowned. 'I had no idea he was planning to marry.'

'Before Christmas if she will have him,' Mrs Stowe said with another look at Jo. 'That's what he said—though I shall say nothing of it outside this room. I thought you must know, ma'am.'

'No, I didn't,' Ellen said. 'Thank you, Mrs Stowe. Jo will pour for us.' She looked at Jo as the door closed behind the housekeeper. 'Did you know anything of this?'

'I know that Chloe Marsham was expecting an offer from him in Bath,' Jo said. 'I think he had other things on his mind—but I dare say he will ask her soon.'

'Oh…I had thought something quite different,' Ellen said and looked doubtful. 'Do you think she will mind us living here?'

'Surely that is up to Hal, isn't it?'

'Yes, but…' Ellen was thoughtful. 'It would change things, Jo. I do not think it could be the same if he were married.'

'No,' Jo agreed. 'I am sure that it would not.'

It would mean that she could not continue to live at Hal's cottage, because Chloe would not put up with it once she knew. Either she would have to go home to Mama or perhaps she and Ellen could find themselves somewhere else to live.

* * *

'It looks as if we may have a fine day for it,' Hal said as he handed Jo into his curricle the next morning. 'George is to come with us. I thought that he could escort you about the town while you do your shopping, Jo. I have some business of my own and George will be pleased to direct you, and to carry any purchases you might make. We shall meet at the Duke's Head afterwards and take some refreshment before we return.'

'That is thoughtful of you, for I have several commissions from Ellen and Mrs Stowe,' Jo said and smiled at the groom, who was standing at the horses' heads. It also made their excursion respectable and would stop tongues clacking, which they might have had she gone with him unescorted. 'I think I shall keep you busy, George.'

'It will be a pleasure, miss. I was born in a cottage just outside Lavenham, and I know it well.'

Hal took the reins, George leapt up behind and they were off, bowling through the pleasant countryside at a good pace. Jo looked about her with interest at the gently undulating parkland, thinking that the estate was larger than she had remembered as they drove here. Soon they were out on the open road, Hal's horses pulling eagerly as if they were pleased to be given their head, their flashing hooves eating up the road.

There was little traffic to be met at first, just a gentleman on a horse, a farm cart and a young lad driving a flock of geese. However, once they began to get near the town they passed several carriages and men on horseback, as well as country folk on foot and in their gigs.

'It is market day,' Hal said. 'I had forgotten that, but no matter. It will make your visit all the more interesting, Jo.'

Jo agreed that it would, a sparkle of excitement in her eyes as she saw all the activity going on. Brightly coloured stalls had been set up on the market place and they were doing a thriving trade as people milled around them, haggling for the wares the traders displayed.

They drove past the inn where they were to meet later, Hal drawing his curricle to a halt at a quieter end of the town. He helped Jo to get down, smiling at her, his hand holding hers for perhaps one second more than he need.

'You have everything you require?' he asked, his brows arched. 'Should you want more money, just ask George and he will advance you what you require.'

'Thank you, but I have sufficient,' Jo said. 'I shall see you here at a little after noon, sir.'

Hal nodded, remounted and set off. George looked at her thoughtfully. 'Where would you like to start, miss? Do you prefer to wander round the market stalls or visit the shops?'

'I think I should like to visit the market first,' Jo told him. 'I have a list of things Mrs Stowe needs for the house. You may know where the best places are to purchase these things.'

George took the list, studied it for a moment and nodded. 'Yes, miss. I can deal with this if you like. I don't know why she gave it to you—this is my department. Now, why don't you have a wander round the market while I do these errands and then I'll meet you—by the bakers just over there.'

Jo followed the direction of his gaze and nodded. 'Yes, that is a very good idea. If you do not know it already, perhaps you might inquire if there is a seamstress in the town, particularly one who has a showroom for her goods.'

'I think I know,' George said, 'but I'll make inquires, miss.'

Jo thanked him and they parted. She began to wander about the market, enjoying the luxury of lingering over the examination of goods she liked instead of being urged to hurry, as she had been in Bath when with Lady Wainwright.

There were all kinds of goods on offer, for it was a large market with more than fifty stalls. Many of them were selling fruit and vegetables, fish, meat and sweetmeats; some had ironmongery, tools and nails and a tin bath; others sold trinkets, and one had leather goods, including shoes and boots. But towards the centre of the market, Jo found the stalls that interested her.

One man had a really good display of material, silks and linens, woollens and fustians, also the cottons and silks needed for sewing. Jo lingered over her purchases for some minutes, deciding at last on some dark green, soft woollen cloth, which would make up into a useful dress for the cold winter evenings to come. Trimmed with silk braid and lace, it would be elegant and charming but understated, which was right for the life she led now. There was no point in buying expensive silk when she would never wear it, though of course there was some wonderful silk in the trunk that had come from the attic.

She had not touched the contents as yet, except for the cloak, which she had worn once or twice when it was very cold. Today it was milder and she had worn a pelisse over her warm skirt and bodice.

Having made her purchase, and seen it wrapped in brown paper, she tucked the parcel under her arm and set out to look for the materials Ellen required. Although one of the market stalls sold some of the things she had asked for, Jo was not satisfied that the silks were of the quality her friend needed and she decided to visit the shop Ellen had told her about next.

As she turned to leave the market, she almost bumped into a man who had been standing very close to her. She apologised, glancing up into his face. She felt an odd quiver of fear as she saw his expression, which was somehow menacing. He said nothing to her, and yet she felt that she knew him. However, it was not until she had reached the baker's shop to find George waiting for her that it came to her. Of course! It was the man from the inn—the one Hal had warned to leave her alone. Mr Carstairs! She had seen him once in Bath. How odd that he should be here in Lavenham, and standing so close to her! He had given her such a cold look, but he had not spoken.

She shook her head as an icy shiver went down her spine. It meant nothing. It was simply a coincidence, of course it was. He probably lived in the district. Nevertheless, she would mention it to Hal when they met later at the inn.

'Let me take that for you,' George offered as she went up to him. 'Now, where did you wish to go next, miss? There is a seamstress just around the corner. She has a little shop, where she sells hats and a few gowns, though most of her work is done to order.'

'I should like to visit her,' Jo said, 'and the haberdashers, which I think is just over there.' She gave him a slightly apprehensive look. 'Will you come with me, please, George?'

'Yes, miss, of course,' he said and frowned. 'Has something upset you, miss?'

'No…at least, I am not sure. There was a man close behind me. I almost bumped into him as I turned.'

'What about your purse, miss?' George said. 'Have you that safe?'

'Yes, it is here on my wrist,' Jo said. 'I do not think it was my purse he wanted.' She gave a little shiver. 'No, it is foolish of me, but he was a little…menacing.'

'If he has harmed you—' George looked fierce '—you point him out to me, miss!'

'No, no, it is quite all right now that you are here,' Jo said. 'Let us go to the haberdasher's shop and then pay a visit to the seamstress. After that, I shall buy some sweet cakes for Ellen and then it will be time to meet Mr Beverley.'

It was half an hour later that they entered the inn and were taken to the private parlour, where Jo waited alone for some minutes for Hal to join her. George had deposited her goods in a safe place for her and then gone off on some errand of his own. She was warming her hands before the fire as she waited for Hal to join her.

She was pleased with her morning's excursion, for the seamstress had been interested in hearing about Ellen's work and expressed an interest in seeing some of it—and, what was more, she had admired Jo's hat. On learning that Jo had fashioned it herself, she had said that she might be willing to buy something similar for her shop.

'We do not have a milliner in town at the moment,' Madame Susanne told her. 'I have considered making a few hats to order—if I had some orders for your work, would you be willing to make up, say, three or four a week?'

'Yes, I think I could manage that,' Jo said. 'I shall return to the haberdashers and purchase a few things I need…oh, but I am not sure when I shall be able to get them to you.'

'I am sure there must be a carrier who comes this way once a week,' Madame Susanne said. 'You must ask your friends, for I am sure they will know.'

Jo had asked George about it when she left the shop, and he had told her that he came into the town at least once every week himself and would be glad to carry out any small commissions she had for him. On the strength of that, Jo had borrowed two books from the local lending library, something new to read to Ellen while she worked on her embroidery.

'Lost in thought? A penny for them?'

Jo turned from her contemplation of the fire as she heard Hal's voice. Her smile lit up her face, making her more lovely than she knew. He stared at her for a moment, his eyes so intent that it made her heart race.

'Is something wrong, Hal?'

'No, nothing,' he said, recovering himself. 'Did you enjoy yourself this morning?'

'Yes, indeed I did, but I did not get as far as the Receiving Office—George said it was at the far end of the town and the time had flown.'

'Then it as well that I went there myself,' Hal said and smiled as he took two letters from his coat pocket and handed them to her. 'These are both for you, Jo.'

'Oh, thank you!' Jo said, and her eyes shone with pleasure. 'One is from Lucy and the other from Mama. They must have had my letters, and I know that it will have set their minds at rest.' She tucked the letters into her reticule for such pleasure was not to be rushed.

'Have you bought everything you need?' Hal asked, a soft smile in his eyes as he saw her innocent pleasure.

'Yes, thank you. I spent more than I had intended, but it

was in a good cause—I believe I may have discovered a means whereby both Ellen and I may earn a little money.'

Hal's brow furrowed. 'I have told you that there is no need for either of you to work. I should by rights be giving you an allowance for looking after Ellen. It was my intention to employ a companion.'

'I should not accept it,' Jo told him, lifting her chin. 'I am very willing to be Ellen's friend and need no remuneration for it—and I love making hats. Marianne and I made them together, and I believe her work was neater than mine, but I can fashion them myself, and I may be able to sell one or two, which will help. Ellen is hoping for commissions for her embroidery, and Madame Susanne says that she will be happy to display her work and take orders for it.'

'I thought you intended to be an author?'

'Oh, yes, I shall do that, too, when I can,' Jo told him. 'But I am not foolish enough to imagine that it will be easy to sell my stories, sir. So I must find something more practical, because my money will not last for ever. And I know that I might ask you for anything I needed, but it would not be right—although I should like to use the materials in your grandmother's trunk, if you are sure that you do not mind?'

'I have told you that you are welcome to use anything you find in the attics,' Hal said. 'I dare say there may be more materials stored in the attics at my house—Grandmother hardly ever threw anything out. I shall ask my housekeeper to discover if there is anything worthwhile and have whatever comes to light sent down to you.'

'That would be wonderful,' Jo said. 'I dare say Ellen would be able to use some of it as well, for it is surprising what can be done if you are good with your needle.'

'Then it shall be done,' Hal said, amused. He thought of his Spanish mistress, who had needed a diamond necklace to please her. 'And now—are you hungry?'

'Yes, I am,' Jo replied. 'Oh, there is one thing…did you know that Mr Carstairs was here in town?'

'Carstairs?' Hal frowned. 'No, I didn't—are you sure?'

'Yes, for I almost bumped into him and he gave me a very odd look. It sent shivers down my spine.'

'Did he say anything to you? Or harm you?'

'No, of course not. Why should he?' Jo smiled. 'He was perhaps annoyed about something that had nothing to do with me.'

'Yes, perhaps,' Hal said, 'but it is odd. I remember hearing something about him. I paid it little heed at the time…but I shall write to a friend of mine and ask what he knows.' He smiled at her. 'Come, let us forget him and have our meal.'

'Oh, yes, these beads are exactly what I wanted,' Ellen said as she undid the paper twist and found some lovely shiny beads, 'and the jet is nice quality, too. I shall be able to make a very good design with these.' She smiled at Jo from the bed. 'What did you buy for yourself?'

'I bought some good quality wool to make into a gown for winter evenings,' Jo said. 'Also some materials to make hats. Madame Susanne complimented me on the one I was wearing, and said that if I made one or two for her to display in her showroom she would take orders for them—so I have decided to try. And I think she was very interested in your embroidery, though she said she could not be sure until she had seen an example of your work.'

'But that sounds very promising,' Ellen said. 'I have some

heavy silk in my trunk, which I shall make up as an evening gown. I shall use you as my model, Jo, for you have a lovely figure, and a lot of young ladies would like to be as slim as you are. It will show the gown to advantage; after all, it is the embroidery that I mainly wish to do—I dare say Madame Susanne has her own girls working for her.'

'Yes, she said as much,' Jo agreed. 'However, she does not have anyone who can do exquisite embroidery or beading, and it was that that interested her, I think.'

'Well, that is good for us both,' Ellen said. 'Did you find any letters waiting for you?'

'I have two,' Jo said. 'Mama says that she is not at all cross with me, but begs me to write whenever I can—and to come home and visit her when you can spare me.' Her eyes were a little moist. 'Do you not think that was kind of her?'

'Yes, for she might have been cross because you went without her permission, but I am glad that she did not scold you. It shows that she loves you very much, Jo.' Ellen looked wistful. 'It would be nice to have a loving mother and father.'

'I am sure that your mother would wish to write to you if she could,' Ellen said. 'But you must not write to her again, in case your father discovers where you are once more.'

'I know…' Ellen shook her head sadly. 'I must try not to mind, Jo. I have you, Hal—and my darling Mattie. It is more than enough. Many people do not have half as much.'

'No, perhaps not,' Jo said, but felt a little sad for her friend, because she had so much more. 'Perhaps one day…'

'Yes, perhaps,' Ellen agreed. 'No more of this, Jo. I made my decision when I ran away to marry my darling Matt and I was very happy. I shall not feel sorry for myself. Instead, we shall plan what we are going to do. You will be busy with your hats and your stories, and I have my embroidery and Mattie.'

'Yes,' Jo said and nodded. They had a great deal to look forward to over the coming months—if both of them had a little sorrow in their lives, they must put it from their minds.

Over the next two weeks Jo worked hard at making three hats to send to Madame Susanne. She fashioned one from some blue velvet that she had found in the trunk from the attic. One was made up from a dark green silk gown that she had cut up to make into a skirt for herself, and another from a small piece of heavy yellow silk that she had also found in Lady Beverley's trunk, right at the bottom. She had bought several lengths of stiffened buckram for the linings and to give the hats their shape, which she formed very cleverly and trimmed with ribbons and artificial flowers, also from the little storehouse of pretty trifles that had belonged to Lady Helena Beverley.

She had also worked on the new evening gown for herself, and she was sitting in the small parlour downstairs one afternoon, surrounded by all her industry when Hal was announced. He walked in, looking surprised and then interested as he picked up each of the bonnets and examined them.

'These are very stylish,' he said. 'Did you make them?'

'Yes. I used some material from your grandmother's trunks to make them,' Jo said. 'I am glad that you approve.'

'I think you have very good taste,' Hal said and smiled as Ellen walked into the room. 'How are you? I must say that you look very well.'

'Oh, I am perfectly well again,' Ellen told him. 'I have just been up to nurse Mattie. She is settled now, but you may see her if you wish.'

'Perhaps another time,' Hal said. 'I came to ask if you would both dine with me tomorrow evening. I have had some trunks brought down from the attics, and if the contents are of use to either or you, I shall have them sent down. To me it all looks sadly dated, but perhaps…' He shook his head as he looked at the hats again. 'You have such good taste, Jo. I think that you might help me decide what I ought to do with my house.'

'You have a lovely house. I have not been inside it, though I have longed to,' Jo said. 'You do not mean to sell it?'

'Oh, good lord, no,' Hal said and grinned. 'I believe I told you that Grandmother never threw anything away?'

'Yes, I think you did.' Jo looked at him inquiringly.

'Well, it is a little overcrowded in parts. I am not certain that it would appeal to a young woman's taste as it is— perhaps one day you would look it over and give me the benefit of your advice?'

'Yes, of course, if you wish it,' Jo said. 'I could come for an hour or so tomorrow, if that would suit you?'

'I do not wish to put you out, for I know you are busy…' his eyes moved over the hats and the sewing she had put down when he arrived '…but I should be grateful for your opinion. It is not a large house by country standards. My father's house is very much bigger, but I prefer Bellingham Park to Beverley House myself. I used to visit my grandmother here when I was a child and fell in love with it.'

'Oh, no, it will be no trouble. I should enjoy it,' Jo said and looked at Ellen. 'You would not mind if I went there for an hour or so tomorrow morning?'

'No, of course not. You know that I do not come down much before noon,' Ellen said. 'And we shall be pleased to dine with you tomorrow evening, Hal.'

'Good, that is settled then,' he said. 'I hoped that you might, for I shall not see you again for a week or so after that, I'm afraid. I must go up to London on business, though I do not intend to stay long.'

'It will be a pleasant occasion for both of us,' Ellen said. 'We are very happy here, Hal, and your visits are a delight— I hope you mean to stay and drink a dish of tea with us?'

'Yes, I should like that,' Hal said. 'I enjoy having you both nearby. I hope you are settled at the cottage?'

'Yes, for the time being at least,' Ellen told him. 'As you know, I do not wish to be found by my father. If he should learn of my whereabouts, I might have to move on, though I should be reluctant to do so.'

'If that happens, I shall talk to him, reason with him,' Hal said. He did not tell her, but one of his reasons for making the journey to London was to discover if there was any way he could legally become her guardian and the guardian of her child. 'But I dare say he will give up when he discovers that you have disappeared again.'

'Yes, I am sure he will,' Jo added her assurances to his— she knew that Ellen was still inclined to worry that her father would arrive and force her to leave with him. 'You are quite safe here, dearest, for how would he know where you are?'

Jo was up early the next morning, because she wanted to put the finishing touches to her new gown, which she intended to wear that evening. She set out for Hal's house at a little after nine, wearing the fur-lined blue cloak that she had taken from Lady Beverley's trunk, because the weather was much colder that day.

When she reached the house, she found that Hal was

standing outside talking to one of his grooms. He turned to watch her as she approached him, his eyes moving over her in silent appreciation. Her hair had blown free of its strict confines, and long tendrils of red-gold tangled about her face. He thought that she looked truly beautiful, something he had not thought when they first met. Perhaps it was because he had come to know her nature, or perhaps it was the blue cloak that seemed to give her a regal presence that she did not always have at other times.

He went to meet her, a smile of welcome on his lips. 'So you have kept your word despite the bitter weather. Come in and take a cup of wine with me to warm you.'

'Thank you,' Jo said. A little tremor went down her spine as he kissed her cheek and she allowed him to hold her hand as he led her into the house. 'Oh, how lovely this is,' she exclaimed. 'It has an immediate feel of warmth and welcoming—as if it were pleased to see one.' She gave a husky laugh. 'That sounds fanciful, I am sure.'

'No, it is exactly as I feel every time I come back to it after being away, as if I were being embraced by a pair of warm arms.'

'Oh, yes, that is exactly right.' Jo's face was alight with pleasure, for she felt so at home here with him.

'Come into the small parlour,' Hal invited. 'My house-keeper has placed the trunks she had brought down there. She says that everything was so well wrapped and preserved with lavender and camomile that it is all in good condition.'

'Just as the trunk was that I already have,' Jo said. 'Your grandmother was a very clever lady—she must have known that such lovely things might be used again, even though she had no use for them.'

Three large trunks had been brought into the parlour. Hal opened the first lid to reveal an array of silk gowns, which had been stored with tissue and herbs to keep them sweet. The second contained all kinds of trinkets, from feathers and lace to bales of unused materials, and the third had evening cloaks, stockings, and many smaller items of clothing. Jo exclaimed over the quality, for much of the contents would be useful to her either for making hats or new gowns for herself and Ellen.

'Are they of any use?' Hal asked as he poured her a glass of wine. 'Or shall we have them returned to the attics?'

'Oh, no, there is a great deal here we may use. We shall enjoy cutting out some new gowns,' Jo said, 'but the lace in that trunk is exquisite, also the silk and ribbons that have as yet been unused. I think Lady Beverley kept all the offcuts from her expensive gowns in case she needed them. I should love to use them for trimmings for my hats.' She took the glass he gave her and sipped from it.

'Then you must do as you wish,' Hal said, and his eyes were soft as he smiled. 'It was strange, but I could not help thinking how well that cloak becomes you. I do not know if my grandmother ever wore it in my presence, but I loved her very much. She was beautiful even when she was old.'

'Then perhaps that is why you thought I looked well in her cloak,' Jo said. She put up a hand to her hair, which she had scraped back from her face in her usual style, though the wind had blown much of it about her face. 'But she must have been a very elegant lady; her clothes are wonderful, even though the styles are dated.'

'Yes, I believe she was much admired, even into her later years.' Hal's eyes glinted with wicked laughter. 'I must warn you that she was a courtesan before my grandfather married her. The clothes in these trunks are from that time and might tell a story if they could. She had several lovers—or protectors—but then she fell in love with Grandfather, and I believe she was faithful to him for the rest of her life, though she still had followers. Another man might have been jealous or suspicious, but I think he took a Machiavellian pleasure in seeing her with her admirers.'

'Oh, no, did he? That is a wonderful story,' Jo said, her face lighting up with laughter. 'Your grandfather must have loved her very much to marry her despite her reputation.'

'Yes, that is just right—Grandfather adored her,' Hal said. 'My father married a woman of good reputation and fortune, and I believe they were content, if not wildly happy. I hardly knew Mama, because she died when I was seven…of childbed fever, I am told. Perhaps that is why I loved Grandmama so much.'

'It must be awful to lose your mother so young,' Jo said and her heart caught. 'We were so lucky, for we had both Mama and Papa until a year ago. Papa died of a fever, which may have been taken from one of his parishioners. He was such a good man, Hal. I wish that you could have met him.'

'Yes, I should have liked that,' Hal said. 'But you have your mama still and your sisters—and one day I should be honoured to meet them, if they will permit?'

'Yes, of course,' Jo said and smothered a sigh. 'I think I miss Marianne the most, for we were very close. Having Ellen as a friend has eased that loss a little, but…'

'You still miss your family, I dare say?'

'Yes, though that does not mean that I wish to go home. I enjoy living with Ellen, and I love little Mattie—she is such a good baby. She sleeps most of the night, though last night she did wake for a while. I took her in with me so that Ellen could rest, and after an hour or so she went back to sleep.'

'Ellen is very fond of you, I know,' Hal said. 'But if you wish to visit your family in a few weeks, you must tell me and I shall arrange it.'

'It is enough for the moment that Mama and Lucy will have my letters,' Jo said. 'And that I have theirs.'

'You must ask George to take your letters with him when he goes to Lavenham while I am away,' Hal said. 'And he will see if there is anything for you whenever he goes in for supplies.'

'Oh, that would be wonderful,' Jo said and smiled at him. 'How kind you are to arrange all this for me, Hal—and I know that I have put you out by coming here, for you did not intend it, did you?'

'No,' Hal said, an odd look in his eyes. 'I had intended something very different, but life has a way of changing a man's plans whether he wishes it or no. However, I am very glad that you came, Jo. Indeed, I am heartily thankful that fate interfered, otherwise I might have made a terrible mistake.' He shook his head as Jo raised her brows. 'No, I must not say more at the moment. My plans are not yet formed. Forgive me—would you care for more wine?'

Jo looked at her glass, which was still full, for she had taken but one sip from it. He had clearly wanted to change the subject.

'Perhaps I might go with your housekeeper now, Hal? I should like to tidy myself—and then to look over the house and give you my opinion. I must say that this room would make a pleasant place to sit during the morning.'

Hal rang the bell and the housekeeper appeared. She smiled at Jo and took her off, saying that she might tidy herself in her apartments before she was conducted over the house.

Hal stared after her as she left the room. He had not intended that Jo should accompany Ellen to his estate, but he knew that it was fortunate that she had done so. Ellen might have died without her friend to care for her. Indeed, she was still weak from the birth, and dependent on Jo—though whether it was fair to keep Jo here with no way of contacting her family other than through letters was another matter.

He was not yet certain of his own mind. His heart was telling him something, but his mind fought against it, for he did not wish to do anything that might hasten his father's death.

Lord Beverley was slowly accustoming himself to the death of his eldest son, and the fact that Hal was now his heir. He had asked that Hal make a good marriage by Christmas—but would he accept the daughter of an impoverished vicar? A girl, moreover, who had left Bath under a cloud of suspicion. Mrs Stowe had suspected that there might be an illicit liaison between him and Jo—and others might also if they knew the way things were here. He had been used to walking down most days, even when Ellen was still confined to bed. He would have to be careful that people did not start to gossip, for Jo's sake as well as his own. It was perhaps as well that he was going away for a few days, because he needed to think about what he truly wanted for the future.

Jo spent almost two hours being shown over Hal's house by his housekeeper, Mrs Baker. She was a plump, friendly, talkative woman and she had been delighted to give Jo a potted history of the house and the lady who had owned it before him.

'She was a delight to know, miss,' she said. 'I was just a girl in those days. My mother was the cook here then and I came to the kitchen to be with her sometimes. Lady Helena Beverley was such a lovely lady. She used to come down to the kitchen to talk to my mother, especially if she was very pleased with a special meal. Sometimes she took me on her knee, for she had wanted a daughter, but had only a son. She gave me a gold ring once for my birthday and I have it still.'

'She must have been wonderful,' Jo said. 'I dare say you miss her?'

'Yes, miss, we all do. She went to live at the big house when she married, of course, but she came to see us sometimes—because she still loved this house.' She looked at Jo oddly. 'Do you know, miss, you remind me of her a little. There is a small portrait of her somewhere—done when she was about your age, and there is something about the eyes…though her colouring was different.'

'I should love to see it!'

'I do not quite know where it has been put,' Mrs Baker said. 'It may have been stored somewhere. I must see if I can locate it for you.'

'It is a very beautiful house,' Jo said, having seen the three parlours and the magnificent drawing room. 'I believe there are ten bedchambers?'

'Yes, miss. The master suite is the main one, of course, but there are six others of good size and three smaller—also the nursery and the servants' rooms above and below stairs.'

'Have we seen all of them?'

'Yes, miss, apart from the servants' quarters.'

'Are they in as good condition as those we have seen?'

'Well, almost, miss—though some could do with a little refurbishment.'

'I did not think that much needed doing elsewhere, other than some decoration that needs freshening and the curtains in several bedchambers. Also in the drawing room I think the curtains and the seat covers might be renewed, but I see little else that needs changing. Perhaps some of the rooms are a little crowded with knickknacks, and they might be stored or moved into other rooms.'

'Yes, miss, just what I have thought myself. You could have knocked me down with a feather when Mr Hal said he was thinking of making changes, for it is not like him—and it would be a shame.'

'Well, perhaps he will not make so very many, though…' She shook her head as the housekeeper looked curious. 'No, it is not for me to say. I have been asked for my advice and shall give it.' She could not picture Chloe here unless sweeping changes were made, and that would be a pity.

'Mr Hal will be in his library, miss,' the housekeeper said. 'You know where to find it?'

'Yes, of course, for you took me there first of all. Thank you for showing me the house, Mrs Baker. I have enjoyed it so much.'

'It is a pleasure, miss. I hope you and the other young lady are happy in the cottage?'

'Yes, we are, thank you.'

Jo left her and walked down the stairs. Hal's library was at the back of the house and overlooked splendid lawns and a rose garden. She knocked and entered as he called out that she might, finding him standing by the long windows, gazing out at the garden.

'I am not disturbing you?'

'No, of course not,' he said, turning to look at her. He had originally intended taking her over the house himself, but decided that it would be better left to his housekeeper. 'What did you think of it?'

'It is a wonderful house, so light and airy,' Jo said. 'I am not surprised that your grandmother loved it. And she had excellent taste. For myself, I would alter very little. A certain amount of decoration is necessary for it has not been done in some years. Curtains in the guest bedrooms need to be renewed, though I would keep the colours much as before—and I think the drawing room will need new curtains and covers for the upholstered furniture. A few bits and pieces could be moved to other rooms, perhaps. However, I would change nothing more. '

His brows rose. 'Nothing more? Tell me truthfully, Jo—if you were to live here would you still change nothing?'

'Only those things I have mentioned, which I am sure your grandmother would do, too, if she were here.'

'That is how I felt myself,' Hal agreed and looked pleased. 'But I thought that it might seem old fashioned to a young lady—and I was willing to pull it all apart if it would please her.'

'Oh…' Jo's heart caught, for she felt distressed to think that this lovely house might be destroyed by an unthinking bride. 'Well, I cannot speak for Miss Marsham, of course, but I think it is lovely as it is. It has an individual charm and it would be a shame to lose it.'

'What has Chloe Marsham to do with my house?' Hal raised his brows at her.

'Forgive me. I know…I thought that perhaps…' Jo's cheeks felt warm. 'But I should not have said…'

'No, it is not my intention to marry Chloe,' Hal told her. 'I have thought of it, I shall not deny it. She would be a suitable bride, in my father's opinion—but I do not think she would please me.'

'I see…' Jo turned away, her heart suddenly racing. She could not look at him for fear that he might see the longing in her eyes. Nothing he had said or done had given her the right to hope. 'You have a beautiful view from here.'

'Yes, I do,' Hal said and his hand was on her shoulder, turning her to face him. She gazed up into his eyes, her throat tight. 'I think you may have sensed that I feel something for you?' Jo moved her head, but did not speak. 'I do feel something, Jo, but at the moment I am not free to speak what is in my heart—do you understand that? And I am not sure of what I feel about that. I hope that you may understand me, because I do not wish to hurt you.'

'You think that your father would not approve?' Her eyes were wide and clear, disturbingly honest.

'Yes.' Hal reached out to touch her cheek, drawn against his will and judgement. He knew that she stirred something inside him he had not felt for any other woman, but he was afraid to examine his feelings too closely. 'Father was badly hurt when Matt married Ellen and went off to join the army against his wishes. I cannot hurt him like that again, because his heart will not stand it. I cannot have his death on my conscience, Jo.'

'No, I see that,' she said. 'It would be a wicked thing to do, Hal—and neither of us could be happy if we were the cause of his demise.'

'No, I do not think we could,' he said. 'So you see…'

'Yes, I do,' she said. 'I think that perhaps I should go now. If I am away too long, Mrs Stowe may start to…' She was close to tears, afraid that she might break down if she stayed.

Before she could finish, Hal pulled her into his arms. He looked down at her hungrily, before lowering his head to take possession of her lips. The kiss was deep and filled with longing, but also sweet and tender, leaving Jo weak and helpless as he let her go. She stared up at him in bewilderment—she felt that he had torn the heart from her with that kiss.

'I should not have done that,' Hal said. 'You had better go now—because if you stay I may never let you go again.'

Jo gave a little cry of dismay and ran from the room. What was he saying to her? He could not offer her marriage because his father would not approve and might be made ill by Hal's disobedience—but even Lord Beverley would not care if he heard that his son had taken a mistress. Indeed, he would probably condone it, providing that they were discreet and it did not affect his marriage to a girl he could approve.

The thought brought tears to Jo's eyes, but she blinked them away. She would not cry! Hal had kissed her, but he had been honest enough to tell her that she must not think of marriage, and it was her own fault if she had foolishly allowed herself to hope.

Chapter Seven

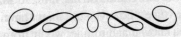

Jo went straight to her room when she got in. She had been crying despite her determination not to as she ran home, and she wanted to wash her face and calm herself before she saw Ellen or, worse still, the housekeeper, whose eyes saw too much. She splashed her face in cold water and brushed her hair, pulling it back tight so that it was flat to her head and made her look very strait-laced. And then she went downstairs, her manner as calm as if she had done nothing more exciting than tidy her room all morning.

'Well,' Ellen said as soon as she entered the small front parlour. 'What was it like? Is it as beautiful as you expected, Jo?'

'Yes, though it is not as grand as the Marlbeck mansion, for that is stuffed full of gilded treasures—but Hal's house is a home. It has its share of treasures, but it is in excellent taste, and so welcoming.' Her heart ached, for she knew that she wanted to live there as its mistress and never would.

'You sound as if you have fallen in love with it,' Ellen teased. 'Or is it the master of the house that you love?'

'Ellen!' Jo looked stricken. 'How could you say such a thing? Of course I am not in love with Hal. It would not be suitable—and you of all people must know that it would be foolish of me to let myself hope for it.'

Ellen's smile disappeared. 'Yes, I know. Forgive me, Jo. I should not have said it—but I know that you like him very well, and I think he likes you, too.'

'Liking is one thing, and I do like him,' Jo admitted, a little wobble in her voice. 'But even if it might have been more, it cannot be. You know that his father would not accept me. Hal is his heir. If your child had been a son, he might have taken that position, but as it is…'

'Lord Beverley would not have accepted my son as his heir, even though the law might have been on our side,' Ellen said and there was a slight hint of bitterness in her voice. 'I am glad that she is a girl. At least I know that she will not be taken away from me—for if Matt's father *had* wanted his son, he would never accept me.'

'He would not have tried to take your child from you,' Jo said. 'No, no, Ellen, I do not think he is an evil man. Hal loves his father very deeply and he would not if he were as bad as you imagine. I know he was unkind to Matt and you—but I think that he might have changed his mind had your husband lived.'

'Perhaps…' Ellen shook her head. 'He would not even meet me. Matt was so angry. He swore that he would never go back to his father's house.'

'I dare say his anger would have cooled in time,' Jo said. 'Hal is not unforgiving, I do not think his father and brother could be so very different.'

'Perhaps not,' Ellen agreed and smiled. 'But a girl is of no use to Lord Beverley. He wants a grandson, which is why Hal must marry. Perhaps this girl you told me of—Chloe something or other?'

'Miss Marsham,' Jo said and frowned. 'He told me that he did not intend to ask her—and yet he told Mrs Stowe that he intends to marry soon. Perhaps there is someone else. He is going away tomorrow. It may be that he will tell us when he returns.'

'Yes, I dare say,' Ellen agreed. 'Tell me, Jo—what are you going to wear this evening?'

'I shall wear my new gown,' Jo said. 'It is cold out today and it will be just right. I finished it this morning before I went up to Hal's house, and I think it looks quite nice.'

'It looked elegant when you tried it on yesterday,' Ellen agreed, 'and those slight adjustments will make it all the better. I think I shall wear my green silk. I have let the waist out a little, though not as much as I thought I might need, for it seems that I have lost some of the weight I put on.'

Jo nodded and smiled, talking with her friend of inconsequential things. Inwardly, her mind was in turmoil—she could not forget the kiss Hal had given her and the words that followed, which had destroyed all her hopes.

The blue gown was a masterpiece of understated elegance. Ellen had helped Jo to pin it so that it fell just right, and as she looked at herself in the mirror she knew that she had never had a dress she liked better, despite the money Aunt Wainwright had spent on her gowns for Bath.

She still had her mama's pearls for she had not wanted to trust them to the trunk that she sent home, and she fastened them about her throat, turning in front of her dressing mirror so that she might see the effect.

She had brushed her hair high on top of her head, letting some curls fall in a little tail at the back, and as always several tendrils had escaped to curl about her face. For once she felt pleased with her appearance, and when she put on the blue cloak with its warm lining, she felt as if she were someone different. A tingling set up inside her and she was excited, as if she were going to meet her lover… Now, where had that thought come from? From somewhere behind her, she heard the sound of laughter, warm, sweet and low, and hauntingly enchanting. Turning, Jo thought for a moment she saw a woman in the shadows at the far side of the room.

'Who are you?' she breathed, her heart racing.

Yet in less than a breath the vision had gone and she laughed at herself for she knew that she had conjured it up in her mind. She touched the pink silk rose at her breast. It had come from Lady Beverley's trunk in the attic here, and it had given a touch of something special to the gown.

Looking at herself in the mirror again, Jo smiled. It was merely her imagination. The stories about Lady Beverley had got into her mind, and she could not get them out. The musky scent of old roses clung to many of Lady Beverley's things, and Jo often thought she could smell it in her room, but that was hardly surprising since she had brought so many bits and pieces here. She had used several bits of lace to trim under-things she had made for herself, and it was hardly surprising that the perfume clung to them.

Jo went downstairs, where Ellen was waiting. She looked very well in her green gown, and she was wearing a velvet cloak that Jo knew had come from the trunks that came down from the house: surprisingly, it did not smell of roses as Jo's did, but a more sophisticated perfume.

'I thought this would go well with my gown,' she told Jo. 'You did not want it for yourself?'

'Oh, no, I have this,' Jo said and smiled. 'It looks well on you, dearest. I am sure we shall both find things we like and we must share them.'

'I think Hal sent them for you,' Ellen said, 'but I do like one or two of the gowns, which I think I could alter to suit me.'

'You must have whatever you want,' Jo agreed. 'They are for both of us. It was such a thoughtful gift, for neither of us could have accepted new clothes from him, and both of us like to make our own things.'

'Yes, it was kind, but then Hal is always generous. I think green suits me better than blue,' Ellen said. 'But yours is just right for you, Jo.'

Smiling and in perfect harmony, the two girls went out to the carriage that Hal had sent for them.

Afterwards, Jo thought that it had been one of the best and one of the worst evenings of her life. Hal had been a generous and caring host, and the meal was excellent. They all three talked and laughed over dinner, enjoying the company.

Hal did not linger over his port, but brought a glass into the drawing room when they had dined. There was an excellent pianoforte by the window and he asked Ellen if she would play something for them.

'I know how well you play,' he said. 'It is a fine instrument, I think—I bought it specially some weeks ago. I enjoy music in the evenings.'

Ellen went to the instrument and sat down, running her fingers over the keys before beginning to play from memory.

'Oh, how lovely,' Jo said. 'I had not realised how well you play, Ellen.'

'You must come here and play sometimes,' Hal said. 'Even if I am not here—and you, Jo. You must come with her—and use my library if you wish.'

'Thank you…' Jo met his eyes, but looked away quickly. He seemed to be telling her something very different to what he had said earlier that day—and she knew she must not listen to her heart, for she might be deceiving herself. Even if Hal liked her well enough to want her as his wife, it could never be—and she was not sure of that, for his kiss meant only that he desired her, and that was not necessarily love.

'I shall not see you again before I leave,' Hal told her softly as Ellen came to the end of her piece. 'I have some thinking to do, Jo.' He applauded as Ellen stood up, and then, in a louder tone, 'Do you play, Jo?'

'Indifferently,' Jo said. 'Not half as well as Ellen, I am afraid—though I sing a little.'

'Then I shall play and you shall sing,' Hal said, going to the instrument. 'What do you know— "A lover and his lass" perhaps?'

'Yes, I know that,' Jo agreed. 'It is an old melody, but always pleasant.'

She waited for him to strike the chord and then joined in with the flirtatious little ditty. It was a merry song and her voice was well suited to it, for, though not strong, the sound was melodious.

Ellen clapped enthusiastically when they had done, asking for an encore, but they declined, and asked her to play one more piece, which after some hesitation she did, her hands moving swiftly and sure over the keys.

'Ellen does everything so well,' Jo said. 'She is an extremely accomplished young lady.'

'Yes, she is,' Hal said and looked thoughtful. 'She would grace any drawing room.'

They listened in silence as the haunting music brought tears to the eyes, and then, when Ellen rose at last, the tea tray was sent for and it was time to leave.

'I hope you will not stay away too long,' Ellen said as they were taking their leave. 'We shall miss you, Hal.'

'I shall miss you—both of you,' he replied with a smile. 'No, I shall not stay away too long. I promise.'

Driving home in the carriage, Jo's throat felt tight and she could barely hold her tears inside. Spending an evening like that with Hal had shown her how good life could be if only... But she must not let herself think of a future that could never be.

Jo lay sleepless for much of the night. Her mind kept going over all the things that Hal had said to her, the kisses he had given her, and the words that had almost broken her heart. He was going away for a few days—would it be better if she were not here when he returned?

If she stayed, it would mean heartbreak, for she knew that Hal must marry to provide his family with an heir. She could just about bear that, because she knew it was right and proper, but she did not think she could stay here, knowing that Hal and his bride were living at the house. Yet how could she think of deserting Ellen?

It was a dilemma that would not leave her and in the end she got up, dressing but leaving her hair loose, pulling on the blue cloak before she left the house. It would keep her warm and the morning was bitter, icicles hanging from the branches of some trees. She began to walk, turning towards the path that led through the trees to the woods, though without any conscious intention to walk that way. Indeed, she was hardly thinking at all, for the tears trickled down her cheeks. She knew that she would have to leave this place sooner rather than later. Perhaps Ellen would accompany her? They might visit Jo's family together and then find an establishment in Truro or somewhere a little nearer Mrs Horne, where they could find work.

Lost in her thoughts, Jo did not notice that she was being followed, until suddenly she heard the cracking of a twig beneath someone's foot and turned. She caught her breath as she found herself looking at the man she had last seen in the marketplace at Lavenham.

'You…' she breathed. 'What are you doing here?'

Carstairs smiled unpleasantly. 'I have been watching you for a while now,' he said. 'I was not sure what was going on here, but now I understand. You are his mistress. How convenient,' he drawled. 'The high-and-mighty Hal Beverley keeps his mistress in a little love nest close to his home. What a fine scandal that would make. I wonder what his father would pay to know that?'

'No!' Jo's heart was pounding. She could not defend herself as she wished, for to deny his accusation and declare that she was here as Ellen's companion would betray her friend and all that Hal had strived for would be lost. If his father learned in such a way of Ellen's child and that she was living here…the shock might kill him! 'You have no right to be here—or to tell your foul lies to Lord Beverley. I am not Hal's mistress, though you may think it and—'

She got no further for he sprang at her like a cat, catching her and pulling her close to him, his greedy mouth fastening on hers in a punishing kiss that bruised her. She wrenched back from him, scrubbing at her mouth with the back of her hand.

'How dare you!'

He sneered, his thick lips ugly to see. 'You have lost all chance of a decent marriage for everyone knows that you are his whore,' he said and grabbed her arm. 'You are soiled goods, but even so I dare say you would be sweet enough to bed. I shall take you with me and see what transpires. Perhaps he will pay to have you back.'

'No!' Jo screamed as she wrestled with him. He was trying to drag her with him, but she fought him, kicking and wriggling as he tried to drag her through the trees.

'I'll soon teach you some better manners, bitch,' Carstairs muttered. 'By God, you will pay for that!' he said as she launched at him and scratched his face. He raised his hand to strike her, but she screamed out and kicked him in the shins once more. 'Damn you…'

'Touch her again and you are a dead man,' a voice said from somewhere to their right. 'Let her go, Carstairs, or I shall shoot you where you stand—right between the eyes. You know I can do it, so let her go.' Hal moved out from the trees so that they could see him. 'Come to me, Jo.'

Jo found herself released and ran to Hal. He pushed her behind him, his eyes never leaving the other man.

'I'll pay you for this,' Carstairs muttered. 'You'd best watch your back, Beverley, for you will never be safe. I paid your brother back for his insults—and I can do the same for you.'

'You…killed Matt? I knew that there was some foul play in his death. He was too excellent a horseman.' Hal's voice had turned to stone. He threw his pistol down and took a flying leap at the other man, bringing him down to the ground. They struggled for some minutes, rolling over and over until Hal was on top, his fists pummelling into Carstairs's face over and over again. 'You evil devil! I'll kill you…'

Now he had his hands round Carstairs's throat, his strength forcing the breath from him, his face an angry mask of hatred that shocked Jo by its ferocity.

'Please, Hal,' she cried, 'do not kill him. He is not worth it. If he killed your brother, he must be tried in a court of law and hanged. I beg you, for my sake, do not take his life, for his blood will always be on your hands! Hal, listen to me…I beg you…do not let him ruin your life and mine.'

Carstairs had lost consciousness and lay still on the ground. Hal still sat astride him, his head bent as if the energy had suddenly drained out of him along with his anger. He stood up and turned to look at her, an expression of horror in his eyes.

'I went mad,' he said. 'God forgive me, I would have killed him if you had not called to me.' She saw that tears were running down his cheeks. 'I do not know what happened to me…it was like being out there all over again…the blood and the dying…'

Jo understood only that he was in some turmoil, remembering things that had hurt him, scarred him. Instinctively, she moved towards him, putting her arms about him, drawing him to her, reaching up to kiss him on the mouth. His response was instant, as he held her to him, pressed so deeply into his body that she might have been a part of him. She responded, melting into him, giving generously of herself, knowing that he felt a need she could not begin to understand.

'Jo…' Hal said brokenly as he withdrew at last. 'Forgive me. I should not…you know that I am not free…'

She put her fingers to his lips. 'Hush, my dearest,' she said. 'We shall not talk of this now. You have something to do…he is stirring…'

'You are right again,' Hal said. He went back to Carstairs, heaving him to his feet, holding him as he swayed. 'I think we shall get you somewhere that you can be tended and then you will be handed over to the law, Carstairs. You are a self-confessed murderer and must pay for your crimes.'

Carstairs was barely able to stand as Hal bore him off. Jo watched them, and then bent down to pick up Hal's abandoned pistol. She followed them, watching like a hawk. If need be she would use the pistol to defend Hal, though she would cripple rather than kill.

However, her heroic thoughts proved unnecessary, for as they left the woods and approached the house, two grooms saw that something was going on and came running. Hal explained what had happened, and they took his prisoner away.

Hal turned to her, accepting the pistol she offered and smiling grimly. 'Were you intending to use this?'

'If he had tried to harm you,' Jo said, 'though I do not know if I would have managed to fire it.'

'Perhaps I should show you,' Hal said. 'It might come in useful if you are ever in danger again.'

'I do not think it will happen, do you?'

'I can only pray that it will not,' Hal said. He took a step closer. 'What you saw…what happened…'

Jo shook her head. 'Do not try to explain. I know there must be things in your life you would rather not speak of—and I shall never speak of it to anyone.'

'It was the way he said…' Hal shook his head. 'I lost my temper…went temporarily mad, but I am sorry that you were forced to witness it.'

'It does not matter,' Jo said. 'Have you not realised that…I care for you, Hal?'

'Jo…' His face twisted with anguish. 'You must know that I feel…want you, care for you…but I can promise nothing. One day it may be different, but until then I can only offer…but I shall not insult you.'

'Hal,' Jo whispered brokenly, 'I can bear anything if I know that you truly care for me.'

'Can you doubt it?' He drew her to him again, looking down at her face. 'You are so lovely, Jo—your wild hair and your eyes…a mountain pool that a man might lose himself in… I need you so and yet…' He groaned as he held her pressed to his chest, his lips moving against her hair. 'I have promised my father to marry a girl he thinks suitable and give him an heir, Jo. It is my duty…the cruellest duty a man can have.'

Jo looked up at him, her eyes dark with emotion. 'I think that if it meant I must leave you or become your mis—' He touched his fingers to her lips, hushing her.

'No, do not say it, Jo, for I might not be able to resist such an offer. God knows, you haunt me—in my dreams and waking. I do not know what I must do.' He looked down at her. 'It may be that I shall have to send you and Ellen to another place, my dear one—but I need to think about this, for it means everything to us both. Promise me that you will be here when I return? You will not disappear?'

'I promise that I shall wait for your return,' Jo said, her voice catching in her throat. 'And now I should go. I have delayed you too long.'

'I was coming to see you, to beg you to be patient,' Hal said. 'I shall try to think of a way that will neither shame you nor break our hearts… Trust me for a little? You know that I would never willingly harm you?'

'Yes, I believe you,' Jo said. 'Go now, before I beg you to stay and never leave me.' She turned and walked away, her head high, the tears unshed.

Jo felt subdued for the rest of that day. She knew that she and Hal had somehow crossed a threshold, for she had seen him with all his defences down, witnessed his private grief. Carstairs's vain boast that he had killed Hal's beloved brother had triggered something, releasing all the pent-up grief and anger inside him.

What had happened afterwards had been brewing for some time. She was sure now that Hal felt a very strong attraction towards her. Had he been free to choose, he might have asked her to marry him, but he was torn between his feelings for her and his duty.

Had Jo been less conscious of duty than she was, she might have blamed him for putting his father first and causing her so much pain. However, she was her papa's daughter, and she knew that her father would have told her that she must accept what could not be changed.

'But I love him so…' she whispered. 'Papa, what am I going to do?'

'Become his mistress if you love him enough.'

The voice Jo heard seemed to come from the air about her,

and had she been superstitious she might have thought it was Hal's notorious grandmother speaking to her from beyond the grave. She had come to know Lady Helena Beverley so well, from her beautiful, elegant clothes to her welcoming home and her sensuous perfume that clung to everything she had worn. But she was a sensible girl and she did not believe in such things. The voice was in her head—because there was a part of her that knew she would give up the world for Hal. What did it matter if she was not recognised in society? She had no wish to gather the elite of this world about her or be acclaimed for her salon or her beauty. Indeed, she did not believe that she was beautiful. All she wanted was to be with the man she loved, to be held in his arms and kissed until her body melted with the pleasure of his loving.

But to cast all aside for love would bring shame on her family. Marianne would have to live with a shadow hanging over her. Even as the wife of the Marquis of Marlbeck, she would feel the shame of her sister's disgrace—and poor Lucy might be forced to remain at home with Mama, for who would wish to marry a girl whose unmarried sister lived as a man's mistress? And what of the girl Hal eventually asked to be his wife? Would his affair with Jo carry on despite that—and could she bear it if it did?

Her thoughts were painful and haunted her throughout the first few days of Hal's absence. When she was in his arms, Jo knew that she would willingly give up everything for his love, but alone in the dark hours she was aware of grief. She knew instinctively that in time one or both of them would feel the shame of such a liaison and that it could end only one way—did she want to live out the rest of her life alone?

Yet it was torture to think of never seeing him again, and in her darker moments she felt that she would rather die. To take her own life was a terrible sin and would hurt her family beyond bearing, and yet she knew that her heart was irrevocably his. She would never love again.

It was only her work that saved her from giving way to her grief. For Ellen's sake, she painted a smile on her face, and when her friend suggested that she ask George to take her into Lavenham with him she was relieved; it would perhaps take her mind from her problems for a while.

'You could take the gown I have made,' Ellen told her. 'And there are two panels of beading that might be used as the front of a bodice. I think that must give Madame Susanne a good idea of the quality of my work—and you have six hats made now, Jo. I think you should take them in and hear what she has to say.'

'Yes, for it is no use continuing if she refuses me,' Jo said. 'But would you not like to come with me, Ellen?'

'Another time, perhaps,' Ellen said. 'Poor little Mattie has not been well today. I think it is just a little fever, but I intend to ask the doctor to call and I shall stay with her. You go and talk to Madame Susanne—and bring me a selection of beads, whatever you think is pretty. Perhaps white and pink…green, too, if you can find them.'

'Yes, of course,' Jo said. 'I need some more materials myself. I used my last piece of stiffened buckram yesterday. I shall need more if I am to continue.'

'Then you must go tomorrow,' Ellen said. 'For though George is very good, I do not think we can expect him to choose beads or buckram, do you?'

Jo smiled at the thought. 'No, I do not think it is quite in his style,' she said. 'I think I may choose some more books.

George is willing to return them, but he begged me not to ask him to choose for he cannot tell one from another.'

And so it was arranged that Jo would go the next day. She sat for a long time at her window, staring out at the moon that night. Hal would be home in two days. It was unlikely that he would decide to abandon his duty—and she ought not to allow it if he did, which left her two choices. She must either leave this cottage or become his mistress.

Hal stared into his wineglass. His business in town was almost finished, but as yet he was no nearer to solving the problem that was foremost in his mind. He had arranged to meet Jack Manton at this club; he thought that his friend would wish to know that Carstairs was in custody, having confessed to the murder of Matt Beverley.

'Ah, there you are,' Jack said, coming upon him unawares. 'Your note intrigued me, Hal. What is this mystery you have uncovered?'

'When Matt died, you told me you thought there was something wrong, that his horse might have been spooked…something under the saddle?'

'Yes, there were marks on the poor beast's back,' Jack said with a frown. 'But we could prove nothing.' His brows rose. 'Do you know something of this?'

'I have reason to believe it was Carstairs. He is in a local prison near Lavenham, Jack. He boasted of it and I damned near killed him. I think I should have had it not been for—' Jack looked at him and he smiled wryly. 'There is a lady in the case. He attacked her.'

'Ah, yes, I have always thought he was not to be trusted in that quarter. I have heard stories of behaviour unbecoming to a gentleman and an officer—that was one of the reasons he was asked to resign his commission. You know that Matt accused him of cheating at cards?'

'No, I did not know that,' Hal said and his eyes sparked with anger. 'What kind of a man is he that—?' He broke off, for his throat had choked with a mixture of anger and grief. 'Matt is dead because of a game of cards!' The thought was doubly bitter—if his brother had lived, Hal would not have considered it necessary to marry to oblige his father. 'Damn Carstairs to hell!'

'That is where he is destined for, I have no doubt,' Jack agreed with a smile. 'I expect you want me to investigate further?'

'If you will,' Hal said. 'I have other things on my mind at the moment—and I know it is something you do well. I should not want him to walk free, for at the moment his confession is all that stands between him and freedom. If he retracts it, he might be released.'

'I shall do my best,' Jack said. 'But I cannot promise. Justice is not always done in these cases, my friend.'

'I should have killed him and been done with it!'

'And then I might have had to arrest you,' Jack said. 'You must give me your word that you will do nothing foolish if he walks free?'

'Yes, if you ask it,' Hal said. 'To tell you the truth, I am in a damned coil and I do not know how to get out of it.'

'Is it anything I can help with?'

'No, for it is a matter of my conscience,' Hal said. 'I can follow my heart or my duty, but not both.'

'A hard choice,' Jack said. 'Your brother chose freely— should you not have the same freedom?'

'It is partly because of my brother's choices that I feel so obliged,' Hal said. 'But we shall forget it for this evening at least, Jack—dine with me. It is good to see you again. I should like to hear about old friends.'

Jo left George at the inn. He had promised to see to the supplies for Mrs Stowe, and she had only two commissions, which would take her no more than an hour or so. It was not a market day and the streets of the town were almost deserted, because it was bitterly cold.

She went first to Madame Susanne's establishment. The seamstress welcomed her with pleasure and exclaimed over the hats, which she said were just right for her clientele.

'You have made them pretty and stylish, but not too modish for country ladies,' she said and smiled. 'I am sure I shall be able to sell these at the price you have asked, plus a commission for myself.' She undid the strings of the parcel containing Ellen's gown and shook it out. She spent several minutes looking at the embroidery and the seaming, and Jo's heart sank.

'Do you not like it, Madame?'

'I have seldom seen finer,' Madame Susanne said. 'I wish that Mrs Beverley might work for me, but I am not sure about the beading. I think it may be too much for my customers. It is beautifully done, of course, but I cannot be sure if it will appeal. I think that your friend should be working in London. Indeed, you would both do well there. Have you considered opening your own establishment?'

'Our own establishment?' Jo stared at her. 'Would that not cost a lot of money? I do not think we could afford it.'

'That is a pity,' Madame said. 'I am willing to try, of

course, but my advice to both of you would be to find someone who would back you. Is there no friend to whom you might apply for a loan?'

'No, I do not think so,' Jo said, for her pride would not allow her to ask Hal for money, though she thought he might give it to her. 'You would not like to be a partner?'

'I should like it very much,' the seamstress replied. 'But my business is here and I have no spare money—at least, not enough to begin in London. However, my advice to you remains the same. Find the money and set up for yourselves. It might take a little time, but I am sure that you could do it.'

'Thank you,' Jo said. She was thoughtful as she left the seamstress's little shop. It would be the very thing for her in the circumstances. If she and Ellen could find a small shop with rooms over the top, much like this—but in a fashionable town, like Bath or London—but it was foolish to dream for she would have to save for a long time to earn enough money to start them off. She had sent off three stories for children to various publishing houses, but as yet she had heard nothing. It was not likely that she would, for she was a mere scribbler and they must have so many manuscripts sent to them. No, she and Ellen must be content to work for others for the time being.

After leaving the seamstress, she visited the haberdashers where she purchased the items Ellen had asked for. She was sorry to have no better news for her friend, because Madame Susanne had not been certain that she would be able to sell the embroidery panels or the gown Ellen had laboured over so lovingly.

George was waiting for Jo at the inn. She had bought some buns to eat on the way home, which she shared with the groom, for she did not wish to waste time eating lunch. She could not rest until she was home and had told Ellen what she had learned that day, because she knew that her friend would be disappointed. She had put so much hope into the idea of supporting herself as a high-class embroideress, and to learn that her work was too exclusive for the ladies of the small town was bound to dash her hopes.

George helped Jo down from the gig, handing her all her parcels with a smile. 'Can you manage all those, miss?'

'Yes, I think so, thank you,' she replied. 'They are bulky, I know, but not heavy. It was very good of you to take me with you today.'

George tipped his cap to her. 'It is always a pleasure to do anything for you, Miss Horne. You have only to ask.'

'Thank you,' Jo said. 'I think it will be a few weeks before I need to visit again.' It might be that she never would, for she knew that her life was bound to change, one way or the other. Either she and Ellen would go away together or she must return home, for she was sure that Hal would tell her he had decided to marry when he returned.

She frowned as she suddenly noticed a travelling carriage drawn up at the side of the house. She had been lost in her thoughts as George handed her down, but now she could see that it was clearly an expensive vehicle and had a crest on the side panel. She felt a chill at the base of her spine and looked back for George, but he had taken the horse and gig round to the back of the cottage.

Who could be calling here in a carriage like that? She did not think that Ellen's father would have such a magnificent crest on his carriage, which must mean…

Mrs Stowe saw her as she entered, and beckoned to her urgently. 'He has been in the small parlour with Mrs Beverley for more than an hour, miss. She hasn't sent for me and I dare not go in, because he looked so angry when he arrived.'

'Is it Lord Beverley?' Jo asked, feeling a little sick as the housekeeper nodded. 'How could he have discovered where she was staying? Hal has been so careful to keep it a secret.'

'Well, I am sure I don't know, miss,' the housekeeper said. 'I haven't spoken of it outside this house—but word gets about. Folk talk and I am sure that someone from the house may have whispered to a friend…you know how it is.'

'Yes, I suppose we might have expected it in time,' Jo said. She had warned Hal that he ought to tell his father from the beginning, but he had made some excuse. Now it seemed that Lord Beverley had discovered it for himself and was angry— perhaps justly so in the circumstances. She took a deep breath. 'I had better go in.'

'Do you think you ought?' Mrs Stowe looked doubtful. 'If his lordship has heard one rumour, he might have heard others.'

'I am not Mr Beverley's mistress, whatever you or others may think, Mrs Stowe, and I shall not cower here in the hall while Ellen is exposed to his anger.'

She walked away from the housekeeper, head high, back straight. She must be careful what she said to Lord Beverley for Hal's sake. It would not do to lose her temper and say hurtful things, because Hal would blame himself if his father's health suffered. However, she would not stand by and see Ellen bullied and reduced to tears.

She knocked and entered the room, then stopped as she saw the domestic scene that greeted her. A rather large man with grey hair was seated in the wing chair by the fire, holding Mattie very carefully in his arms. Ellen was standing by his side, smiling tenderly down at her little girl.

'Ellen,' Jo said, moving slowly towards her. 'Is everything all right, dearest?'

Ellen looked at her. 'Mattie's grandfather has come to visit us,' she said. 'She was fretful, though the doctor told me there was nothing wrong other than a little chill. I had her in her cot by the fire as I worked on my sewing when Lord Beverley arrived. She cried when I picked her up, but quietened in her grandfather's arms—is that not amazing?'

'Yes, it is, truly amazing,' Jo said, hardly knowing what to say. 'You must have the knack, sir. I know that Papa was often able to comfort a crying child when we visited his parishioners, but it is not given to everyone.'

Lord Beverley looked at her, a frown creasing his brow. 'And you are, young woman?'

Jo took a deep breath—his behaviour towards the child was tender enough, but his eyes were cold as he looked at her. 'I am Miss Josephine Horne, and I am Ellen's friend.'

'You are the one who helped her when the babe was born, I understand,' Lord Beverley said and nodded, but his expression did not lighten. 'I dare say I owe you a debt of gratitude, for Ellen assures me that she might have died had you not been here.'

'I did very little…'

'Oh, Jo, that is not true,' Ellen said. 'You have been a constant comfort to me and a good friend. Indeed, I do not know what I should have done without you. I have told Lord Beverley that you came because I was afraid that my father might force me to return to him—and that he would have made me give my child up, because he believes her a child of sin.'

'Stuff and nonsense!' Lord Beverley said. 'I may not have approved of the idea, but a marriage over the anvil is legal enough, and Ellen tells me it was blessed by the padre out in Spain. So everything is all right and tight, and little Mattie will be acknowledged as my granddaughter.' He glared at Jo. 'I have told her that she must come and live with me. I shall give her all the things she is entitled to as Matt's widow. He had money of his own—at least, he would have had once I restored what was due to him—and I see no reason why Hal would object to her living at the house. Damn it, he does not care for the estate as he ought, even though he remains my heir.'

'I am sure that Hal cares for it as much as he ought,' Jo said, defending him. 'I know that he cares very much for you, sir.'

'Indeed!' Lord Beverley glared at her again. 'And how do you know what my son thinks, miss?'

For a moment Jo was tempted to tell him, but she held the angry words inside. 'He has told me that he worries for your health, sir.'

'Stuff and nonsense,' Lord Beverley replied, forgetting that he had played on his son's concern to oblige him to come home from the army and to make the kind of marriage he desired. 'I am not about to shuffle off this earth just yet—and had he cared for my peace of mind more he might have told me that he had found Ellen and that she had a beautiful baby. I have been employing agents to look for her for months. I had hopes that she was in Bath, but when I sent someone to fetch her to me, she had gone. When I heard she was here, I decided to come myself this time. Hal might have brought her to me and saved me a journey.'

Jo stared at him. 'You sent someone to Bath to find her… It was *your* agent that stood outside the house and followed her, not her father's.'

'I was informed of your whereabouts quite recently. Had my thoughtless son told me where she was when he visited, I should have been saved a lot of time and trouble.'

'I am sure he would have done had he thought you wished to see her,' Jo said, her head up, expression proud as she met his fearful gaze. 'He was afraid that the shock might be too much for you, sir. If he kept it from you, it was for your sake, my lord.'

'The shock of knowing that Matt left a daughter…' he growled. 'God knows I wish she might have been a son, but a daughter is sometimes more of a comfort to a man in his advanced years.' He looked at Ellen. 'You will take pity on me, m'dear? I know I behaved badly, but I didn't know you. I was told your father was in trade and I thought—'

'That I was an adventuress?' Ellen asked and smiled oddly. 'Perhaps had we been braver, you might have accepted me in time—but my father was against the marriage as much and more than you, sir. We felt that we had no choice but to run away together.'

'Well, well, that part of it is best forgot,' Lord Beverley said. 'You must not worry about your father. If he comes here, I shall know how to deal with him—and once you are living with me he will not be allowed near you unless he gives me his promise of good faith.'

'You are very kind,' Ellen said. 'May I think about it, please? I must talk to Jo—we had plans of our own. I was hoping to become independent and to work as an embroideress.'

'My daughter-in-law has no need to work,' Lord Beverley

said. 'Come, take the child, Ellen. I must go up to the house. You tell me that my son is not here, but I shall wait until he returns. We have much to talk about.' He looked directly at Jo. 'Will you take my arm, help me to my carriage, miss?'

'Yes, if you wish it,' Jo said and offered her arm. He held on to it and she felt his weight, which told her that he truly needed her assistance.

'Been sitting too long,' he told her as she walked him out to the front door. Mrs Stowe was hovering and opened it for him, giving Jo an odd look as she went out with him. 'Not as fit as I used to be—but I'll last a few years yet.' He frowned at her. 'What is this I hear about you, miss? I hope there is no truth in these stories?'

'If you have heard that I am Hal's mistress, then you have been told lies,' Jo said. 'I have been nothing more than a friend to him.'

'But you would like to be, I dare say?' Lord Beverley said. 'No, no, don't tell me. It is not my business. You know that I require an heir from my son, and that his wife must be a girl of good family?'

'Yes, Hal has told me.'

'Has he, be damned?' Lord Beverley glared at her. 'Think yourself the right girl for him, do you?'

'It is not a matter of what I think, is it, sir?' Jo gave him a straight look.

He stared at her for a moment, shook his head and made a guttural sound that might mean anything. 'Good day to you, Miss Horne. You've plenty to say for yourself, and that's a fact.'

Jo stood back as one of his grooms came to help him, assisting him into the carriage. She stood watching as the door was closed after him, turning to go back into the house as it was driven away. The message could not have been clearer. Lord Beverley did not approve of her.

How could she expect Hal to defy his father and marry her now?

Chapter Eight

'Well,' Ellen said as Jo went back into the parlour. 'I was never more shocked in my life than when he arrived. I thought he was going to rage at me for daring to come here, but he seemed more angry with Hal than me. He asked why I had not come to him, and I told him that I did not expect him to accept me. He apologised to me, Jo—and there were tears in his eyes. He truly wants me to go and live with him at his estate.'

'Yes, I think he does,' Jo said. 'He was very good with Mattie. I think it would be a fine thing for you, dearest. You would not have to worry about your father finding you, for I am sure that Lord Beverley would set him to rights if he tried to make you go with him, and he will never tell you that you must give the child up.'

'No, for he clearly loves her,' Ellen said. 'I am in such a state, I do not know what to do for the best.'

'Surely you must do as he asks,' Jo told her. 'I know we have been comfortable here, but it would be a better arrangement. Once Lord Beverley acknowledges you, which he clearly intends, you will be accepted everywhere. I dare say he will entertain and introduce you to his friends. You may even visit London and mix in society, as you ought.'

'I am not sure that that appeals to me,' Ellen said. 'To live in his house and entertain a few friends, yes, I should enjoy that, I think—especially if some of Matt's friends come to visit…but what of you?'

'What of me?' Jo asked. 'You know that I could not come with you, don't you? I do not think that Lord Beverley would accept me—besides, Mama and Lucy would be hurt. They understood when you needed me, but you will not need me once you are living with your husband's father.'

'You are my very best friend. I should miss you, Jo.'

'Yes, I know, and I shall miss you,' Jo said. 'But I might be able to visit sometimes, just for a week or so, if Lord Beverley permits…but you know it is the right thing, Ellen.'

'We had such plans…'

'Which may come to nothing,' Jo said. 'Madame Susanne said she might be able to sell my hats, but she thinks your work is too fine for a provincial clientele.' She kept Madame's other opinions to herself, for she did not wish to raise false hopes, especially now that Ellen had been offered the kind of home she was entitled to expect as Matt's wife.

'Oh, I see.' Ellen looked disappointed. 'That makes a difference. I am determined not to live on Hal's charity all my life—but if I am entitled to Matt's own money…'

'Yes, of course you are,' Jo told her. 'It should always have been yours. Besides, you want Mattie to know her family, don't you? Think of her future—what is best for her. She can either be the daughter of a seamstress or the granddaughter of a lord. Think about when she grows up, Ellen. You want her to have the best in life, don't you?'

'Yes, of course I do,' Ellen said. 'It is for her sake that I have considered it. I do not think I can deny her both her heritage and her family, Jo. Had there been no alternative, I must have done the best I could, but now…'

'You must make up your mind to go with him,' Jo said. 'I shall go home to Mama and Lucy. I know from their letters that they miss me.' She smiled at Ellen, hiding the hurt inside her. It was the right decision and it had been made for her. She could not stay at the cottage alone, and Ellen must do what was right for her and her child. 'I shall begin to pack my trunks at once—I am sure that Hal will allow me to take the trunk that was stored here. He gave me the contents and they may still be of use to me.'

'Yes, of course you must,' Ellen said. 'I shall tell Lord Beverley when he calls tomorrow, for he says he must rest today and will see me in the morning. But do you not think you should wait to talk to Hal? He will be back soon and it cannot make any difference to you, for your mama does not expect you.'

'No, I shall go as soon as I am ready,' Jo said. 'I do not imagine that Lord Beverley will want to delay for longer than a day or so, and I can be ready by tomorrow. I shall ask George if he will take me into Lavenham early in the morning, and arrange for my trunks to be sent by the carrier as soon as possible.'

'Do you have enough money for your fare?'

'I have enough for the mail coach,' Jo said. 'Madame Susanne paid me for two hats immediately, for she liked them so much—but I dare say she will send me the money on for the others if I write to her.'

'Oh, Jo…' Ellen moved to embrace her. 'I had such plans. I thought that things would be very different. You and Hal—'

'Please do not,' Jo said. 'Lord Beverley does not consider me a suitable wife for his son. He made his position quite clear before he left. I dare say that was why he asked me to accompany him to the door. I shall not break Hal's heart by making him choose. Once I have gone he will forget me and do his duty, as he ought. You know that he has no choice, Ellen.'

'Oh, Jo,' Ellen said, and there were tears in her eyes. 'I feel very fortunate, but I shall miss you so.'

'You must not cry,' Jo said and hugged her. 'You have everything to look forward to, Ellen—and so have I. Mama will be so pleased to have me home, and I shall have more time for my writing.'

'Well, if it is what you want.' Ellen looked uncertain. 'I think you should wait for Hal, but you must do as you wish.'

'It is not what I wish for,' Jo said, her face proud. 'But it is what I ought to do. Papa would say it was the right thing.'

Ellen nodded. She knew that once Jo had made up her mind there was no stopping her. 'Then I shall say—' She broke off as they heard loud voices in the hall and then the parlour door was thrown open. The colour drained from her face as a man walked in. 'Father…'

'So there you are at last! A fine chase you have led me,' her father said angrily. 'All the lies and the false reports—but this one was right. I have found you and now I am taking you home with me.'

'I shall not go with you,' Ellen said, raising her head proudly. 'Have you come to see your granddaughter, Father? She is beautiful and—'

'She is no kin of mine,' he thundered at her. 'Be damned to the little bastard—she will never be welcome to me. As for you, you will behave yourself in future, for you will not be allowed out without your mother.'

'No, Father,' Ellen said proudly. 'I have this day received a visit from my father-in-law, Lord Beverley. He has invited me to live with him on his estate. He will acknowledge my daughter as his grandchild, as she is…and I am to have all the honour and position accorded as his son's widow.' Her voice was cold. 'He is a good kind man and he held Mattie in his arms. He loves her. Why should I come with you to a house where I have never known love? In Lord Beverley's house I shall be loved and respected. You have no power to make me come with you—and I am no longer afraid of you. Lord Beverley has powerful friends. I think that he would not hesitate to ruin you if you harmed me—and he could.'

'I am aware of that, for I have just come from him,' her father said and there was a mixture of rage and defeat in his tone. 'So you will not come home to your mother?'

'My mother is welcome to come to me. I dare say there would be a home for her if she wished it.'

'Your mother will do as I bid her. Well, that is your final answer?'

'Yes, sir. As far as I am concerned, I have no father.'

For a moment longer, he stared at her, then turned and strode from the room, slamming the door as he went out. Ellen sagged and then sat down abruptly.

'Well done,' Jo applauded her. 'You were so brave, Ellie.'

'I have learned it from you,' Ellen told her with a smile. 'I am not sure I could have done it had you not been here— and if Lord Beverley had not stood by me.' She drew a shuddering breath. 'My father must have gone to the house first…'

'I dread to think what Lord Beverley said to him,' Jo said and laughed. 'Well, I think you may rest easy now, Ellen. You have faced your worst fears and won.'

'Yes, I have,' Ellen said and looked pleased with herself. 'I would not have dared to stand up to him like that before—but it made me so angry because he would not even look at Mattie.'

'But Lord Beverley loves her,' Jo said. 'Now you can see you have made the right choice.'

'Yes, I have, Ellen said. 'But I still wish that you were coming with me, Jo.'

'It cannot be,' Jo said. 'You have made the right choice, Ellen—and so must I.'

It was much easier to say it than to carry out her decision. Jo wept long and hard as she began to pack her trunk. She was able to get all her own things into Lady Beverley's trunk, though she would carry one small bag with her for the journey.

'Forgive me, my darling Hal,' she whispered as she closed the lid of her trunk. 'You may think me a coward to run away from you, but it is for the best. I cannot be your mistress, and your father would not accept me…but I love you so.'

She seemed to smell the scent of roses, and felt a presence, wrapping her about, comforting her. She knew that it was a woman's presence and it seemed to be telling her that she too had known the pain of unrequited love.

'One day…' the voice in her head was saying, 'one day you will find happiness.'

'Yes, I shall be happy one day,' Jo said aloud, though she knew that there was no one there. 'I shall learn to forget him and do all the things I meant to do. I shall write my stories…perhaps I shall write your story.'

She seemed to hear husky laughter and it lifted her spirits, though of course it was all in her mind. Yet she was comforted by the thought of the lady who had been rather wicked in her youth, but a faithful and loving wife at the end.

'I wonder why you became some man's mistress,' she murmured. 'Did you love unwisely or too well?' There was no answer to her question, for of course it was all in her mind, and yet she knew that she had the beginnings of a story.

Jo changed into her favourite gown for the evening and went down to join Ellen in the parlour. It was her last day at the cottage and she intended to make the most of it. In the lonely days and nights ahead, when she had time to dwell on her broken dreams, she would have time enough to cry. This evening she would smile and pretend that everything was as it should be.

'You will write to me,' Ellen said the next morning when Jo was preparing to leave. 'You will keep in touch?'

'Yes, of course I shall,' Jo said. 'You have my address and you must write to me as soon as you are settled, and I shall reply.'

'I can never thank you for all you have done for me,' Ellen said. She handed Jo a package, looking a little shy. 'This is for you. I have been working on it for a while. I thought it might come in useful one day.'

'Oh, Ellie,' Jo said. 'I have nothing for you. I was going

to make you a hat, but I did not have time.' She opened the package and found a piece of ivory silk heavily embroidered with pink and pearl beads. 'This is so beautiful…I shall treasure it always.'

'I found the silk in one of the trunks from the house,' Ellen told her. 'I thought it might make a panel in…an evening dress.' She had intended it for Jo's wedding dress, but refrained from saying what was in her mind. She had hoped that Hal would marry Jo and that they might all visit one another often, but Jo was so sure that it was hopeless.

'I think it is lovely,' Jo told her. 'When I am a renowned author, I shall have it made up into a splendid ballgown.'

'Oh, yes, you must,' Ellen said and hugged her. 'I shall miss you, dearest Jo.'

'As I shall miss you—and darling little Mattie. Give her a big kiss for me everyday, Ellie…' Jo's composure almost broke, but she recovered it and smiled through the mist of tears. 'I shall send her a book of my fairy stories when it is published.'

'Yes, please do,' Ellen said, joining in the game. 'Please come and see me sometimes, Jo.'

They embraced once more and Jo went outside to where George was waiting with the gig. He was driving her to Lavenham, where she could take the mail coach to her home. He had her trunk strapped on the back and would send it on to her by carrier.

'I am sorry you are going, miss, and that's a fact,' George said. 'I don't know what Mr Hal will say, I am sure.'

'Oh, I don't suppose he will mind too much,' Jo said, keeping her smile in place. 'I was merely Mrs Beverley's friend, George.'

'Well, that's not how I saw it,' George said. 'You will be missed and that's not just my opinion.'

Jo nodded, but did not say anything more. It was very hard, because her throat felt tight with tears, and she could not resist turning her head to look back at the cottage before it disappeared from sight. Her heart was breaking, but she must be brave. If she were too distressed when she got home, Mama and Lucy would be upset. She had small gifts for both of them in her trunk, for she had been making things to take home with her when she visited—but she had expected to return to the cottage and Ellen. And Hal, her heart was telling her, but she shut out the small, insistent voice.

She would not see Hal again, never hear his voice, and enjoy the way his eyes lit up with devilment when he teased her—and she would never be kissed so deeply that she felt like swooning. It was a memory she must treasure, something that she could remember when the days seemed dark—to be kept in a secret part of her heart and told to no one.

Hal was eager to see Jo. He had made up his mind that he would tell his father that he did not wish to marry just yet, and then find some way of introducing him to Jo. Surely when they met, Lord Beverley would see what an attractive, clever and lovely girl she was? He could only pray that it would be so, for he knew that he must provide an heir for the estate, but he did not see how he could marry anyone else.

He dismounted, tying his horse to a pole near to the cottage and sprinting the last few yards. He rapped at the door knocker, feeling as if he had come to life—he had felt the parting from Jo keenly and he knew that he wanted to be with her more than anything else in the world.

Mrs Stowe opened the door to him. She looked at him oddly.

'Oh, it is you, sir. I am afraid there is no one home. Did they not tell you up at the house?'

'Tell me what, Mrs Stowe?'

'They have gone, sir. Miss Horne left two days ago and Mrs Beverley went this morning…'

'Gone! Jo has gone—where?' he demanded, too stunned to think what he was saying. 'How could she have gone without telling me?'

'I am not sure, sir. She did not tell me where she was going—just said thank you for looking after her. Mrs Beverley went with your father—' She broke off as she saw the wild look in his eyes. 'I was wondering what you wanted me to do about the cottage now.'

'Damn the cottage!' Hal said with a strangled oath. 'Did he turn her out? Did Ellen go willingly? For God's sake, tell me what has been going on here!'

'Had you better come in, sir? You look quite queer.'

'No, I do not wish to come in,' Hal said. 'I wish to know where Ellen and Jo have gone.'

'Mrs Beverley has gone to live with your father at his estate,' Mrs Stowe said. 'She seemed quite excited about it—though she was upset to part with Miss Horne, naturally.'

'Jo did not go with them?' Hal asked and cursed as she shook her head. 'No, I dare say he did not wish it. But where did she go? Has no one any idea?'

'George took her to Lavenham to catch the mail coach,' Mrs Stowe said and gasped as she saw the anger in his eyes. 'He may know something…'

'I shall ask him,' Hal said and turned away. 'Damn him for

this! To send her on the mail coach. He might at least have paid for her to travel by post chaise.' It was his father he was speaking of, the anger so bitter that he could barely hold it in check.

'What about the cottage?' Mrs Stowe called after him.

Hal turned to look at her, his eyes as chill as the winter wind. 'You may keep it clean as always, but it shall never be let to a tenant again.'

'Well, I never…' Mrs Stowe said, watching as he mounted his horse and rode away, clearly out of sorts. 'It makes you wonder.' She went back inside and closed the door. It seemed that she would have the cottage to herself for the time being at least, which suited her very well.

Hal rode away without a backward glance. He knew that he must find Jo for he would have no peace until he had spoken to her—but what had made her run away like that? Had his father thrown her out? It seemed likely that he had heard some tale of Jo being Hal's mistress, for he knew that people might think it, because of the way she had left Bath so abruptly with him as her escort. Anyone who understood the situation would know it was a lie, but his father had probably made the worst of it. Had he been unkind to Jo, called her names and driven her from the cottage with threats?

Hal was frustrated and fearful as he went in search of his groom. He would not easily forgive his father if anything had happened to Jo.

'What are you saying?' Hal asked, staring at the young lad he found in the stables brushing out the soiled straw. 'Why isn't George here?'

'He had to visit his married sister in Devon, sir,' the lad

said. 'He'll be back in a few days, but she's ill, you see, and she wrote and asked George to come. He took the gig, sir—said as he was sure you wouldn't mind. He'll bring it back right and tight.'

'Yes, well, that isn't the point,' Hal said, feeling the rising frustration. 'I wanted to know where—but no matter.'

He walked back to the house, his sense of frustration becoming almost unbearable. Why had Jo run off without a word to him? She must have known that he would at least take her home, if nothing else. Why had she not waited for him to return?

Of course he knew the answer. She had believed that he intended to marry a girl of his father's choosing. He had allowed her to believe it, because it was what he had believed himself. Now he saw that it was impossible. He could not go through with what would be a sham just to please Lord Beverley—and his father should not demand it of him. It was all wrong. Even if he put Jo aside, if he resisted the need to make love to her, it would still be a mistake—and unfair to the girl he married.

All he could offer was his name and the promise of a title and wealth, but nothing more. He would seek his wife's bed only for the getting of an heir. How unfair that would be to her, and to himself—but most of all to Jo. He had kissed her, taught her to love him, and then told her he could not marry her. What a damned prig he had been! It was a wonder that she had not told him to go to hell—but she would not, because she was all that was good and honest, all that he loved and needed. He had been a fool and it would be his fault if she no longer cared for him.

He would seek her out wherever she was, but first he must

speak to his father. He must speak his piece, gently, with care for Lord Beverley's health, but firmly, because he could not lose Jo. He knew now that without her his life would be empty, an endless stretch of years with no hope of love or happiness.

'Mama, there is a gig stopping outside in the drive,' Lucy said. She had been standing in the window for some minutes, staring out at a grey day and wishing that she had someone to keep her company. Her mama and Aunt Bertha were very dear, but they did not laugh and play silly games with her the way her sisters had. 'Mama! It is Jo.'

'Jo—are you sure?' Mrs Horne put down her mending and got up to join her daughter in the window. She saw a woman wearing a very elegant blue cloak that seemed to be luxuriously lined with fur, at least about the hood that framed her face. For a moment she wasn't sure if it was her daughter, for there seemed to be an aura of…mystery…around the woman, but then as she spoke and laughed with the man who had handed her down, Mrs Horne saw that it was indeed her beloved Jo. 'Yes, it is darling Jo—go and greet her, Lucy.'

She had no need to urge her youngest daughter—Lucy was already flying through the hall to the door, which Lady Edgeworthy's obliging footman opened for her.

'Jo! Jo dearest!' Lucy cried and flung herself at her sister, hugging her as if she would never let her go, until Jo laughed and kissed her. 'Why didn't you let us know you were coming?'

'It was meant to be a surprise,' Jo said. 'I thought I might have been here yesterday, but I was too late to catch the mail coach and George brought me all the way here in the gig. We had to stop one night with his sister in Devon.'

Lucy looked at the man who was bringing in Jo's trunk, which had been strapped to the back of the gig. He was a man in his thirties, not at all handsome in her opinion but with a friendly face, especially when he smiled and tipped his cap to her.

'Who is he?' she whispered to Jo as she drew her through the hall.

'Mr Beverley's groom,' Jo said. 'It was so kind of him to bring me for he knew that I did not wish to wait two days for the next coach.'

'Was it not uncomfortable to drive such a long way in the gig?' Lucy asked in awe.

'Yes, a little, but I was not cold in this,' Jo said, though it had not been a pleasant journey. 'But at least I am here—and poor George has to drive all the way back. Though I think he means to stay with his sister for a day or two this time.'

'Jo, my dearest!' Mrs Horne put an end to their conversation as she came forward to greet her daughter. 'I am so glad to have you home—but why did you not let us know you were coming?'

'It was a surprise,' Lucy said. 'Oh, I don't care! I am just so glad that you are home, Jo. I have missed you so very much.'

'And I have missed you and Mama—and you, Aunt Bertha,' Jo said as she saw Lady Edgeworthy enter the parlour. 'It seems so long since I saw you all!'

Mrs Horne nodded, her eyes noticing the difference in Jo. She had been a girl when she went to Bath with her Aunt Wainwright, but she was most definitely a woman now. Something had happened to her, and she was not sure that it was a good thing, but, being the wise woman she was, she would not press her daughter. Jo would tell her what she wanted to know in her own time.

'I shall instruct Cook to give your groom a decent meal, for to drive all this way in such weather was noble of him, though I think your friend would have done better to send you by post chaise,' Aunt Bertha said. 'You should have known that I would pay the fare when you got here, Jo. You must be frozen to the bone.'

'No, for my cloak kept out the bitter wind,' Jo said and took it off, laying it down on a chair. Lucy pounced on it and stroked the lining, exclaiming how soft and warm it was. 'It was fortunate that I had it—but I fear poor George must be chilled. I should be grateful if he could stay the night, Aunt, for it looks as if it might snow.'

'I shall instruct my housekeeper,' Lady Edgeworthy said and went out to make sure that the groom was made welcome and given both food and shelter for the night.

'Your aunt is right,' Mrs Horne said with a frown. 'The least they could have done was to send you by post chaise, dearest.'

'Oh, I meant to travel by the mail coach, but we were delayed on our way and missed it by a few minutes. George saw that I was distressed and offered to bring me himself. It was exceedingly good of him, Mama. We had to change horses several times and he paid for it from his own pocket. I offered, but he would not hear of it.'

'At least *he* is a gentleman,' Mrs Horne said and frowned. She might have said a lot more for she was angry at the way her daughter had been treated by her friends, and suspected that there was a lot more that Jo had not told her. 'Where did you get your cloak, Jo? It looks very expensive. I do not think that my sister bought you that…'

'No, she did not,' Jo said with a smile. 'Feel the quality, Mama. Is it not lovely? It belonged to Mr Beverley's grand-mother and was stored in the attic at the cottage where we stayed. As you know, I sent my trunk home and was a little short of clothing. Hal…Mr Beverley said that I might have some things that had been stored and this was my favourite thing. It looks so well.'

'Yes, it does,' Mrs Horne agreed. She did not know why, but Jo had seemed almost a stranger wearing the cloak, but now she was her darling child again, come back to her—and if she was not quite as she had been, the love of her family would restore her. 'Come and sit down, my love. Are you hungry?'

'No, for George's sister Maudie prepared us a basket of food to bring with us,' Jo said. 'We stayed there last night, and she was very kind to me, Mama. She made such a fuss of me. I think she hoped that George had brought me home to meet her at first, but she was no less kind when she understood the truth.'

'The truth, Jo?'

'That he was merely bringing me home to my family.'

'Your decision was a little sudden, I think?'

'Yes,' Jo said and looked her in the eyes. 'I am not in any sort of trouble, Mama. Lord Beverley came to the cottage and begged Ellen to make her home with him. He nursed his granddaughter and begged Ellen's pardon for his unkind-ness when Matt ran off to marry her—and she decided that it was the best thing for her daughter. She did not wish to live on Hal's charity for ever, and was determined to earn what she could to support herself and Mattie—but Lord Beverley told her that she was entitled to her husband's estate, which is quite a considerable sum. That changed things, naturally. She did ask if I would go with her, but I did not think that would be right—besides, I preferred to come home to you and Lucy, Mama. I went with Ellen because she needed me. At that time she was alone and frightened, and even though Hal came just as we were about to leave Bath, she begged me to accompany her.' Jo hesitated. 'I know that I ought not to have deserted my aunt, but…'

'Say no more on that score, dearest,' her mother bid her. 'Your aunt wrote me a most unkind letter and it will be some time before I am able to forgive her. I should never have allowed you to go to Bath with her. Bertha has given us a home and we shall visit London or Bath occasionally with her—and neither you nor Lucy shall be exposed to my sister's unkindness again.'

'Oh, Mama, how good you are to take my side,' Jo said and moved to kiss her cheek. 'But I know that I was reckless and ought not to have behaved as I did. It was from the best of motives, though that may not excuse me. I can only hope that I have not done anything that might affect Lucy's chances when she comes out.'

'If anyone was unkind enough to think ill of you, it will be forgot by then,' Mrs Horne said. 'We shall say no more of it, Jo. What I should like to know is what you have been doing all this time?'

'Making hats,' Jo said, and told her how she had been thinking of selling her hats through Madame Susanne. 'She told me that Ellen and I should set up our own establishment—but of course Ellen will not need to work for her living now. I shall make hats for myself and Lucy, but I dare say there is no chance of my selling them here.'

'What about your writing?' Lucy asked. 'I read the pages you sent home in your trunk and I liked the wicked earl, because he wasn't wicked anymore.'

'Oh…' Jo laughed. 'I gave that one up in despair, Lucy, for he would not do as I wanted—but I have written several children's stories, which I shall let you read. If they are good enough, I may send them to a magazine or a publisher—but I have another idea for a love story.'

'A love story?' Mrs Horne looked at her with interest. The Jo who had gone to Bath had not believed in romantic love.

'Yes, I think so,' Jo said and her cheeks were pink as she met her mother's gaze. 'While I was at the cottage I heard a lot of stories about Hal's grandmother and gradually a story began to grow in my head. I have not tried to set it down yet, but I shall…though of course it will not truly be about her.'

'What I do not understand is where Mr Beverley was when you left,' Mrs Horne said. 'You wrote of his kindness to you and Ellen, but it seems odd that he would let you come all this way in a gig.'

'Hal…Mr Beverley was away,' Jo said, her cheeks flushed as she felt the curiosity in her mother's eyes. 'Would you mind if I went upstairs now, Mama? I should like to make myself comfortable after the journey.'

'Yes, of course,' Mrs Horne said and watched her daughter walk from the room. Clearly she did not wish to talk about her real reasons for leaving. The fact that she had chosen to do so while Mr Beverley was away was revealing, and Mrs Horne sensed at least one of the reasons for the change in her daughter. However, she would not push the point—Jo would tell her when she was ready.

Upstairs, alone in her room, Jo sat down on the bed,

feeling the weight of her unhappiness suddenly descend on her. She had forced herself to think of practical things, and there had been the need to hide her distress from others: first Ellen, then George and now her family—but here, alone, she knew that her heart was breaking. She loved Hal so very much and she knew that she would not see him again.

He might be angry or upset at first when he discovered that she had gone, but then he would see it was for the best and he would learn to forget her—as she must forget him.

Hal dismounted, gave the reins of his curricle to a groom and strode up to the house. He had driven straight here from his estate, stopping only to change his horses once, and he was in a frenzy of frustrated anger and despair. It had done his temper no good to reflect on the fact that it was his own fault that Jo had run away from him. Had he behaved better, she would not have left without a word.

'Mr Hal, sir,' the butler greeted him as he entered the hall with its magnificent curved staircase and the marble-tiled floor. 'I am glad you came, sir. We were about to send for you.'

'Send for me? What do you mean…Father?'

'Lord Beverley had one of his turns when he arrived,' Jenkins told him. 'We sent for the doctor, sir. He says there is no cause for immediate alarm, but his lordship must rest and take care not to upset himself. It was the journey, I dare say.'

'Is he in his bedchamber?'

'I believe so, sir,' Jenkins replied. 'He did not want to go, but Mrs Beverley insisted. I think she may be with him now. I must say it is good to have her here at last, sir—and the baby.'

'Yes, it is high time she was given her rightful place,' Hal agreed. 'I shall go up to my father. Excuse me…'

Hal walked up the stairs. His anger had abated a little, though his frustration was, if anything, increased by the news of his father's illness. It was impossible to say the things he wanted—needed!—to say, because if Lord Beverley was badly distressed it might bring on a fatal attack. Clearly the journey to Hal's estate had been too much for him.

It was a damned stupid thing to do! Why had he gone down there anyway? If he had discovered Ellen's whereabouts, he had only to send for his son and ask for an explanation.

Pausing outside his father's rooms, he took a deep breath to steady his temper and then entered the little sitting room. Ellen was there, looking through the small bookcase. She turned with a book in her hand, smiling as she saw him.

'Hal,' she said. 'I am glad you came. I dare say you know your father has had another little turn? It wasn't so very bad. Indeed, he did not wish to rest, but I persuaded him. I was about to read to him for a while—but I shall leave you alone with him and come back in a little.'

'You are all right, Ellen? You were not forced to come here?'

'No, certainly not,' Ellen replied. 'I was invited to make my home here and I accepted—but surely you had my letter? It was taken up to your house by one of the grooms.'

'I did not go to the house,' Hal said. 'When I learned what had happened I came straight here. What of Jo?'

'She decided that she would return home,' Ellen said. 'I asked if she would come, even if only for a short visit—but she said that her mama would expect her to return home now that I did not need her.'

'Yes, I dare say she would say that…' Hal frowned. 'My father did not…say anything to her?'

'Nothing to my knowledge. I believe it was her own decision, Hal.'

He nodded, frowning because it confirmed his opinion that it was his fault that Jo had left so abruptly. 'I shall go in to him now, Ellen.'

'Yes, of course—be gentle with him, Hal. He is not a bad man, even though I once thought so.'

'I know…that is the problem,' Hal said and sighed.

He went through into the bedroom. Lord Beverley was lying with his eyes shut, but he opened them and looked at his son.

'So you've come, then.' He grunted. 'What have you to say for yourself, sir? I do not think that I deserved such treatment from you, Hal.'

'If you mean that I ought to have told you about Ellen and the child sooner, then I am perhaps at fault,' Hal said. 'Jo said that I should trust you, that you might wish to know your grandchild—but I was afraid you would be angry and that it might bring on one of your attacks.'

'So it is all my fault?' Lord Beverley glared at him. 'Well, perhaps you are right. I did not treat Ellen well—refusing to meet her when Matt asked me to *was* wrong. Had I done so, I should have realised that despite her father—who is everything I knew him to be!—she is a lady.'

'Yes, Father, she is. I believe her mother was county gentry, but no money—but Ellen's father is in trade, of course. I understand he is quite rich.'

'As he so rudely told me,' Lord Beverley said. 'He assured me that his daughter would not get a penny of his money, and

I am afraid I…was rather rude to him, Hal. I shall not repeat what was said, but I think he understood that Ellen did not need his money. However, he went to try to force her to go with him, but she told him that she would never set foot in his house again. Apparently, that girl—Jo, was it?—Ellen told me that she had learned to stand up for herself from Jo…quite a spunky gel, that. Pity she went off so suddenly. I should have liked to see her again.'

'Jo is wonderful,' Hal told him. 'I really think Ellen might have died had she not been there when Mattie was born. Ellen has been very low, but she is better now—and much of that was due to Jo.'

'Yes, well…' Lord Beverley grunted. 'I may have been wrong about a few things, but I am not a fool, Hal.'

'No, Father, I know that you are not,' Hal said. 'If you have heard gossip, you should ignore it, for it is not true. Jo has done nothing to be ashamed of I promise you.'

'As I said, I am not a fool,' Lord Beverley said. 'And now, if you don't mind, I should like to rest, Hal. I am very tired. Perhaps we may speak again soon? I think we must have a proper talk, but I confess I am not up to it just yet. I trust you mean to stay here for a few days at least?'

'Yes…' Hal said reluctantly, for he could do no other. 'Yes, sir. I shall certainly stay until you are on your feet again.'

'Speak to Greaves. He has some business that needs attention. It is your duty to see to the estate, Hal. I think it is time I gave the reins to you, for if I do not take things easily I shall not live long enough to see my grandchildren grow up.'

'Yes, of course, I understand,' Hal said. Lord Beverley was

looking rather pale and frail as he lay back and closed his eyes.

Hal left his room with a heavy heart. For a moment he had thought that it might be possible to talk to his father, to tell him how he felt about Jo—that she was the only girl he could bear to marry. It was obvious that this latest attack had brought Lord Beverley low, but despite his illness he had a strong constitution and with rest and care would probably recover to live for some years yet.

And Hal wanted him to live. He was aware of a lump in his throat as he realised that he cared deeply for his father. To do anything that might precipitate his death would be shocking—but what was the alternative?

He could not give Jo up entirely! Yet he could not go haring after her immediately, even now that he knew she had gone home, for his father had asked him to take over the estate and it was undoubtedly his duty to do so.

He could write to Jo, of course, but what could he say? Until he found the right opportunity to tell his father what was in his heart, there was nothing meaningful that he could say to the girl he loved.

Chapter Nine

'Oh, I loved all those stories,' Lucy said as she curled up on her sister's bed that morning. 'Especially the one about the fairy grotto and the prince…it was funny and exciting, too. I loved the way the wicked witch kept changing the prince into all kinds of horrid things and the good fairy changed him back again, and each time she did he became handsomer and handsomer.'

'Well, he started off with spots and a crooked nose and the princess thought he was ugly, but every time he did a good deed he got better and better looking.'

'Oh, yes, it was so amusing,' Lucy said, 'because in the end she fell in love with him—but he went off with the poor girl who had been kind to him.'

'It is a very moral tale.' Jo said and laughed. 'I think Papa might have approved, don't you?'

'Oh, yes, he would,' Lucy said and giggled. 'It is so lovely having you home, Jo. I sometimes wish that Marianne was with us, but I am sure she is happy with Drew, aren't you?'

'Yes, very happy,' Jo said. 'She has sent Mama a lovely

long letter and enclosed her love to us. I dare say she will write to both of us when she has the time.'

'I do hope so,' Lucy said and wrinkled her brow. 'I read all your letters to us, Jo, for Mama let me read hers as well— I thought that perhaps you liked Hal very much, because you mentioned him so often. You have not heard from him or Ellen since you came home, have you?'

'No, but it is only a few days,' Jo said. 'I dare say that Ellen has a great deal to do. She will need time to accustom herself to her new home and all the people she will meet. I expect she will have duties as Lord Beverley's hostess.'

'Do you think they will entertain a lot?' Lucy asked, her eyes wide. 'Is Lord Beverley very rich—as rich as Drew?'

'I am not sure. No, perhaps not quite, for Drew is very rich, Lucy—but Hal's father is a wealthy and important man, I am sure.'

'I am not certain that he is a very nice man,' Lucy said. 'He did not treat Ellen very well, did he? Refusing to meet her and disowning his son when he ran off and married her.'

'Well, perhaps he was entitled to be angry,' Jo said. 'Ellen's father was not a gentleman—in fact, he really is most unpleasant. I expect Lord Beverley imagined that Ellen might not be a lady, but she is, of course—you would like her very much, Lucy.'

'I should if she is nice to you,' Lucy said. 'But if she forgets to write to you now that she is living in a grand house I shall not like her at all.'

'Oh, you wretch,' Jo said. 'Off with you, now. I must get up, because I have decided to walk down to the village. I want to make a new hat for Mama—and perhaps I shall make you a bonnet, too, if you help me. There are some bits and pieces

I want from the shop in Sawlebridge. Would you like to come with me?'

'I should love it of all things,' Lucy said, 'but I have two friends coming to have nuncheon with us today. Sarah and Jane Henley. They live in Truro and their father is bringing them specially, so I must be here to greet them.'

'Yes, of course you must,' Jo agreed. 'And we can walk to the village another day. We have plenty of time now.'

She sighed as her sister hugged her and then ran off. After a moment, she threw off the bedcovers. Jo was happy to be with her family again, but in this well-run house there was often not enough to keep her busy. She spent some hours each day writing in her notebooks and had already written two chapters of her new novel, which was the story of a beautiful young girl who fell in love with a handsome rogue who would give her a child and desert her. After becoming a courtesan, she fell in love and married a man who adored her.

Washing and dressing, Jo let herself remember the way she had felt at the cottage, and the warm feeling she had every time she wore the blue cloak. She did not know how much of her story might be true, but she had a clear picture in her mind of everything that she intended to write. And at least it stopped her moping, which she was determined not to do, because it would distress Mama. Besides, she was quite sure that she had made the right decision, for had Hal wanted to see her he would have come long before this—and if he had not come he might have written. Neither he or Ellen had written to her, and, despite the excuses she had made to Lucy, that hurt.

Jo lifted her head. She was not going to give way to self-pity! She had made her decision and she would not falter.

Even though she made herself useful to her mama and Aunt Bertha, Jo knew that she was not needed here—not as she had been at the cottage. She was loved and wanted, but only Lucy truly needed her—and Lucy was making friends here, which was a good thing. Mama and Aunt Bertha were very comfortable together, which was wonderful because poor Mama had been so uncomfortable when she was forced to live on her sister's charity.

Jo looked at herself when she was dressed. She picked up her brush and was about to scrape her hair back in her usual style, but something made her change her mind. Instead of securing it all at the nape of her neck, she drew the sides back and tied them with a ribbon, letting her hair fall down her back. One or two tendrils escaped to curl about her face, but the effect was much less severe than usual. She smiled at herself as she picked up her cloak and took it downstairs. She had been brought a pot of chocolate in bed, which she and Lucy had shared, and she wanted nothing more for the moment. She would walk down to the village now and buy what she wanted, and then she could spend the rest of the day working on the hats she was planning to make for her mama and her sister.

Jo spent a happy hour choosing silks, cottons, beads, materials for stiffening, ribbons and a pretty spray of cherries that would suit the hat she was making for her mama. For Lucy she chose a spray of yellow primroses made of a silk velvet, for she had found some more of the lovely yellow brocade that she had used once before, and knew that it would suit her sister very well.

She left the shop carrying her parcels by the string the

obliging assistant had tied for her, and began to stroll towards the road that led up towards the cliffs, intending to walk home by the longer route. The fresh air was bracing and she needed some time for thinking.

'Miss Horne! Is it really you?'

Jo turned as she heard the gentleman speak, giving a little exclamation of surprise as she saw who it was. 'Mr Browne—how very nice to see you again. I had not expected it. When did you leave Bath, sir?'

'Shortly after you, Miss Horne,' the Reverend Browne said. 'My family comes from Truro, you know—at least my mother's family live there still. I came to visit and was told of some deserving cases here amongst the families of the miners. I decided to visit and see for myself what could be done. It is my intention to set up a school for the children of miners and seamen who have met with bad times. I have been looking at various properties in the district.'

'Oh, how worthy that sounds,' Jo said, her eyes sparkling. The fresh air had given her some colour and she looked truly beautiful. 'May I be of some assistance to you, sir? If you are looking for property it may be that my aunt—Lady Edgeworthy—could help you. She knows everyone, of course, and will be able to put you in touch with anyone you need to see. I am sure she would be delighted if you were to come for tea at Sawlebridge House. Anyone will tell you where it is to be found.'

The Reverend Browne looked at her for a moment. He had spoken to her on impulse, though he was aware of all the speculation that had surrounded her departure from Bath.

'Are you here with your aunt?'

'Mama, my sister Lucy and I live with Lady Edgeworthy,'

Jo told him. 'I visited Bath with Mama's sister—but I am afraid we do not get on very well. I dare say it has been my fault, for I am a little outspoken—and I think she will never forgive me for leaving her as I did.'

'You went to stay with a friend, I believe?'

'Oh, yes, Mrs Ellen Beverley. She is the daughter-in-law of Lord Beverley, and now resides with him. There had been a disagreement and she was living alone when I met her—but it is all resolved now and she is settled with her father-in-law. Her husband was killed while with the army in Spain, you know.'

'No, I did not know,' the Reverend said. 'There was some false tale circulating after you left, Miss Horne—but you have set my mind at rest. You asked if you might be of assistance to me, and I am happy to say that you may. I shall be holding a little gathering at the church hall here later this week. I want to get local people interested in the welfare of these poor families, and you might wish to attend, because we shall need ideas about what may be done to raise funds from the good people of the district. My fund will purchase the property, but we need a new fund to maintain and run it.'

'Yes, I should enjoy that,' Jo told him with enthusiasm. 'I should be happy to help, as I did before.'

'Yes, you did very well at the bazaar, I remember,' he said and gave her a look of approval. He tipped his hat to her. 'I shall certainly call on your mother and aunt, Miss Horne. It is a great pleasure to meet you again.'

Jo nodded and walked on, feeling a little better in her mind. She would enjoy helping Mr Browne with his various projects, because he was a good man in his way and reminded her of her father. It would enable her to meet more people, for she must make up her mind to settle here and get on with her life. There was no prospect of her marrying now, but with all her interests she could be content enough if she tried. If there was a little voice at the back of her mind that told her she would never be happy without the man she loved, she would not let herself listen to it. Hal did not love her. He would not have let her go so easily if he had.

'Good morning,' Ellen said as Hal entered the nursery, where she had been comforting a tearful Mattie before laying her down. 'I think Mattie finds it a little strange here. The cottage was so much smaller, and she was more often with me. I come up as often as I can, but there has been so much to do. People have been calling to see how your father is, and I like to sit with him as much as I can. He says I should bring Mattie with me, and I shall once he is more himself. But I think he is much better now, don't you?'

'Yes, he seems better,' Hal said. 'He is sitting in a chair and talks of coming down this afternoon, but he still seems a little frail.'

'Yes, he is not as strong as one would like,' Ellen admitted. 'But I believe he is not as frail as he looks, Hal. You must not think it…' She hesitated, then, 'You seem unlike yourself, Hal. Is something troubling you?'

'No…' He sighed and bent over the cot. 'The babe is thriving and I see signs of Matt in her sometimes. Father dotes on her. He was talking about buying her a pony when she is old enough.'

'Oh, dear, I am afraid that is a long way off,' Ellen said and smiled. 'I believe he loves her, though he wishes that she had been a boy.'

'Yes, I know. He wants an heir.' Hal sighed. 'I shall have to do something about it.'

'Why don't you tell him?' Ellen said. 'I know it is not my business to speak of it, Hal—but Jo loves you and I think you love her.'

'Was it so obvious?'

'To me, yes,' Ellen said with a smile, 'because I loved you both. You were my friends and you gave me the strength to go on—and now I have so much. Your father made me very happy when he brought me here, Hal. Not because of the house or the money—or even my place in society—but because of his love for Mattie. He has become the father I never had, and he cannot do enough for me. I know you are afraid of upsetting him, but I think you ought to tell him the truth. You could never be happy with an arranged marriage, and Jo must be breaking her heart for you.'

'Do you truly think it? I wondered if she had decided that it was all a mistake.'

'Did you really? Or were you making excuses because you cannot face speaking to your father?'

Hal pulled a wry face. 'I would face the French with a smile on my face any day,' he told her. 'But telling my father that I want to marry a girl he will not approve of makes me feel like a little boy. I am not afraid of him…only of disappointing him.'

'Then tell him,' Ellen said. 'Go and do it straight away, Hal. He is well enough to listen now, providing neither of you loses your temper. Delay no longer—it is not fair to anyone.'

'You are right,' Hal said with a rueful smile. I must say what I have to say—though, as you asked me, I shall be gentle.'

He left the nursery, turning towards the main wing of the house where his father's apartments were situated. It was time that he spoke out, told his father exactly what was in his mind. He would not quarrel with Lord Beverley whatever the outcome, but this thing must be settled one way or the other now.

'It is very nice to meet you, Mr Browne,' Lady Edgeworthy said. 'Jo told us what you were planning and I am very pleased to hear of it. I have a list of people I should like you to meet—Dr Thompson and his wife, Jane, in particular. Doctor Thompson has long been aware of a need for something of the sort, especially if the children were to be given milk and a proper meal at school. It would be one way of making sure that they had some decent food inside them, and would not be seen as charity, I think.'

'Now that is exactly what was in my mind,' the Reverend said. He looked at Jo as she brought him his tea, accepting it with a smile. 'It was an excellent suggestion of yours to invite me to meet your aunt, Miss Horne. This is just what we need—people of standing to take an interest in the school.'

'I am glad you are pleased,' Jo said. 'I know Jane and Dr Thompson do as much as they can, but the miners and their families are very proud. They will not accept money, though Lucy and I have taken a few clothes to the church hall. They will accept from the church what they will not take from us—Papa taught me that.'

'Mr Horne was clearly an excellent man,' the Reverend said with a smile. 'I wish it had been my good fortune to meet him.'

'My husband loved people,' Mrs Horne said. She was not sure why, but something in his manner was not right. He spoke well and undoubtedly he worked hard for his various funds, but she could not quite like him, which was unfair of her. 'He did what he did out of genuine concern and love for others.'

'Yes, of course.' Mr Browne looked at her, unsettled by something in her eyes. He put down his cup. 'I think I should be going now. You will come to the meeting tomorrow, Miss Horne?'

'Yes, certainly,' Jo said. 'I shall be very interested to hear you speak, sir—and of course to help the children when I can.'

'I am so pleased to have met you, Lady Edgeworthy—Mrs Horne. Goodbye.'

'You must come again,' Lady Edgeworthy said and wondered why Jo's mother frowned at her. 'We shall be pleased to help all we can. Take Mr Browne to the door, Jo.' She waited until they had gone out and they could no longer hear voices, and then looked at her niece. 'Well, Cynthia—why did you not like him?'

'I hope it did not show,' Mrs Horne said. 'I know he seems a very worthy man—but there is something…' She sighed and shook her head. 'I do not know, but he is not like my dear husband…not at all.'

'He is perhaps a little proud of his good works,' Lady Edgeworthy said. 'Few gentlemen are truly as good as Mr Horne, my dear. You must not judge everyone by his standards.'

'You are right, I know,' Mrs Horne said. 'But Drew loved Marianne so much and I just knew that he would make her happy. I wanted something of the sort for Jo.'

'You do not think…' Lady Edgeworthy was thunderstruck. 'She would not! Oh, no, my dear, I cannot think it. He is very well in his way—but as a husband for Jo…it would never work. She is too spirited—too outspoken!'

'She is also very conscious of duty,' Mrs Horne said. 'Her papa always said that she had a very caring nature. I am afraid that she might—' She broke off as Jo came back into the room. 'Has he gone, dearest?'

'Yes, Mama,' Jo said. 'Did you approve of him and what he is trying to do? I know Jane and Dr Thompson feel that something is necessary. The poorest folk in the district cannot afford to pay for their children to be schooled, and that means they can never rise above what they were born to. It would be such a fine thing if even a few of them could learn to read and write and take up trades, would it not?'

'Yes, my love, it would,' her mother told her. 'I have every admiration for what Mr Browne is trying to do—but I am not sure of his reasons.'

'What do you mean, Mama?' Jo was surprised, because she had not thought about his motives. 'Surely it is for the good of others—which is what Papa always told us we should consider in our lives.'

'Yes, indeed he did,' Mrs Horne said. 'And I am proud of you for what you have offered to do, my love. You are always so busy anyway, to give up your pleasures in order to raise money is a good thing—but you do it because you sincerely care about those children. I am not sure that Mr Browne does. I believe he is more concerned with appearing to be a good man than actually being one.'

'Mama!' Jo was shocked, for she had not seen him in that light. 'I know he can sound a little pompous, but I think he means well.'

'He is well enough as an acquaintance, but…you would not think of marrying him, Jo?'

'Marry Mr Browne?' Jo stared at her and then burst into laughter. 'Oh, Mama, how could you think it? I like him well enough—but I would not consider being his wife, even though Aunt Wainwright was convinced that it was the best offer I should receive. She said that, if I did not take him, I should never marry.'

'Did she, indeed?' Mrs Horne was angry. 'And who is she to be the judge of that, I should like to know? I do not consider him a fit husband for my daughter, Jo. If you had set your heart on him, I might have allowed it in time, but I am very glad you have not.'

'No, Mama, I have not,' Jo said, but the laughter had gone from her face. 'My heart very definitely does not belong to Mr Browne.'

'Jo…' her mother said, but Jo fled from the room before she could burst into tears.

'Oh, this is beautiful,' Lucy said as she tried on the hat Jo had made for her. 'Marianne made me some lovely bonnets, as you know—but this is such a pretty colour.'

'I am glad you like it,' Jo said. 'It was some material that I found in Lady Beverley's trunk. I think she must have had a gown made from it and saved the offcuts. I have found her things so useful.'

Lucy took the hat off and waved it under her nose. 'It smells gorgeous as well…old roses, the ones with the musky scent, I think.'

'Yes, it is the smell of roses, but with something else added,' Jo said. 'I have wondered about it many times, for it clings to all her things and I would like some for myself if I could buy it.'

'But you smell of it all the time,' Lucy said. 'I thought it was a new perfume you had bought somewhere.'

'No, I do not have the perfume,' Jo said and looked thoughtful. 'It must come from the cloak, I think.'

'Oh, yes, that wonderful cloak. It suits you so well, Jo. You look different when you wear it, especially when you let your hair hang loose. I like it so much better that way. You always said it was awful, but I think it is pretty—mine is so pale besides yours.'

'Oh, no, Lucy darling,' her sister said and kissed her. 'Your hair is beautiful. I am going to walk down to the village now for the meeting. Would you like to come with me?'

'Do you mind if I do not?' Lucy said. 'I have a new book to read that Aunt Bertha subscribed for me—and I do not like that man very much. I know it is wrong of me, but I think he is false. He says things and he laughs, but his eyes do not smile.'

'Oh, Lucy!' Jo laughed at her sister's expression. 'Well, do not look so guilty, my love. Mama does not like him much either—but I am interested in helping him, and I think Papa would approve of what he is doing.'

'Oh, yes, of course,' Lucy said. 'I shall help when you have bazaars and things, but I don't want to listen to him making speeches—if you don't mind?'

'Of course not, dearest,' Jo said. 'You must do as you wish, but I shall go. Mr Browne is relying on it, and I do not know how many people will attend the meeting. I hope there will be several, but one cannot always tell—and now I must go.'

Jo wrapped herself in her warm cloak, for it was bitterly cold out. There had been a frost overnight, and her toes felt like ice as she walked to the village. It was a long way, but she walked briskly and arrived in plenty of time. The meeting had not yet begun, though some ten others had arrived and were finding seats in the front row. A black iron pot-bellied stove was making the room pleasantly comfortable, and a table with sandwiches and cakes had been set out at the back of the hall. Jo had been responsible for making most of the cakes in her aunt's kitchen, but someone else had supplied the sandwiches.

She took her seat in the fifth row, leaving the front ones to fill up, which they gradually did until there were perhaps thirty ladies and gentlemen, which, considering the weather, was excellent in Jo's opinion.

She waited patiently until Mr Browne arrived. After greeting his audience and some hesitation, he began his speech about the poverty of children living in hovels, and malnutrition. He spoke of the need for education and about it being the duty of everyone to do what they could, but as his speech went on, Jo sensed that his audience was losing interest. He made it all sound so dull, as if it were a duty that must be done despite the inconvenience it caused. She was surprised, for she had expected something more inspirational—something that touched hearts.

However, he was given a round of applause when the speech finished and several of the ladies went up to him, a dainty cake plate in one hand, clearly more interested in the man than they had been in his cause. Jo watched thoughtfully as he preened and smirked, realising that her mother and Lucy had seen him very clearly. She had confused him with her papa, but they were indeed very different men.

She was tempted to leave without speaking to him, but

even as she thought about it, he left his little group of admirers and came to her.

'These cakes are very good, Miss Horne. I am told that you made them?'

'Yes, I did—with Lily's help,' Jo said. 'I am glad they meet with your approval.'

'Not only mine,' he said. 'I believe everything went very well. I think we shall have as many willing helpers as we need.'

'Yes, I am sure you will,' Jo said. 'And now, if you will excuse me, I think I must leave.'

'I shall call on you soon,' he said. 'We have things to discuss, Miss Horne.'

Jo nodded as he was reclaimed by one of his new admirers. She was lost in thought as she went out into the chill of a very cold day. Looking up at the sky, she wondered if it might snow. Suddenly, she was in a hurry to be home and to get warm by her aunt's fire.

'Someone has arrived,' Lady Edgeworthy said to Mrs Horne about an hour after Jo had left for the village. 'I think it is a gentleman, though I do not know his carriage.' She listened as the knocker sounded and then heard the voice of her housekeeper as she admitted the caller. 'I do not know his voice either.' She took her seat next to the fire, waiting in anticipation as the door was opened and their visitor was announced.

'Mr Beverley to see Mrs Horne, my lady,' the woman said. 'Please go in, sir. Shall I bring some refreshment, my lady? It is bitter cold out and the gentleman has travelled a long way.'

'Yes, please do,' Lady Edgeworthy said. 'Hot chocolate for us—and brandy or Madeira for our guest, I think.'

'Brandy would be welcome on such a day,' Hal said and entered the room, where he was greeted by the curious gaze of two ladies. He smiled and advanced towards his hostess. 'You must be Lady Edgeworthy, I believe? And Mrs Horne— I would know you anywhere, ma'am, for you have the look of your daughter about your eyes. '

Mrs Horne stood up and gave him her hand. He bowed over it, kissing it gallantly. 'I am very pleased to see you here, sir,' she said, for all at once she thought she understood the sadness she had seen in Jo's eyes at times. 'I speak for all of us when I say that you are very welcome.'

'That is kind of you, ma'am,' Hal said. 'I came straight here, though I ought perhaps to have sent some warning— but I was not sure of my whereabouts and asked for directions here. Finding myself nearer than to the inn I am told is reasonably equipped for accommodation, I thought to visit you first.' He looked about the large room with interest, noticing that it was comfortable rather than elegant, though everything was of good quality. 'Jo is not here?'

'She has gone to a meeting to help poor children,' Lucy said from the doorway. She looked at him curiously. 'Oh, you must be the wicked earl—the one that Jo says kept getting nicer and nicer so in the end she had to give him up.'

'I beg your pardon,' Hal said, a twinkle in his eyes as he looked at the girl. By heaven, she would set the town by its ears in a year or two! 'I am not sure that I understand you?'

'Oh…' Lucy blushed. 'Didn't you know that Jo was writing a book? It was about a wicked earl who did lots of terrible things to Miranda, but Jo said that it went wrong and she couldn't make him do anything bad any more. He kept rescuing the heroine, which he was not meant to do.'

'Ah, yes, I see,' Hal said. 'He fetched her in out of the snow and fed her, I suppose, instead of leaving her to starve.'

'Something like that,' Lucy said with a giggle, for she had taken to him immediately. 'But she is writing a much better book now—about a young woman who is betrayed by her lover and nearly dies. However, she is saved by her friend and begins to get better—and then she is offered *carte blanche* by a rich lord who wants her to be his mistress.'

'Lucy!' Mrs Horne said, alarmed. 'Are you certain that Jo is writing something of that nature?'

'Yes, Mama, for she lets me read every chapter when it is finished,' Lucy said. 'It is very good, much better than the one about the wicked earl—and I like it as much as the fairy stories, though they are good, too.'

'I wish she would let me read them,' Hal said. Lady Edgeworthy indicated that he should sit and he did, his eyes still on Lucy's face. 'Perhaps you will tell me about them. Jo was going to let me send them to a publisher for her, but then she went away.'

'Oh, I think they should be published, even if one had to pay for them,' Lucy said. 'Jo makes them so funny. I have read lots of fairy stories, you see, but most of them are not so amusing. I particularly like the one about the prince who starts off ugly and gets handsomer and handsomer every time the good fairy turns him back from a toad or a snake or whatever the witch turned him into.' She blushed and looked at her mama. 'I am talking too much and I should not.'

'Oh, but you should,' Hal said and his eyes were filled with gentle laughter. 'I do so much want to hear more about Jo's stories—and you are very good at telling them.'

'Not as good as Jo,' Lucy said loyally. 'But she is good at

everything, isn't she, Mama? She has gone to a boring old lecture with the Reverend Browne. He came here to tea, but I didn't like him much. I do like you, though. Have you come to see Jo?'

'Yes, I have,' Hal said. 'Do you think she will be pleased?'

'She might,' Lucy said. 'She was a little sad when she came home—and I thought it might be your fault, but she is much better now.'

'Is she?' Hal was thoughtful. 'I never wanted to make her sad, Lucy.' He delved into his jacket pocket. 'I have brought a present for you.'

'For me?' Lucy was surprised. 'Are you sure it is for me?'

'Yes, quite sure. Jo saw it in a shop window in Bath. She told me that she thought you would love it, but she did not know if she could afford to buy it. I thought you might like it, too, so I bought it for you.'

'Oh…' Lucy's eyes widened as she took the little velvet pouch and undid the strings. She was amazed as she took out the beautiful silver box and opened it. When the little bird popped up and started to sing she cried out in delight, 'How lovely! See how beautiful it is, Mama. I may keep it—please say that I may have it, Mama?'

'It was bought especially for you,' Mrs Horne said looking on with approval. 'It would be very rude to refuse it.' She met Hal's amused gaze. 'It was very kind of you to think of it, sir.'

'I admit it was bribery,' Hal told her honestly, but with such a wicked grin that she was charmed. 'I wanted to get into Lucy's good books—and Jo's through her. I know how much Jo loves her sisters and her family.'

'Do you need our help to win Jo over?'

'Yes, I think I may,' Hal said. 'I may have hurt her deeply—though it was never my intention.'

'I see…' Mrs Horne held up her hand as he would have gone on. 'Give me no explanations, sir. You may keep those for my daughter. You have hurt her, for I have seen it in her eyes, though she tried to hide it from us. Jo is very outspoken and brave. She does not weep easily—nor does she tell anyone what is in her heart. At least, we who love her may guess or sense her feelings, but she does not speak of them. I hope you do not mean to hurt her again?'

'No, I believe not,' Hal said and smiled. 'I hope that she will be pleased to hear what I have to say—'

He broke off for they heard a voice in the hall and then the door opened and Jo came in. She had taken off her cloak and was wearing a dark green, velvet walking gown, which suited her well, her hair drawn back from her face and tied with a ribbon, fine tendrils curling about her face. The cold air had given her a fresh colour and he thought he had never seen her look so lovely.

'It is bitterly cold out. I am sure it will snow before…' Her words drained away as she saw Hal rise to his feet. 'Hal…Mr Beverley. I did not know you were here.'

'How should you, for I sent no word of my coming,' he said. 'I thought that by the time a letter arrived I could be here myself.'

Jo advanced to the fire, making a show of warming her hands before the fire. She was shocked, taken completely off guard, and she did not know how she had kept from throwing herself into his arms.

'How is Ellen?' she asked, her back still turned to him. 'And your father…and little Mattie?'

'They are all well now,' Hal said. 'My father was taken ill as soon as he got home, and Mattie has had a nasty chill. Ellen asked me to apologise for not writing to you sooner, but I have a long letter from her.'

Jo took a deep breath and turned to face him. 'I am sorry to hear of Lord Beverley's illness,' she said. 'I dare say it was the journey.'

'Yes, it was too much for him. I should have told him sooner—as you bid me, Jo.'

'Yes, it might have been better,' Jo admitted. 'He seemed a kind enough man, and he certainly loves Mattie.'

'Yes, indeed he does,' Hal said. He saw that she was apprehensive. 'Perhaps I should have written first, Jo?'

'Perhaps…' Her eyes fell on Lucy, who was playing with her silver box. 'What have you there, dearest?'

'Is it not lovely?' Lucy said. 'Mr Beverley bought it for me—and I have been telling him about your stories. He wants to read them for himself. May I give them to him?'

'Oh…I suppose…if he really wishes.'

'Perhaps I should go and call tomorrow?' Hal said, for he could see that Jo was uneasy. 'I must in any case find somewhere to stay for the night.'

'Oh, no, I shall not hear of it,' Lady Edgeworthy said at once. 'You will stay here, Mr Beverley. We have plenty of room—and Jo was perfectly right, it has started to snow. I shall direct one of the servants to show your groom where the stables are. He may lodge here, too—and my housekeeper will prepare a room for you.'

She got up and left the room. Mrs Horne glanced at Jo and then at Lucy. She got to her feet, holding out her hand to her youngest daughter.

'Come along, Lucy. I have something I want to show you.'

'But, Mama…' Lucy saw her mother's expression and then looked at Hal. 'Oh, I see…yes, I am coming.'

Silence filled the room after they had gone. Jo moved away to the window, looking out at the few flakes of snow now falling. She was not certain how she felt at this moment. She had longed to see Hal, but finding him with her family, seemingly perfectly at home, had thrown her off balance.

'I am sorry if I came at an awkward moment…'

'No, of course not,' she said without turning to look at him. 'You are very welcome, as I believe my family have shown you. You were very generous to me. I am still using the material in your grandmother's trunk.'

'Nonsense!' he said harshly. 'Trifles! I have given you nothing—and you must know that I want to give you everything?'

Jo turned to face him then, a feeling that she recognised as anger coming to the fore. 'How should I know? You have told me nothing—other than that I am not suitable to be your wife.'

'That was stupid of me,' Hal said. 'I should not have said anything until I had spoken to my father.'

'And have you spoken to your father?' Jo asked, and seeing the answer in his eyes, 'What did he say?'

'He said that he would be pleased if you would come for a visit with Ellen and—'

'So I am to be looked over to see if I will suit?' For some reason Jo was furiously angry. In a more reasonable mood, she would have realised that this was an encouraging sign, but she was too angry to think clearly and it felt as if she were a prize filly being considered for purchase. 'Please thank

Lord Beverley for his kind invitation, but I have only just returned to my family and cannot be spared for the moment.' Without giving Hal a chance to answer, she walked swiftly from the room, picking up her cloak and going out of the front door.

Coming down the stairs at that moment, Mrs Horne called to her daughter but Jo either did not hear or ignored her, the door closing behind her with an ominous slam.

'Jo went out rather suddenly,' Mrs Horne said to Hal as she entered the parlour where he was still standing, looking rather stunned. 'Forgive me for asking, but have you quarrelled?'

'I think Jo is angry with me,' Hal said and looked rueful. 'It is all my fault, Mrs Horne. You must not think any blame attaches to Jo, for it does not.'

'Well, I shall not ask for details,' Mrs Horne told him with a smile. 'But I shall tell you something you may be well aware of—my daughter is both proud and sometimes hasty of temper. She will calm down and be her reasonable self if you give her a little time.'

'So you do not think I should follow her?'

'That is not for me to say,' Mrs Horne replied. 'I do not know your intentions towards Jo, sir.'

'I love her desperately,' Hal said. 'But I have been foolish and I think I have hurt her too many times.'

'Then give her a little time to think things over, Mr Beverley, for I am sure that if she loves you she will give you another chance once she has regained her composure.'

'Yes, perhaps that might be for the best,' Hal said. 'I have some business for my father. I came here first, but in the circumstances I think it would be best if I did not stay. I do not wish to distress Jo. My father has written to her and I should be grateful if you would give her the letter, Mrs Horne. I shall return in a few days and perhaps Jo will feel more inclined to talk to me then.'

'I think that is very sensible,' Mrs Horne said and smiled at him. 'If you are sure that you will not stay? I know my daughter and her moods never last long.'

'I do not give up easily,' Hal said. 'I have hesitated, because I was afraid of causing my father distress, but I should never have allowed him to part us. It was merely a case of being patient...but he has told me that he likes Jo. It was his suggestion that she should come for a visit, even before he knew that I wanted to marry her.'

'Does Jo understand that?'

'I may have put it badly,' Hal said with a rueful look. 'Please tell Jo that I shall return very soon, ma'am. And if Lady Edgeworthy's offer still stands, I shall leave my groom here. It looks to be a foul night and he has no need to accompany me for I shall be back in a day or so.'

'Yes, of course, that is considerate of you. And I shall give Jo your father's letter,' Mrs Horne promised. 'Also that you intend to return in a few days.'

Jo walked very fast until she was out of sight of the house. The angry tears trickled down her cheeks and she was breathing very hard. It was humiliating to know that Hal had asked his father for permission to marry her and had been told that he wished to look her over first. If Hal had loved her as she loved him, he would simply have told his father and then married her against any opposition, as his brother had Ellen! And yet...almost immediately she began to realise that she was being unfair. Hal was concerned for his father's health and that was as it should be, of course. Had the situation been reversed, she could never have done anything to wound Mama or Papa. It just hurt to know that Hal's love for her was not the kind that would sweep everything else before it—how could it be when he had made it clear that his father would not think her suitable?

Jo's hurt pride carried her as far as the path leading to the cliffs, and it was there that she saw a gentleman walking towards her. Had there been any way of avoiding him, she would have done so, for she had no wish to talk to anyone. However, he had seen her and it was clear that he meant to come up with her.

'Miss Horne, how fortunate,' the Reverend Browne said and smiled at her. 'I was on my way to call on you and this is an excellent opportunity to have a few minutes alone with you.'

'I am sorry,' Jo said, feeling trapped. 'I was about to return to the house, for it is cold. Perhaps you would care to walk with me? Have you come to ask me about the bazaar you were planning?'

'I have had several offers of help,' he told her with a self-satisfied expression that she found irritating for some reason. 'No, it was something more important…more personal that I wished to discuss.'

Jo stared at him. Something warned her that she would not like what he was about to say and she wished that she might avoid it, but she could not simply walk away.

'I do not think we have anything of a personal nature to discuss, sir.'

'I dare say you do not, for I have remarked that you are a modest girl, and it may not have crossed your mind that I would admire you or consider you worthy to be my wife.'

She felt an overwhelming desire to giggle at his announcement, because it was made in such a pompous manner. However, she struggled to control her sense of the ridiculous and took a deep breath before replying.

'You are very good to say so, sir, but correct in assuming that I would not have thought of it—indeed, it had not entered my mind.'

He gave her an approving look. 'As I thought, you are far too modest to think it, but I assure you it is so. I have often remarked your selflessness and concern for others, and, after some deliberation—because, of course, there was some scandal attached to your name when you left Bath—I have decided that I shall disregard it. So I have the honour to ask you to be my wife and join me in my work, which I am persuaded you believe to be as important as I do.'

'You do me honour, sir,' Jo said, deciding that she would not allow herself to show the contempt that she felt for the manner in which he had made his proposal. 'However, I am sorry, but I must refuse your very obliging offer.'

'I beg your pardon?' He was staring at her in such astonishment that Jo's amusement turned to anger. 'Are you sure that you understood me, Miss Horne? I am offering you an opportunity that is hardly likely to come your way again, for your reputation was sadly tarnished.'

Now Jo was angry again. 'I beg your pardon, sir, but I have done nothing that anyone with even a vestige of common sense could censure me for.' Her temper had led her astray, and she realised it almost at once. 'I beg your pardon—that was rude. But you should not listen to gossip.'

'I saw you leaving Bath in the company of a gentleman…and Lady Wainwright told me that you had run off without a word to her.'

'If you believed that, I wonder that you considered me a fit person to be your wife,' Jo said. 'I left a letter for my aunt, as you must know, and if you saw me leave Bath, you must have seen that Mrs Beverley was with us. She is the daughter-in-law of Lord Beverley. I do not think that there was anything improper in Mr Hal Beverley accompanying his sister-in-law and her friend to her new home.'

'Lord Beverley's daughter-in-law, yes, you told me so.' The Reverend Browne looked at her hard. 'But even so, the manner of your departure occasioned gossip. My understanding from Lady Wainwright was very different at the time… and others believed the stories circulating.'

'I have no idea what my aunt said to you, sir—or your understanding of her comments. She may well have been angry with me for leaving her, but we were to have parted in a day or so in any case—but I believe you should be careful before making careless comments that may reflect on another's good name.'

'Indeed. If I have said too much, I apologise…but no matter the truth, your reputation has suffered.'

'I believe it would be better if no more were said on either side,' Jo said and lifted her head proudly. 'Excuse me, I must go home or I shall be missed.' She walked away from him, feeling an extreme irritation of the nerves. Hal's announce-ment that he had spoken to his father, who had then invited her to visit Ellen, had made her feel that she was to be in-spected to discover whether or not she was fit to marry Hal—but the Reverend Browne's qualified proposal had been nothing short of insulting!

Against that, Hal's very natural concern for his father's health became perfectly acceptable. Now that she was calmer, she realised that Hal's news was excellent indeed, for his father might have demanded that he have nothing more to do with a girl who was so far below him in rank—and, moreover, if Mr Browne were to be believed, had a somewhat tarnished reputation.

It was so very cold out and the snow had begun to fall in earnest now. Jo hurried towards the house, feeling that she could not wait to be at home and to listen to what Hal had to say to her.

She went straight to the parlour, feeling a little disappointed to discover only her mother and Aunt Bertha.

'Has Mr Beverley gone upstairs?' she asked, struggling to keep her voice even. 'I have something to say to him.'

'He was afraid that he had upset you,' Mrs Horne told her. 'He has gone, Jo. He had some business for his father, but he said that he would return within a few days—and he left a letter for you from Lord Beverley. It is on the table in the hall.'

'Hal has gone…' Jo stared at her in disbelief. 'But he had only just arrived—and it is snowing outside.'

'We thought that you might wish for a little time to compose your thoughts,' her mother said and frowned at her. 'It was a little foolish of you to rush off like that, Jo—and rude, my dear. Whatever you feel about Mr Beverley, you might have listened to what he had to say in a proper manner.'

'I did not mean to…' Jo caught back a sob, because it was impossible to explain all the doubts and fears she had experienced over the past few weeks. 'I just wanted a few minutes alone. I was ready to talk to him now.'

'Then I am sorry I advised him to give you some time,'

Mrs Horne told her. 'Had you told me how you felt, I might have known whether you truly wished to see him or not.'

'I like him very much,' Jo said, and then, 'I love him, Mama—but I am not sure he loves me…at least not enough.'

'I think you will find that he does care for you,' her mama said with a smile. 'But why do you not open your letter and read what his father has to say?'

Jo went out into the hall and picked up the letter Hal had left for her. She broke the seal and read the few lines written in a neat, strong hand.

My dear Miss Horne, Lord Beverley had written. *My son tells me that he believes you to be the only young lady he could ever contemplate marriage with and I am sorry that he did not think fit to tell me sooner. We are not much acquainted, as you know, but I hope to rectify that immediately. Ellen has told me a great deal about you, and I look forward to a visit from you very soon. Whatever opinion you may have formed of me, I am not an ogre, and I wish only the best for my son. Please do me the honour of being my guest in the near future. I know Ellen would love to see you. Yours sincerely, Beverley.*

Jo took the letter into the parlour and gave it to her mother. Mrs Horne studied it in silence for a moment, before looking at her daughter.

'It seems to be a perfectly pleasant letter, my dear,' Mrs Horne said. 'At least he has not condemned you out of hand, but you must expect that a man in Lord Beverley's position would not be overjoyed to hear such news from his only son. I dare say he had hoped for a more prestigious match, dearest. We have no fortune and we are not of the aristocracy, though we are of good country families.'

'You are my family, and Beverley has no need to look down his nose at my niece,' Aunt Bertha said. 'I should tell him so if I saw him!'

'No, no, Bertha,' Mrs Horne said with her gentle smile. 'I never expected my children to marry above their station. I see nothing to be offended at in this letter. It is up to Jo whether or not she wishes to visit Lord Beverley, of course—but if she loves Hal…' She looked at her daughter. 'If he had ignored his father's wishes and caused another fatal attack… I think you would not have been happy with that outcome, dearest?'

'No, I should not,' Jo said and bit her lip. 'But when I left Bath with Ellen and Hal there was some gossip. If it were to come to Lord Beverly's ears…'

'I dare say he would make nothing of it if he knew the truth,' Mrs Horne said. 'He seems a sensible man to me—and there has been nothing of which he would be justified in his disapproval, I think?'

'No.' Jo's cheeks were a little pink, for she could not forget the way Hal had kissed her and her response. 'We kissed…'

'As we all do when young and in love,' Mrs Horne said, a reminiscent smile on her lips. 'But I know my daughter and I hold you blameless, Jo. You must make up your own mind—but be sure that you are certain of your heart when Mr Beverley returns.'

'Yes, Mama,' Jo said. She took her letter, refolding it as she walked upstairs. Alone in her room, she read it over and over again, trying to fathom the meaning in Lord Beverley's words. He wanted only the best for his son… Now, did that mean that he thought Jo was not worthy of Hal…or was he going to make his decision when they met again?

She put the letter away, wishing that she had not run away when Hal was here. She had been so upset to see him, apparently at home with her family, and yet ready to give her up at his father's behest, that she had not thought things through. It was the fault of her hasty temper!

Going over to the window, she saw that the snow was falling thickly now, covering the garden and drifting so that it lay deep in some places. A cold shiver ran down her spine—she did not like to think of Hal out on such a night. If she had been more sensible, he would still be here in the house instead of alone in a snowstorm.

Chapter Ten

Hal hunched his shoulders against the thickly falling snow; his hat was pulled down low on his head, the cold biting deep into his flesh. He had passed an inn a short distance back and was beginning to think that he ought to have stopped and taken a room for the night. Indeed, he wished now that he had waited until the morning to travel, for it was a foul night. He had left Sawlebridge House because he did not wish to distress Jo further, and he cursed himself for not making his meaning clearer. He ought to have told her at the start that, no matter what his father said, he would marry her in time. His sense of duty had held him back, but he had realised soon after Jo's departure that he could not contemplate life without her—and now he was very much afraid that he might have lost her.

She was angry and he could not blame her, for how might he have felt if the situation had been reversed? He knew that he would have raged against it and demanded that she come away with him, forcing her to choose—but she had never tried to influence his decision. Indeed, he believed that, had he asked her, she might have given up all for love, because she was brave and beautiful and he loved her more than he could ever say.

Lost in his own thoughts, head down against the driving snow, Hal was unaware that he had been followed ever since he passed the inn. When the shot whistled past his head, he was startled, too slow to stop the headlong charge of his horses. Waking from his reverie, Hal fought valiantly to calm the terrified beasts, but the terrain was difficult, and snow hid the ruts that caught the wheels of his curricle, overturning it so that he was thrown to the side of the road, striking his head against a hard object.

He lay still, unaware of the man who bent over him, stripping him of his gold signet ring, his watch and fob, and the guineas in his pocket, before walking callously away, leaving Hal lying unconscious by the side of the road, the snow beginning to cover his body.

'A letter has come from Marianne,' Mrs Horne said as Jo went into the front parlour two days later. 'She says that she is very happy and is enjoying their trip. They have been to Paris and when she wrote the letter they were about to board a ship, which was to take them to Venice.'

'She does not say when they will be home, I suppose?' Jo asked. She was missing her sister so much, for she could have told Marianne things that she could not say to either Lucy or Mama.

'I dare say it will not be much before the spring,' Mrs Horne said and glanced at her. 'Have you thought about Lord Beverley's letter, Jo?'

'Yes, I have. I believe I shall go—if you will allow it, Mama?'

'Yes, of course,' her mother said and smiled. 'You must understand that Mr Beverley has behaved just as he ought in waiting to speak to his father first, dearest. It may not be romantic, but it is perfectly proper.'

'Yes, Mama,' Jo said. 'Only I wish he would come so that we can talk.'

'Well, he did say he would be a few days,' Mrs Horne said. 'You must learn to control your impatience, Jo. Had you not run off in a temper, he would not have thought it best to leave.'

'I know—' Jo broke off as they heard voices outside the parlour door. Her heart raced as she heard a man's voice, though it did not sound like Hal. The door opened and a maid came in, looking at Mrs Horne.

'A gentleman has called, ma'am. He says that he has an urgent message for Mr Beverley.'

'A gentleman looking for Hal?' Jo said, her heart fluttering.

'Ask him to come in,' Mrs Horne said. 'I do hope it is not bad news.' She looked at the tall, attractive man who had entered the room in the wake of the maidservant. 'Sir, I hope it is not Lord Beverley's health that brings you here?'

'No, he was well enough when I last saw him, which was three days ago,' Jack Manton said, and offered his hand. 'Captain Manton, ma'am—and a friend of Mr Hal Beverley. I had something urgent to tell Hal, but his father said I would find him here.'

'I am afraid he is not,' Mrs Horne said. 'He did call briefly two days ago, but said that he had business for his father and would return in a few days.'

'Damn!' Captain Manton frowned. 'Forgive me. I had

hoped to find him here. May I write a letter for him, ma'am? I shall go to Truro and see if I can find him, but there is something he needs to know…because he may be in some danger.'

Jo's heart jerked with fright. 'Does it concern a man called Mr Ralph Carstairs?' she asked. 'Hal said that he was going to talk to a friend about that wicked man who killed his brother.'

'What do you know of that?' Captain Manton asked, looking puzzled.

'I was there when Carstairs confessed to his crime,' Jo said. 'He tried…he accosted me and when Hal warned him off, he boasted of having caused the accident that took Matt Beverley's life.'

'Then you must be Jo,' Captain Manton said and smiled at her. 'Hal spoke about you. Yes, it does concern that rogue. He was supposed to be under lock and key, but he was taken before the magistrates without reference to me or Hal and they let him go…because no evidence was presented. I dare say he found some way of bribing the idiot who took the case. I shall have something to say about that, you may be sure—but in the meantime Carstairs is free and I think he may do Hal an injury if he can.'

'No! He must not,' Jo cried. 'You must warn him somehow, sir. Please find him and tell him that he is in danger.'

'That is my intention,' Captain Manton told her. 'I shall write my letter in case he comes here, but I shall not leave it at that, Miss Horne. I intend to look for him. I believe the business he had for Lord Beverley was in Truro—so I shall begin my search there.'

'If you find him…if something has happened…you will let us know?' Jo's face was white and strained. 'Please…'

He nodded, understanding everything from the look in her eyes. 'Yes, I shall send word at once. But I dare say there is nothing to worry about, Miss Horne. Hal knows how to take care of himself.'

'Come, sir, you may write your letter here,' Mrs Horne said, indicating a small writing desk near the window. 'There is ink, pen and paper in the drawer.'

'Thank you,' he said and sat down to write a brief note to Hal, sanding it but not sealing it as he left it lying on the desk top. 'Excuse me, I shall not delay. The sooner I find Hal, the better it will be for all of us.'

Jo looked at her mother as he left them. 'If anything happens to him, Mama…' Tears caught in her throat. 'I shall never forgive myself. If I had been sensible he might still be with us.'

'Stop that at once,' Mrs Horne said in what was for her a sharp voice. 'I am sure Mr Beverley is quite all right and that nothing has happened to him. After all, why should it? I dare say this man is nowhere in the district.'

'You do not know what happened, Mama,' Jo said, a feeling of dread inside. 'Hal thrashed him and I think…he might have killed him had I not called to him to stop. If this man had the chance, I think he would not hesitate to take his revenge on Hal.'

Alone in her bedchamber, Jo stood at the window, looking out. The snow had gone now, but she knew that it had been heavy the night Hal left them and she was anxious because something inside her was telling her that he had had an accident. She had no good reason for thinking it, but a night and day had passed since Captain Manton left them to look for Hal. He could have been to Truro and back by now and yet he had sent them no news.

She felt her throat closing with fear as she thought about what might have happened that night. His curricle could have overturned in the snow or he might have… Her mind shied away from all the things that could have happened.

'Please do not be dead, my darling,' she whispered, the tears building in her eyes. 'I cannot bear it if I never see you in this life again. Come back to me. I beg you, come back to me.'

'Ma! Ma, I think the gentleman is waking,' the girl went to the top of the cottage stairs and called down to her mother. She had been told to watch over him for signs that he was coming to himself, and she had seen his eyelids flutter—and he had muttered something rude!

Sally Reed came to the foot of the stairs, wiping her hands on her apron. She had been busy baking, but came instantly to her daughter's call, because the child sounded anxious.

'Well, then, Rosie,' she said in her calm tones, 'what has he been saying to you then?'

'I think he swore, Ma,' Rosie said and a cheeky grin peeped out at her mother. 'You'd best come and see to him, for I think he needs help.'

'Aye, well, I'll take a look at the poor gentleman,' her mother said. 'I feared we should lose him, so I did—but the fever broke first thing this morning and I dare say he'll mend now.'

Mrs Reed went into the bedroom ahead of her daughter. She was just in time to see her patient attempt to get out of bed and fall back again with a curse.

'Now then, sir, that will not do,' she said, clucking like a mother hen as she went to his assistance. 'The doctor said I was to keep you in bed for some days. You was lucky Mr Reed came along with his wagon when he did—lying there in the snow like you was, you would have been dead afore morning.'

Hal looked at her. His head was going round and round like a spinning top and it ached abominably. Where the devil was he? He seemed to have been looked after wherever he might be, and clearly that was due to this good woman.

'I must thank you, ma'am, and Mr Reed for all his good offices…whoever he might be.'

'Mr Reed is my husband, sir, and the carrier in these parts. He brought your horses into the stables, but he says the curricle may be beyond repair, for it was near smashed to pieces in the accident, and lies by the roadside still.'

'Well, I dare say I had better buy a new one,' Hal said with a rueful look. 'Are the horses all right? I care more for them than the rig.'

'Aye, Mr Reed says they have a bit of bruising and some cuts, but he is a good man with horses, sir. He will look after them for you.'

'I have been fortunate,' Hal said, realising as memory returned that had Mr Reed not stopped to help him he would probably have died of the bitter cold while he lay out of his senses. 'I thank you for looking after me, ma'am. I shall repay your kindness somehow. I have only a little money on me and—' Hal was conscious that the gold ring he wore on his little finger was missing. 'Damn! My ring must have come off in the accident.'

'Mr Reed says as he thinks you may have been robbed, sir.

We looked though your pockets to try and find out who you were, but there was no money—and no watch or any valuables.'

'I have lost my signet ring, too,' Hal said and frowned. 'Now I think of it, there was a shot…it was what caused me to lose control of the horses. Curse it! Forgive me, ma'am, but I think your husband is right. It means I have nothing to pay you with—except my horses. Would your husband accept them in payment for all you have done?'

'Now that's foolish talk, sir,' Sally Reed said. 'A gentleman like you knows them horses are worth far more than you could ever owe us. You look honest enough to me and I dare say you'll make it right with Mr Reed when you get home again.'

'Home… Good grief!' Hal said as his thoughts cleared and he remembered what had happened shortly before his accident. 'How long have I been here?'

'Three days and four nights, sir.'

'Then I must leave at once. Jo will be anxious about me.'

'Is that your wife, sir?'

'No, but I hope she will be very soon,' Hal said. 'I must go to her.' He swung his legs over the side of the bed, but fell back again as his head swam, cursing at his own weakness. 'I think you are right, ma'am. I must rest for a bit longer— but perhaps your husband could send a message for me?'

'Aye, he'll do that right and tight,' she said. 'I'll send Rosie up with pen and ink—and I'll bring you some of my chicken soup up in a few minutes, sir. Once you've some good food inside you, you will do well enough.' She ushered Rosie from the door. 'We'll leave you alone to make yourself comfortable, like the gentleman you are.'

Hal smiled at her. 'Thank God your husband came when he did, ma'am, for I have both of you to thank for my life.'

'It was only what any decent folk would do, sir,' she said and went out, closing the door behind her.

Jo was standing by the window when she saw the man dismount from what was obviously a carrier's wagon. He stood at the front of the house and looked at it doubtfully, lifting his rather worn hat to scratch his head. She went to the door, her instincts alert for any news, because there had been none from Captain Manton in two days.

'May I help you, sir?' she asked as she went out of the door. 'Have you a message for us?'

'Well, bless my soul, miss,' the man said and grinned at her. 'Now how on earth did you know that? Would you by any chance be Miss Josephine Horne?'

'Yes, I am.' Jo's heart gave a great leap. 'Is it news of Mr Hal Beverley?'

'He has been right poorly since the accident, the poor lad,' Mr Reed said. 'But he begged me to bring a letter.'

'Hal had an accident?' Jo moved towards him, her expression one of fear and anxiety. 'Oh, I knew something was wrong! What happened to him? Is he all right?'

'He's on the mend,' Mr Reed assured her, 'but his head is still in a whirl and he can't stand for more than a minute or two, or I've no doubt he would be here in my stead.'

'Where is he?' Jo asked, feeling near to hysterics. 'I must see him. I must go to him! Will you take me back with you, sir?'

'Well, I don't rightly know,' the carrier said, scratching his head. 'My old wagon ain't the right thing for a lady like you, miss.'

'What is it, Jo?' Mrs Horne had come out to see what was going on. 'Is something wrong?'

'Hal has been in an accident and still cannot leave his bed,' Jo told her. 'I must go to him, Mama. I must! But this gentleman thinks it would not be fitting for me to ride on his wagon.'

'It would be very uncomfortable,' her mother said. 'I am sure your aunt would allow you to take the carriage, Jo. Besides, if Hal is still a little unwell, it would be best to bring him here as soon as he can travel.'

'Ah, that's what I were thinking,' the carrier told her with a smile. 'I'll give your coachman my direction, for the gentleman is lodged with me, Tom Reed. My home is just two miles this side of Truro, see. 'Tis I that found him by the roadside, half-frozen he were, poor lad, but my missus has fixed him up right and tight. I dare say as he'll be fit to travel in a few hours. Here, you take the letter, miss, and I'll go round to the stable and have a word with your man.'

'Oh, thank you, thank you so much for coming here,' Jo said. 'Please, I must give you something for your trouble.'

'Weren't no trouble, miss. I were coming this way and Mr Beverley will make it right when he's in funds again.' He nodded his head to her, remounted his wagon and drove round to the back of the house.

Jo had torn open Hal's letter and was scanning the brief lines written there. 'Hal says someone shot at him during the snowstorm. He wasn't hit, but his horses bolted and the wheels of his curricle caught in a deep rut, overturning and throwing him out. He says he remembers nothing more until waking in Mr Reed's cottage. Apparently, he owes his life to him and his wife.'

'Well, we must assume that it was that rogue Mr Beverley's friend told us of,' Mrs Horne said. 'Unless it was a highwayman, of course—but whatever, I agree that you must go to fetch him here, and you must take some money with you so that he can settle his debt to these good people.'

'Oh, yes,' Jo said. 'I must get ready, Mama. Hal may be thinking as you do that it was just a highwayman—but if that awful creature who murdered his brother is lurking out there somewhere, it may be that he might try again.'

Hal had managed to rise, shave and dress himself at last. He was still feeling a little light-headed, but much better than he had since he first came to his senses in Mrs Reed's bed. A bowl of her chicken soup and some freshly baked bread had restored some of the strength he had lost while in a fever. He was just about to attempt the stairs when he heard a loud knocking at the front door and in another moment a girl's voice speaking urgently. He went out to the landing and was at the head of the stairs just as Jo came to the bottom of them.

'Hal!' she cried and came running up them before he could attempt the descent. 'Hal, my dearest—how are you? We have been so worried about you!'

'Jo?' Hal saw the passionate look in her face and reached out to put his arms around her. 'Why have you come? You had my letter of course—I told you that I would return as soon as I was able.'

'I had to come,' Jo said, gazing up at him, her eyes ablaze with all the passion and love that was in her. 'Mama agreed that I should, especially when we heard what had happened. Your friend Captain Manton called two days ago. He is looking for you, because that man…Carstairs…the magistrates let him go because there was no one to present evidence in the case.'

'The devil they have!' Hal was angry at the blunder. 'I cannot say with any certainty that it was he, for I did not see who shot at me. It could well have been a highwayman. I had passed a rather seedy-looking inn perhaps ten minutes earlier and someone must have seen me and followed.' He looked down at her. 'You should not have come here, dearest. You heard Carstairs confess to killing my brother—it is very possible that he might attempt to kill you as well as me.'

'I had to come,' Jo said. 'I was so foolish, Hal…I am so sorry for running away like that.'

He stopped her with a kiss that took her breath away, stroking her cheek and looking down at her so tenderly that she felt her throat closing with an overwhelming rush of love.

'It was my fault,' he told her softly. 'I should never have made love to you and then left you guessing, Jo. I told you that my father would not approve of a marriage between us, because it was what I believed. He had demanded that I make a good match with a girl of breeding and fortune and threatened to cut me off if I flouted his wishes. I cared nothing for the money, but I do care for my father. He suffered greatly after the estrangement with Matt and I did not want it to happen again. I considered making a marriage of convenience, but then I realised that it was impossible. I could never have married anyone but you. I wanted to tell you, but he was ill and I could not leave him, nor could I write to you until I had spoken to him. I had to choose the right time to tell him.'

'I do understand,' Jo replied, tears shimmering in her eyes. 'Had it been my papa opposed to the marriage, I think

I should have been torn apart, for I could not have hurt him for the world—and yet to lose you…'

Hal smiled at her. 'Then you know exactly how I have felt, my darling. It would have hurt me to be the cause of more grief or even the death of my father. After you left the cottage I wondered if perhaps I had misjudged your feelings, but Ellen told me that I was a fool to delay. I told my father that I loved you and would not marry any other, but I begged him to meet you before he dismissed the idea.' He touched her lips with his finger as she would have spoken. 'Do you know what he said?' Jo shook her head wordlessly. 'He said that he believed I might have come to my senses at last and asked me to bring you to visit so that he could get to know you better.'

'What did he mean?' Jo said. 'He told me in his letter that he wanted only the best for his son.'

'I do not know what you may have said to him at the cottage,' Hal said, 'but it seems that he thought you a sensible girl. He approves of you, Jo—and he wants to meet you again. Not to give his consent or his approval, but simply as a gesture of friendship.'

'Oh.' Jo felt the tears begin to trickle down her cheeks. 'I think I have been foolish. I thought when you brought me the letter…'

Hal lifted her chin as she hung her head, laughter in his eyes. 'I know what you thought, dearest Jo. You have never been able to hide your feelings from me, my love. When we were at the cottage, you thought that I would offer you the chance to be my mistress, did you not?' She nodded, a faint flush in her cheeks. 'And I think at one point you might have said yes?'

Jo's eyes flashed with pride. 'Oh, do not shame me! You know that I would.'

'Yes, I did believe it,' Hal said, 'and I wanted you so badly that I was tempted to take advantage of your generosity. I felt that I was trapped, unable to speak to my father or ask you to be my wife, for fear of making him ill…but I knew that it would never be enough. I did not want you as my mistress, but as my wife.' He gave her a look of tenderness and love. 'You will be my wife, won't you, Jo?'

Hearing a giggle from below them, Jo looked down and saw a young girl watching them curiously.

'I believe we have an audience,' she told Hal with a smothered laugh. 'But I do not care. Yes, my darling, I shall marry you, because I cannot contemplate my life without you. I do love you so very much.'

'Then I am the happiest man alive,' Hal told her with a grin. He drew her into his arms, kissing her once more to the huge delight of the watching child until her mother came and took her away.

'Oh, Hal,' Jo said. 'I do not know what I should have done if anything had happened to you.'

'Hush, my love,' Hal said. 'We shall not speak of it again.' However, there was a grim look in his eyes, for out there somewhere was a man who had killed his brother and he knew he would not rest until Carstairs was caught and punished.

'So there you are,' Mrs Horne said welcoming them back to the house that evening. 'Come in, Mr Beverley, and get warm by the fire. How are you? I am so sorry for what happened to you after you left us. I have wished that I had prevented you from leaving that day.'

'It was an unfortunate incident that could have happened

to anyone,' Hal said. 'I dare say I was attacked by a highway-man, for I was robbed as I lay on the ground, but my attacker did not finish his work, and I have lived to tell my tale. So we must be thankful that it was no worse.'

'Yes, that is the best way to think of it,' Mrs Horne said approvingly. 'I must tell you that Captain Manton called here after Jo left this morning. I told him what had happened and he said that he had something to do, but would call on you in the morning.'

'That is welcome news,' Hal said. 'I think I must enlist his help in the matter of my brother's murderer—but enough of that.' He glanced at Jo and held his hand out to her. She took it, gazing up at him trustingly. 'I must tell you that I have asked Jo to be my wife and she has accepted me. I shall write to my father tomorrow, and with your permission I shall take Jo to stay with him in a few days' time.'

'Jo, my dearest,' Mrs Horne said and opened her arms to embrace her daughter. 'I am so happy for you both. I do not know what Lord Beverley will wish, but I think my aunt would like you to be married from this house.'

'It is very kind of her to offer,' Jo said. 'However, I think we must ask Lord Beverley what will suit him, Mama. It would be quite a journey for him to come here, and I think he would wish to be present at our wedding. If he prefers to have the wedding there, we must agree.'

'Yes, perhaps that would be best,' her mother agreed. 'I shall leave it to you and Mr Beverley to decide—but you may come here if you wish.'

'I should be happy if you would call me Hal,' he said. 'I think my father would appreciate the chance to give us a wedding at Beverley House—but if Jo wants to be married here, she must have her way.'

'All that matters to me is that we shall be married,' Jo said, gazing up at him with love in her eyes. 'If your father is kind enough to offer us a wedding reception, we shall accept, Hal. Mama is able to travel, as are Lucy and Aunt Bertha. I would not force your father to travel unnecessarily.'

Hal's eyes were warm with love. 'It is no wonder that I love you,' he said. 'You are all that is generous and good— and I am fortunate that you have given me your promise.'

Jo's eyes went over him, noticing the signs of tiredness he was trying to hide. 'I believe Mama and my aunt will excuse you if you should wish to go up and rest. A supper tray may be brought up to you if you wish.'

'Thank you, my dearest,' Hal said. 'But if I may go up and change, I should like to join you all for supper.'

'I shall show you to your room. We have kept it ready for you,' Mrs Horne said. 'I shall come in and talk to you while you change, Jo.'

'Yes, Mama, of course,' Jo said and gave her a brilliant smile. 'I shall go up at once.'

'So,' Mrs Horne said as her daughter left the room, 'it is all settled then. I must say that Jo is everything that makes a mother proud,' Mrs Horne continued. 'I have wondered if she would ever give her heart, but she has and I believe she has chosen wisely.'

'You are as generous as your daughter, ma'am,' Hal replied. 'I am not sure that I deserve such a compliment, but you may be sure that I love Jo and shall do everything in my power to make her happy.'

'Then I am content,' Mrs Horne said. 'Should Lord

Beverley not wish the wedding to take place at his home, you will remember that you are always welcome here?'

'Yes, of course,' Hal said, 'but I believe my father has learned a lesson, and I am sure that he will fall in love with Jo when he knows her.'

'Then there is nothing more to be said, except to wish you happy. And now I shall take you upstairs…'

'I believe this belongs to you,' Jack said and laid a gold signet ring on the table. They were in the small parlour at Sawlebridge House, the family having left them to talk alone. 'I was shown it when I made inquiries at an inn about five miles from Truro and I recognised it at once. I redeemed it from the host, who had taken it against his bill. His description fits my memory of Carstairs very well.'

'I feared as much,' Hal said and frowned. 'I have no idea why he did not kill me, unless he thought that I was already dead.'

'It was a terrible night by all accounts.' Jack said. 'He may have been in a hurry to get into the warm. Or he might have been disturbed…we may never know—unless he shows himself again, it may not be possible to trace him.'

'He is a self-confessed murderer,' Hal said and his eyes darkened with grief. 'He boasted of being the cause of my brother's death. I am determined to bring him to justice for that alone.'

'It might be difficult to prove, for your testimony might not be enough. You know I investigated the accident in Spain, because I had my suspicions at the time, but I found nothing conclusive, Hal—though he could hang for what he did to you.'

'I could not swear that it was he who shot at me. But he took more than this.' Hal picked up his ring and slipped it on to his little finger. 'Thank you for restoring it to me. I was sorry to lose it—my brother gave it to me on my eighteenth birthday. I shall repay you anything you have paid out when I have had a chance to visit my bank, of course. In the meantime, I would like to ask another favour.' Hal explained about the people who had helped him when he was ill, and arranged for them to be paid a hundred guineas. 'The thief took money, my watch and a chain with an unusual gold fob in the shape of a castle. It is very distinctive and if he still had that on him it might be proof enough of his crime.'

'Then we should have him,' Jack said. 'Don't worry, Hal. I shall put some of my best men on this, but unless he makes a mistake we may never be able to bring him to justice.'

'We can only hope that luck is with us. And now—wish me happy, Jack, for I am to be married.'

'I hope you mean to invite me to the wedding,' Jack said, a smile in his dark eyes.

'I hope that you will stand up with me,' Hal said. 'Had Matt lived I should have asked him, but there is no one I would rather have in his stead, Jack, if you are able to spare the time from your duties.'

'Then of course I shall be there,' his friend replied. 'My role is more of an investigative nature these days. We are not yet free of Bonaparte's shadow, Hal, and I shall return to the army when I am needed, but his Majesty has been pleased to commission me for other work for the moment.'

'Drew told me something about French spies,' Hal said with a frown. 'I believe you were successful in that affair?'

'Yes, at least in part,' Jack replied. 'But there are many

others to take his place, Hal—and other matters concerning the security of the nation that I may not discuss even with you.'

'Yes, I dare say,' Hal said. 'You live a dangerous life, Jack.'

Jack smiled enigmatically. 'No more so than when we faced the enemy's fire. I must leave you now, but send word to my house in London if you need me—and do not forget that invitation to your wedding.'

They shook hands and Hal went to the door with him. As he turned back, he saw Lucy coming down the stairs carrying a box in her arms.

'We are going to make decorations for Christmas,' she told him. 'Would you like to help me put them up in the drawing room?'

'Yes, certainly, if I can be of help,' Hal said. 'Where is Jo?'

'Oh, she went out a few minutes ago to cut some holly,' Lucy said. 'It has beautiful red berries and grows at the bottom of the garden. At the Vicarage, we always made pretty wreaths of greenery and decorated them with ribbons and silver baubles. Aunt Bertha says we may do the same here.'

'Then, if you will forgive me, I shall go and find Jo,' Hal said. 'We shall return and then we may all do the decorations together.'

He walked out of the house and down through the shrubbery to the end of the garden where several holly bushes grew. Jo had been cutting them and now had several bunches tied and ready to take back to the house. Hal called to her and she turned and saw him, her hair windblown, and a deep flame colour in the clear morning light as it curled about her face.

'I came to help you,' he said, smiling easily. He would not

tell her that while they remained at this house he was anxious to protect her lest Carstairs was still in the area, waiting for his chance to strike against them again. 'Let me carry some of that for you.'

Jo waited for him to come up to her. Instead of bending to pick up the holly at once, he took her into his arms, kissing her tenderly.

'You look so beautiful,' Hal said. 'You should always wear your hair loose this way, it suits you—my winsome gypsy.'

'Oh, Hal!' Jo cried, but she laughed, because she did not mind if he thought her a gypsy. He loved her and she loved him, and nothing else truly mattered any more. 'You are a wicked tease, but I do not mind, for you make me so happy.'

'I hope that I shall always make you happy, my love,' he said and bent to kiss her once more.

'I wish that you were to spend Christmas with us,' Lucy said, hugging her sister as Jo prepared to leave with Hal one morning later that week. 'It will not be the same without you.'

'I shall see you again very soon,' Jo told her and kissed her cheek. 'You will find your present with the others on Christmas morning, dearest Lucy—and I believe you may find something special from Hal. We did some shopping when he took me into Truro to draw money from his bank.'

'I was so frightened that that awful highwayman might attack you again,' Lucy said. 'You will write to me as soon as you reach Hal's home?'

'Yes, of course, dearest. It will not be so very long until we are together again, and you have made so many friends here, Lucy. You will be invited to parties and you can have your friends to visit here, for I believe Aunt Bertha is planning to give a large affair this year.'

'Yes, I know,' Lucy agreed. 'But this is the first year I have spent Christmas without you and Marianne.'

'Yes, I understand that,' Jo said. 'It will seem a little strange for all of us, but I dare say Marianne has sent you something—and she will be home again in the spring.'

Jo hugged her again and then went to climb into the carriage with Hal. They were to travel post chaise—he had not yet made arrangements for a new curricle to replace the one that had been so badly damaged on the night of the snow-storm.

'You look a little sad, dearest,' he said looking at her face. 'Does something trouble you?'

'Lucy was clinging a little,' Jo told him. 'She had hoped we would be here for Christmas.'

'She will see you quite soon. And perhaps next year she and your mama may come to us for the festive season.'

'Yes, perhaps,' Jo said and smiled at him a little apprehensively. 'But where shall we be living, Hal? At your house, which I like so very much—or at your father's?'

'I dare say he may wish us to live with him,' Hal said and frowned. 'And we must certainly visit him often, for he finds travelling tiring, as you know—but I prefer my own estate, and I hope that we shall be there for much of the time.'

Jo nodded. 'It was so odd, but I felt at home there from the very first…almost as if the house had been waiting for me.'

'Yes,' Hal said and nodded his agreement. 'I have often felt that too.' He looked at the cloak she was wearing and smiled. 'I am glad you still choose to wear that, even though you have your own things now. It becomes you so well, darling Jo.'

'The first time I wore it I felt I became someone else,' Jo told him with a smile. 'I was no longer the plain Miss Josephine Horne, but a woman who might love and be loved.' Her eyes sparkled up at him. 'I think your grandmother's spirit lives on in her things, Hal.'

'I have always sensed her at the house,' Hal said. 'She wore a wonderful perfume…like roses and lavender…and you sometimes wear it, too.'

'Only when I wear something of hers,' Jo said. 'But it is a perfume I like and, if I knew where to buy it, I should always wear it, I think.'

'Then you will like the gift I bought for you when we were in Truro,' Hal said. 'I bought several things I thought you might like, but I decided to keep them until Christmas.'

Jo looked at the sapphire and diamond ring that he had purchased in Truro. It was not an engagement ring, for he had told her that he wanted her to have a special ring that had belonged to his grandmother. The ring he had given her for now was a love token and pretty, but of no great value in Hal's eyes.

'You bought me this,' she said. 'I love it—it is just right and suits me well. I hope you do not mean to spoil me, Hal. I do not need presents to make me happy.'

'No, you don't,' he said. 'A trunk of old clothes is your idea of heaven for it gives you employment, does it not? But you will have lots of pretty new clothes for your wedding, Jo, and your choice of the family jewels that were left me by my grandmother and mother. I suppose you are entitled to the Beverley heirlooms, too, but we shall leave them for

Ellen, I think, because she never had her chance to wear them as Matt's bride. Besides, I believe you may prefer something more personal—and my grandmother had some wonderful jewels, given to her by her lovers, I dare say.' His eyes held wicked laughter, for he knew that most of the jewellery had been gifts from his grandfather, but it made a good story—and he knew how much Jo adored stories.

'Oh, how well you know me,' Jo said and leaned over to kiss his cheek. 'I would not want to deprive Ellen of the things that ought to have been hers had your brother lived.' For a moment the smile left her face. 'Do you mean to tell Ellen—and your father—that Matt was murdered?'

'Not until it becomes necessary,' Hal said. 'It is my hope that Ellen may never need to know, though I may be forced to tell my father if…'

'If they catch that terrible man?' Jo said and looked at him anxiously. 'I pray they do, Hal, for he tried to kill you once and he may try again.'

'You must not worry,' Hal said and reached for her hand. 'Jack has men looking for him, and, though he has said nothing, I dare say he has men watching over us, too, my love.'

Jo nodded. 'We are fortunate that you have such a friend, Hal. I shall never be completely at ease until that man has been brought to justice.'

'If anyone can do it, Jack will,' Hal said. 'And now, my love, we shall forget all about that unpleasant business. It is nearly Christmas and I intend to enjoy it with the woman I love.'

Chapter Eleven

'So we meet again, miss,' Lord Beverley said, his gaze narrowed as he looked at Jo. 'Yes, I see that my eyes did not deceive me the last time. There is something of a likeness about the mouth and a certain look...pride, I dare say. You remind me of a picture of my mother, painted when she was a young woman.' He looked at Hal. 'You should have it somewhere, Harry. Have you not remarked it?'

'I do not think I can have seen it, Father,' Hal said. They were sitting in the family parlour, which was used mostly in the afternoons, but never for entertaining. Ellen had not yet come down, for she was in the nursery. 'I have never thought of Jo as anything but herself—because she is lovely in nature as well as appearance.'

'Indeed?' His father grunted and looked at her, a speculative gleam in his eyes. 'You had more to say for yourself last time, miss. Have you nothing to say to me now?'

'I am pleased to meet you, sir,' Jo told him. 'It is interesting that you see a likeness to Lady Helena. Hal's housekeeper saw it, too, and said she would see if she could find the portrait you spoke of, but I do not know if she did. I expect it has been hidden away somewhere, as things often are.'

'She was wearing a cloak very like that when she was painted,' Lord Beverley said. 'Sit down and take it off, girl. You cannot be cold in here?'

'No, sir, I am not,' Jo said and took off her cloak. 'I kept it on to give me courage. It belonged to your mama, sir, and was stored in a trunk at the cottage.'

'Did you need courage to face me?' His eyes were intent, suspiciously bright with what she suspected was humour.

'I thought I should,' Jo told him frankly and then she smiled, her eyes alight with laughter as she understood that her fears had been for nothing. 'But that was foolish of me, was it not?'

In that moment, Lord Beverley saw the reason why his son had fallen so deeply in love with this girl. 'Perhaps, though I can be a tyrant when I choose, young lady.'

'I dare say you are strict sometimes,' Jo told him. 'Papa expected his daughters to behave in a proper manner and he could be stern if he thought someone had neglected their duty—but in his heart he was the kindest of men, and I think perhaps you are, too, sir—but perhaps you do not always show it?'

'Your young lady sees a lot, Hal,' his father said, and there was definitely laughter in his eyes, though his expression did not change. 'I shall want to hear more of Mr Horne, miss. You will come and talk to me again, on your own mind. Hal, you may sit down and talk to me. Mrs Royston will take Jo upstairs…' The door opened and Ellen came in. He smiled his satisfaction. 'Ah, here *she* is. No need to ring for the house-keeper. I dare say Ellen will want Jo to herself for a while.'

'Jo!' Ellen cried. 'How good it is to have you here, dearest. I was telling Beverley that I was sure you would come very soon and here you are.'

'Ellen, how are you?' Jo said and stood up to embrace her. 'You look wonderful. It must suit you to live here.'

'I have been utterly spoiled,' Ellen said and looked at Lord Beverley with affection. 'I shall take Jo upstairs so that we can talk, dear Papa. You may wish to have a little time alone with Hal.' She tucked her arm through Jo's and led her from the room.

The hall was large and impressive, with a high ceiling, decorated with huge gilt-framed mirrors and matching pier tables on which stood magnificent silver-gilt candelabra. The floors in the hall were laid with marble tiles, and the stairway was carved of solid marble, but the landing was covered in a rich Persian carpet in shades of blue and red.

'It is all very grand,' Jo said. 'How do you like living here, Ellen—truly?'

'I like it very well,' Ellen told her. 'It is true that the main reception rooms are grand, and the large drawing room is cold unless the fire is kept going continuously, but we only use them when we have a big occasion—such as the Christmas party. The family rooms are much more comfortable, as you have already seen.'

'Oh, yes,' Jo said. 'Well, I suppose I shall get used to it in time.' She smiled at her friend. 'How is my darling Mattie? I am looking forward to seeing her again.'

Downstairs in the parlour, Lord Beverley looked at his son. 'Well, have you asked Miss Horne to be your wife, sir?'

'Yes, Father. I hope you approve, for I do not wish to disappoint you—but Jo is the only girl I could be happy with, because I love her.'

'Humph,' his father said. 'Why didn't you tell me in the first place? She is a lady, anyone can see that in an instant. The family is of no consequence, of course, but they are respectable—I ask no more. You don't need to marry for money, unless you've landed yourself in Queer Street?'

'No, Father, I have not.'

'I wronged Matt by refusing to see Ellen and I have never ceased to regret it. Her father is despicable, but we shall have as little to do with him as possible. I dare say Mrs Horne and her daughters will visit us from time to time?'

'Mrs Horne has sent you a letter, Father. I think you would like her.'

'If she is anything like her daughter, I dare say I may,' his father said. 'I hope you do not intend a long engagement? Never seen the sense in that myself. Marry her and bring her here to live—at least, make this your home for a part of the year, Hal. The estate will be yours and there's no one else to care for it, because I cannot see to it as I ought these days.'

'We shall visit often, and I shall make sure that the estate is run as it ought to be, sir,' Hal said. 'But my house will be our home. Jo feels happy there. Besides, Ellen is with you now and her daughter. You will not be lonely in their company.'

'True enough,' Lord Beverley said. 'They have brought life to this house when it seemed all was lost—but you are my heir, Hal. I like your Jo and it would please me if you would visit as often as you can.'

'I should have known that he would like you. How could he fail to when I love you?' Hal said when he and Jo were alone later that evening. He had taken her on a tour of the house after they dined, and they were in the picture gallery. 'This is my mother, Jo…and this is my grandmother when she was past seventy.'

Jo paused to look at the woman she felt she knew so well from using her things. Even in advanced years, she was still lovely, her face proud but not cold, her eyes filled with warmth and a hint of laughter.

'Yes, she was very lovely,' Jo said. 'But I should like to see that picture your father spoke of, Hal.'

'Yes,' he said and smiled down at her. He bent his head to kiss her on the lips. Soft at first, it became deeper, more passionate as he drew her to him, pressing her close to his eager body, feeling her willing response to the urgent need they both experienced. 'I think we should marry quite soon, my darling, because I am not sure how much longer I can wait to make you mine.' He was breathing hard, his face expressing a deep desire that was echoed in hers.

'I will marry you as soon as the banns are read,' Jo said. 'Ellen and I could sew my gown together. We could be married almost as soon as the twelve days of Christmas are out.'

'You do not wish me to employ a fashionable seamstress?'

'No, for no one is better than Ellen, and we shall enjoy fashioning it together—besides, I should need fittings and possibly a trip to town, and that means delay. Whereas if we do it ourselves we can be married much sooner.'

'Which means that Lucy and your mama may come to us as soon as they wish after their own Christmas entertaining is done,' Hal said. 'I shall arrange it at once, dearest Jo. And you may write to your family…for no doubt Lucy will also need a new gown or possibly more. I shall send your mama some money for her.'

'You are in danger of spoiling us all, Hal,' Jo told him, but received only a smile and a shake of the head. She could not find it in her heart to scold him, because it was exactly what she would have done herself. It would give her great pleasure to spoil her sister now that she was to have a generous allowance for herself.

'Oh, Jo,' Lucy cried, hugging her sister when they were alone in Jo's bedroom. 'This is such a huge house. I think I should get lost—and it is colder than Aunt Bertha's house, but very impressive. I think Lord Beverley must be very rich.'

'Yes, perhaps he is, but I do not care for that,' Jo said. 'I do like him, because underneath that growling bear image is a very kind and gentle man—much like Hal, really.'

'Yes, I think I like him, but not his house,' Lucy said. She was wandering around Jo's room, picking up her sister's things to examine them, because Jo had so many new trinkets. She opened a Bristol-blue glass flask of perfume and sniffed it. 'Oh, this is gorgeous!'

'Hal bought it for me for Christmas,' Jo said and looked at the magnificent sapphire and diamond ring on her engagement finger. 'He has given me so many things, Lucy—and Lord Beverley gave me the family sapphires. Ellen has the emeralds and the diamonds, but I am to have the sapphires, because he says they are my colour.'

'They are magnificent,' Lucy said, for she had already been shown them. 'I wonder what Hal will give you tomorrow for your wedding?'

'Oh, I don't know,' Jo said. 'I already have so many lovely things. I need nothing more.'

'But Hal likes spoiling you,' Lucy said. 'And he is very kind to me. Did you see what he bought me for Christmas? I have never seen anything so wonderful in my life. It is what they call an automaton, Jo. It is a group of monkeys dressed in fashionable clothes and they play music—at least it appears that they do, though the music comes from a box underneath.'

'I am so pleased that you liked it,' Jo said. 'Hal chose it—but asked me if I thought it would please you.' She put out a hand to caress her sister's cheek. 'I wish that Marianne could be here for our wedding, but Hal says that he shall invite them to stay when they return from their wedding trip. We do not wish to go abroad, as they did. We shall go to Scotland for two weeks and then go home for a while, before returning here for a visit, because Hal has so much to do looking after both his own and his father's estate.'

Alone in her room a little later, Jo smiled dreamily as she thought about the next day. She would marry Hal and be happy ever after. Wandering towards the window, she glanced out towards the shrubbery, catching sight of someone standing there. For a moment the man stood staring at the house before turning and walking away.

A cold shiver went down Jo's spine and for a moment she felt the threat of a dark cloud over her happiness. She had not seen the face of the man she had glimpsed in the shrubbery, and yet she had sensed something…a hidden menace that threatened all she held dear. She must warn Hal of what she had seen, because it could mean danger for him.

Jo sat down to pen a letter to Hal, telling him that she had seen a man watching the house that night. She would not see him again before the wedding the next day, but at least she could let him know that someone—perhaps his enemy—had been lingering in the shrubbery.

She rang the bell, giving the note to the maid who came, asking that it might be delivered to Mr Beverley as soon as possible. Satisfied that she had done all she could, Jo went to bed. For a while she lay restless, then at last she drifted into sleep.

A maid bringing in a tray of chocolate and sweet biscuits woke Jo the next morning. A few moments later, Lucy came in and sat on the bed to share them, as she had used to at home. Mrs Horne knocked and entered the room a quarter of an hour later, bringing a small gift she had kept for her daughter's wedding day.

'Papa gave me this when we were first married, Jo,' she said, presenting her with a small box. Inside was a large heavy cross made out of gold and engraved with a pattern. 'I thought you might like to have it, though I know you have many jewels to choose from now, my love.'

'Yes, of course I should like to have it,' Jo said, looking at the beautiful trinket as it lay in the palm of her hand. 'I shall wear it inside my bodice close to my heart and think of Papa as I am married.'

'He would have been so proud,' Mrs Horne said, the shine of tears in her eyes. 'As I am…of all my girls.' She smiled at Lucy. 'You had best leave your sister to dress now, my dearest.' She nodded her approval as her youngest daughter obeyed, and then looked at Jo. 'Is there anything you need to ask me, Jo?'

'No, Mama, I am very happy to be marrying Hal,' Jo told her. 'I do not fear it, I long to be his wife.'

'That is as it should be,' her mama said and kissed her. 'I shall leave you to your maid now, my love. I have no doubt that you will be very happy—you have made a wise choice.'

Jo smiled as her mother left her. She got out of bed and was dressing when Ellen entered the room. The dress that she and Jo had made together was lying on the bed, ready for Jo to put on at the last moment. Ellen helped her to slip it over her head, admiring the fit when it was buttoned up at the back. The front panel was thick with beading, a froth of pretty lace about the neck and shoulders.

'Oh, yes, that looks well on you,' Ellen said. 'I was afraid the beading might be too heavy for the silk, but it is just right.'

'It is lovely,' Jo said and smiled at her. Her maid had helped her to fasten the Beverley sapphires about her throat, but Jo refused her help with her hair. She had decided that she would wear it loose the way Hal liked it, fastening it with a spray of simple white flowers at the crown. 'There—shall I do?' she asked Ellen as she picked up the posy of pink roses Hal had sent her. He had also sent her a pretty bangle set with sapphires and diamonds, which she was wearing on her left wrist. At the last moment she remembered her mama's cross and picked it up, slipping it inside the bodice of her gown. 'It was a wedding present from Papa to my mother,' she told Ellen. 'I wanted to have him near me during my wedding.'

'You look lovely,' Ellen said and kissed her cheek. 'Shall we go down now? Lord Beverley is waiting.'

As Jo had no father to give her away, Lord Beverley had said that he would stand with her in his stead. He was waiting downstairs for her with her mama and sister, everyone else having left for the church, apart from those servants who were needed at the house, most of whom had crowded outside the front door to watch her leave and clapped her as she came out.

Hal's father smiled at her and came forward to meet her at the door, kissing her cheek. 'You look beautiful, young lady. I hope my son appreciates his good fortune.'

'Oh, I am sure he does,' Jo said, her eyes bright as she smiled at him. 'Are you ready to leave, sir?'

'Yes. We must not keep Hal waiting,' his father said as they went outside to the carriages.

It was rather chilly outside, for there was a cool breeze. One of the grooms had moved forward to open the carriage door for them. Lord Beverley paused to look back and say something to Mrs Horne just as the man came dashing forward. Lucy screamed, for she was the first to see the knife in his hand as he struck at Jo, his blade piercing her breast through the panel of heavy beading.

Suddenly aware of the danger, Lord Beverley whirled round and struck out at the assassin with his knobbly, silver-topped cane before he could use his weapon again. He knocked the rogue to the floor with one blow, and the next moment three of the grooms were on him, overpowering him after a short struggle and dragging him off as he cursed and shouted angry threats. Jo was swaying, a small crimson patch appearing through the bodice of her gown.

'Jo!' Lucy screamed and ran to her. 'My darling Jo! Are you hurt?'

'My dearest one…' Ellen and Mrs Horne were on either side of her, holding her as she stood there, her face pale.

Clearly stunned by what had happened, she was unable to answer for the moment. 'Are you badly hurt, my love?'

Jo slipped a finger inside her gown, feeling the small cut and the blood that had stained her gown, also the heavy cross, which had deflected the knife thrust and saved her life.

'It is just a scratch,' she said as her mind cleared and she realised that she was not badly wounded. 'I am all right, I promise you. Papa's cross…' She took it out and showed her mother the indentation in the gold where it had taken the brunt of the knife thrust. 'But Lord Beverley…is he all right?' One of the grooms had come to his master's assistance, for Lord Beverley was looking a little odd and rather yellow.

'Are you ill, sir? Is it one of your turns?' she asked, concerned for him now rather than herself.

'No, no, my dear,' he said and shook off the groom's hand. 'I was a little shaken, but I am well enough—but what of you, my dear? That wicked rogue has hurt you.'

'It is nothing,' Jo told him, 'a mere scratch, for my papa was watching over me and Ellen's beading helped to deflect the blow.' She took a linen kerchief from her purse and placed it inside her bodice over the small cut. 'There, I shall do now…oh, my dress…' She looked at the small patch of blood on the bodice. 'What shall I do?'

'You do not mean to go ahead with the wedding?' Mrs Horne asked, looking horrified. 'Are you sure, Jo? We could postpone it for a day or even an hour or two.'

'No, there is no need,' Jo said. 'I am perfectly all right. I just need something to cover this stain. I do not wish Hal to know what happened until after the ceremony, because it would upset him.'

'But, Jo—'

'Let the gel have her way,' Lord Beverley said. 'If she has the pluck to go on with it, I'll not deny her. Here, my dear…' He reached into his coat pocket and brought out a large diamond brooch in the shape of a star. 'This belonged to my mother. I was going to give it to you later. Pin it over the mark and then no one will know anything has happened.'

'Thank you so much,' Jo said and took the brooch, pinning it into place. 'I hope your men have that wicked man under lock and key, sir. Hal will have something to tell you about him later.'

'Indeed?' Lord Beverley looked at her hard. 'Well, I shall not say anything now, for you've had enough upset for one day—but I may have something to say to that son of mine later!'

Jo walked down the aisle to stand by Hal's side. She was trembling inwardly—although she had brushed the frightening incident aside, it had deeply distressed her. However, she was determined not to make a fuss or let any of the guests guess what had happened. Her wedding must go ahead as if the incident had never occurred, though of course Hal would need to be told later.

She was conscious of a soreness just above her left breast, but bore it bravely, for she knew that only her papa's cross and perhaps the thickness of Ellen's beading had saved her life. She had no idea why Carstairs had decided to attack her on her wedding day, but presumed that it was some malicious attempt to cause Hal grief—which it would have, had he succeeded. And Lord Beverley had saved her from further attack, which was quick-witted and courageous of him.

It seemed to her then that her darling papa was standing

by her side. She could feel his presence, and the warmth of his approval as she repeated her vows in a firm, clear voice, and she was proud of the fact that her hand did not tremble as she gave it to Hal and he slipped his ring on her finger. She smiled up at him as he bent his head to kiss her, and then it seemed that before she knew it the bells were ringing and she was walking from the church on Hal's arm to be greeted with showers of dried rose petals.

They received the congratulations of friends and villagers, but did not delay long for the wind was bitter. Hal took her hand and they ran to the waiting carriage, which was to take them up to the house.

'You look so beautiful, my darling,' Hal said and drew her to him to kiss her. Jo could not hold back the slight wince, for she felt the soreness sting her as he held her tight. 'What is the matter, my love?'

'Nothing,' she said. 'It was just this brooch. It pressed into me.'

'Let me look,' Hal said and bent to look at the brooch. He saw the stain of blood and gave a startled oath. 'Forgive me! Did I do this?'

'No…' Jo took the kerchief out and showed him. 'The blood is dry, Hal. It happened before we came. It was Carstairs, but you must not worry, for your father knocked him down and the grooms overpowered him. I do not think he will escape from them, and this time there were witnesses to his crime.'

Hal pulled the bodice back, discovering the small cut made by Carstairs's knife. 'Jo! What happened? Did he attack you?'

'Papa's cross took the force of the blade,' Jo said and caught his hand as he clenched it. 'And Ellen's beading helped to deflect it—and your father struck him before he could use his knife again. No, no, do not look like that, dearest. As you see, I am perfectly all right.'

'You should have sent word. We could have postponed the wedding… Jo, my love,' Hal said, his voice breaking, 'I would far rather he had attacked me…my poor darling. It must hurt you…' He bent his head, kissing the mark gently. 'You are so brave.'

'It is only a little sore,' Jo told him softly. 'It will be better once I have put some of Mama's soothing lotion on it. I did not wish to postpone our wedding, Hal. Why should we let that wicked man spoil our lovely wedding day?'

'Oh, Jo, my dearest Jo,' Hal said. 'You put me to shame. I want to weep and rage at what has been done to you—but you will have none of it, will you?'

'Our guests must not know,' she said. 'I shall go upstairs and bathe it and apply a little lotion, and then I shall come down and we shall forget that it ever happened—though your papa will want to know why that man attacked me.'

'Yes, he will,' Hal said. 'He will say that I should have told him, and blame me for not taking more precautions to protect you, I dare say—but I did not imagine that Carstairs would dare to attack you on our own estate.'

'I saw something in the garden last night—a man lurking in the shrubbery. I wrote you a letter, but perhaps it never came to your hand?'

'No, it did not.' Hal frowned. 'Even if it had, I should not have expected him to attack you like that.'

'He must be desperate,' Jo said. 'How can anyone know what goes on in the mind of a man like that?'

'He chose a moment when I was not near,' Hal said. 'But

he made a great mistake, Jo, for he will hang for what he has done—you may be sure of that.'

A shiver went through her. 'I dare say he deserves it, Hal—but do not let us speak of it today.'

'We shall not speak of him again,' Hal said. 'We have him now and I promise you that Jack will know exactly how to deal with him.'

Jo felt very much better after she had bathed the cut and applied soothing lotion. For the next few hours she was able to enjoy greeting her guests and thanking them for all the lovely gifts she and Hal had been given. If her wound was a little sore no one would have known from the way she laughed and smiled at her friends and Hal's.

'Are you feeling all right, dearest?' Jo's mother asked when she helped her change into another gown that evening. Lord Beverley was giving an evening party as well as the wedding reception, and Hal had decided that they would stay overnight in their own apartments at the house, leaving for their wedding trip in the morning. 'Not too uncomfortable?'

'No, Mama, it is more comfortable now,' Jo told her. 'I promise you it looked much worse than it was. Had I not placed Papa's cross inside my gown, it might have been different. I am sorry it has been spoiled, but I shall still treasure it.'

'Oh, my dear one,' Mrs Horne said, tears in her eyes. 'You have made so little of it, for which I must thank you. I thought Lucy would have hysterics, but because you remained calm she has taken her lead from you.'

'I should not want her to have nightmares,' Jo said. 'There is nothing more for her to worry about. I promise it is all over now.'

'She will say goodnight to you before the end of the party. Perhaps you would take her up to bed and say goodnight before retiring yourself?'

'Yes, of course, Mama,' Jo said. 'And now we should go down.'

Jo was able to dance with her husband as much as she liked, and as he waltzed her around the ballroom she felt as if she were in a dream. Once upon a time she had believed there was no hope for them, but now, after both she and Hal had been attacked by that wicked rogue, and against all expectation, they were married.

At just after ten that night Jo took her sister up to her room and saw her into bed, kissing her cheek before she said goodnight.

'Are you really all right, Jo?' Lucy asked anxiously.

'Yes, my dearest sister. I promise you I am not in terrible pain. It was sore, but it has stopped hurting now. Go to sleep now and I shall see you before we leave in the morning.'

'Good night, Jo,' Lucy said. 'I am so glad you married Hal. I like him very much. Thank him for the pearl necklace he gave me. I already have, but he only smiled—the way he always does.'

'Yes, I shall,' Jo said. 'Goodnight, my love.'

After leaving Lucy, she went back downstairs, saying goodnight to Ellen, Lord Beverley and a few guests who had not yet retired or gone home.

'You are a very brave young lady,' Lord Beverley told her. 'I was proud of the way you conducted yourself today, Jo. I am honoured to have you as my daughter-in-law.'

'Thank you, sir,' Jo said, a wicked smile in her eyes. 'I

thought you were rather brave yourself, sir—and very strong, too.'

'Found me out, have you?' he said. 'Well, I think I could not have done otherwise in the circumstances. We shall do very well together, miss.'

Jo went to her husband's side. She whispered to him that she was going upstairs and he nodded his head, indicating that he understood. Her maid was waiting to help her undress, but Jo sent her away as soon as she had taken off her gown. She sat at the dressing table in her night chemise, brushing her long hair, waiting for the moment when Hal would come to her.

He did not keep her long, knocking softly before entering. He stood just inside the door looking at her, his eyes dwelling on her hungrily for a moment or two before he came to her.

'I love you so much, my darling,' he said. 'Are you well enough…not in pain…?' He drew the flimsy material aside to look at the red mark. 'My poor love, he hurt you so.'

'It hardly hurts at all,' Jo said, moving towards him, lifting her face for his kiss. 'Yes, of course I am sure. I have longed for this moment…wanted to be your wife for so long now.'

And then she was in his arms. He was kissing her, carrying her to the bed, laying her carefully down. Jo went joyfully to him as he lay beside her, kissing her, stroking her hair, touching her, discovering all the secrets of her lovely body. Abandoning their clothing, they lay flesh to flesh, enjoying the sensation of being so close that they had become almost one. Their loving was sweet and tender, Hal taking her slowly with consideration for her virgin innocence, but as she surrendered to him sweetly, eagerly, they were swept away on a tide of passion. If there was some pain at the first Jo hardly knew it; she had discovered that there was so much more to loving than she had ever guessed, and that she was made for loving and to be loved.

Jo woke from her sleep. Hal was still sleeping at her side as she rose and went into the dressing room for a moment. It was cold as she left the bed, and she picked up her blue cloak, putting it about her shoulders as she paused by the window to look out at the moon.

'So you are happy at last...'

Jo heard the soft voice, smelled the perfume of roses and lavender and turned, but there was nothing to see. Yet she felt that she was wrapped in love and she heard the sound of husky laughter, but as she ran to the bed, throwing off the cloak to snuggle into her husband's warmth again, it had gone as if it were never there. She knew somehow that she would not hear it again.

'Jo, darling?' Hal stirred at her side. 'Are you all right, my love?'

'Yes, I am very happy,' she said and kissed his shoulder. 'I love you, Hal.'

'Love you, too,' he whispered huskily, pulling her closer. 'You smell wonderful...really wonderful...'

'It is the perfume you gave me,' Jo said and smiled.

Afterword

Lucy stood watching as the carriage drove away. She had hugged her sister and kissed Hal, wishing them good fortune and happiness. Hal had given her another small parcel before he got into the carriage.

'Do not open it yet,' he told her. 'It is a surprise for Jo, but I knew she would want you to have one, too.'

Lucy had smiled, but said nothing. She liked surprises and she had a good idea of what might be in the parcel. She waited until the carriage was out of sight before opening it to discover the small book of fairy stories—written, it said in big gold letters, by Miss Josephine Horne.

Lucy could not have been more delighted if he had given her the crown jewels, for the book had a beautiful leather cover and was worthy of the stories her sister had written. She thought it was a pity that Jo probably would not have time to write more stories, for she was so good at it—but then, Jo was good at everything, as was Marianne. It was only she, Lucy, who had no real talent, and perhaps that was because she was a dreamer and did not try hard enough at her studies.

Mama was always telling her that she must work at her sewing or her music, but the trouble was that her mind kept drifting away and she became lost in her daydreams.

Both Jo and Marianne had fallen in love. Lucy wanted that, too. She wasn't as clever as Jo or as beautiful as Marianne…but she did hope that one day she might fall in love just as they had. In fact, she had once met a gentleman she liked an awful lot, but he was older than her and she did not think that he had even noticed her.

She smiled as she remembered that he had come to Marianne's wedding. She had hoped that he might come to Jo's, too, but he hadn't…she wasn't sure why, for she knew that his name had been amongst those who sent wedding gifts.

Realising that she was daydreaming again, Lucy put all thoughts of her secret beau out of her head and ran into the house to show her mother the gift Hal had given her before he left. Jo would be so thrilled to see her name on the cover of the book, and perhaps she would write some more stories one day.

𝔐edieval
LORDS & LADIES
COLLECTION

VOLUME FOUR
CHRISTMAS KNIGHTS
Share the magic of a Medieval Christmas!

King's Pawn by Joanna Makepeace

The handsome Earl of Wroxeter, powerful and commanding, had no intention of marriage. But when the king ordered him to take a bride, he had no choice but to obey. Cressida, a beautiful innocent, caused fireworks at court. It was the Earl's task to rescue her…and make her every Christmas wish come true!

The Alchemist's Daughter by Elaine Knighton

A chance meeting in the Holy Land gave Isidora a means of escape. But she would have to watch her beloved Lucien continue the experiments that claimed her father's life. And how would such an exotic flower fare in the cold depths of an English winter?

Available 5th October 2007

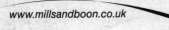

www.millsandboon.co.uk

2 FREE

BOOKS AND A SURPRISE GIFT!

We would like to take this opportunity to thank you for reading this Mills & Boon® book by offering you the chance to take TWO more specially selected titles from the Historical series absolutely FREE! We're also making this offer to introduce you to the benefits of the Mills & Boon® Reader Service™—

- ★ **FREE home delivery**
- ★ **FREE gifts and competitions**
- ★ **FREE monthly Newsletter**
- ★ **Exclusive Reader Service offers**
- ★ **Books available before they're in the shops**

Accepting these FREE books and gift places you under no obligation to buy, you may cancel at any time, even after receiving your free shipment. Simply complete your details below and return the entire page to the address below. You don't even need a stamp!

YES! Please send me 2 free Historical books and a surprise gift. I understand that unless you hear from me, I will receive 4 superb new titles every month for just £3.69 each, postage and packing free. I am under no obligation to purchase any books and may cancel my subscription at any time. The free books and gift will be mine to keep in any case.

H7ZED

Ms/Mrs/Miss/Mr .... Initials ....

BLOCK CAPITALS PLEASE

Surname ....

Address ....

....

.... Postcode ....

Send this whole page to:
UK: FREEPOST CN81, Croydon, CR9 3WZ